NIGHT DREW HER SABLE CLOAK

A Novel by Joel Bowman

Night Drew Her Sable Cloak
Copyright © 2023 Joel Bowman

ISBN: 978-1-7368381-3-6 (Hardcover)
ISBN: 978-1-7368381-4-3 (Paperback)
ISBN: 978-1-7368381-5-0 (E-Book)

The following is a work of autobiographical fiction; inspired by true events, and fictionalized to protect the names of the living.

Cover art and design by Alejandro Baigorri
Layout and Text Design by James Jabonero

First Edition Printing, 2023
JoelBowman.Substack.Com

For Anya and Frida

Table of Contents

Vitae summa brevis spem nos vetat incohare longam
By Ernest Dowson

They are not long, the weeping and the laughter.
Love and desire and hate:
I think they have no portion in us after
We pass the gate.

They are not long, the days of wine and roses:
Out of a misty dream
Our path emerges for a while, then closes
Within a dream.

Preface...

All literature is, finally, autobiographical. So observed the incomparable giant of twentieth century letters, Jorge Luis Borges. Dear readers will kindly forgive our presumption in offering an addendum to Sr. Borges's after all truthful words: All autobiography is, finally, fictional.

Owing to the poverty of pure recollection, that conniving membrane through which all memory escapes its historical setting, wherein it is pick-pocketed, molested, exaggerated and distorted to Procrustean proportions, the past appears to us as an impression of an impression (of an impression, *ad infinitum*), a reflection in a hall of mirrors, a vaguely familiar juncture, buried deep in a Borgesian labyrinth. Vainly do we grasp at an image, a smell, a sensation. And as our fist clenches the sweet seawater of youth, freely does it flow from our palms, into time's limitless ocean, eternally one with past, present and future.

Inspired by his famous "madeleine moment," the mighty Marcel Proust spent thirteen years "in search of lost time," reanimating the events of a life over a million and a half words spanning seven weighty volumes. And yet, from the finest grain of Balbec sand to the coquettish glint in Odette's eye to the feel of the letter sent from Albertine's aunt, even the penetrating exactitude of the author's pen can but hope to emulate those now timeless moments. (To say nothing of the impressions on impressions wrought by subsequent translators, skilled though they undoubtedly were.)

All autobiography is, finally, fictional.

And yet, we do not create from nothing, but rather remake the world around us. We do not invent, only rearrange. We do not ourselves cease to be, only yield to the constant, universal change around us. This phenomenon the ancients knew well. "Nothing comes from nothing," declared Empedocles. "The totality of things was always such as it is now, and always will be," stated Epicurus. "Change is the only constant," observed Heraclitus.

Modern physicists, too, have agreed on as much, as formulated in the principle of mass conservation. But what say our metaphysicians? What of the world behind the world, that mysterious governing realm of universal laws, concepts and murky abstractions? When we summon the past, or fragments thereof, conscripting soldierly facts for our stories, our wild tales and world building fantasies, are we not merely shuffling memories from one place to another, rearranging experiences, plumbing perpetual permutations, filtering them through our imperfect minds, rusty from disuse and dark as a dead end in Minos's bewildering maze?

Whether by sleights of commission or omission, all attempts at faithful recollection are mere simulacrums of a discrete moment in time, unique and unrepeatable, a transmogrification unrecognizable to the denizens of that other realm, no less abstruse to them as our own future is to us.

So it is with some hesitation that we attempt to categorize the work that follows, which in its present form is both autobiographical fiction and fictional autobiography. We become a part of our stories just as our stories become part of us. Metaphysical caveats aside, this braided narrative owes a great debt of gratitude to histories both recent and distant, personal and familial, primary and secondary. A postface, following the text, will serve to avoid any untimely spoilers.

Joel Bowman
Buenos Aires, Argentina ~ April, 2023

* * *

NIGHT DREW HER
SABLE CLOAK

Chapter 1

FIRST LIGHT

I awoke with the sun, the first light of a new day cradling tiny dust particles as it peered through the shutters in soft, golden shafts. Our modest bedroom, suffused with a steadily growing energy, felt warm and safe and homely. As the fog of sleep receded, a clear date, sharp and immovable, formed in my mind: Exactly two months from today.

Blinking my eyes open, I focused on the ambient sounds; muffled voices carried up from the street corner, five stories below our apartment in the historic Recoleta *barrio* in Buenos Aires; a delivery van, unloading produce for the fruit and vegetable stand across the way, the men calling to one another in their friendly and familiar *Porteño* slang; a child, somewhere off in the distance, crying (or perhaps laughing?); and the slow, gentle breathing of my dear wife, Evelyn, lying beside me, full of her own energy and promise and light.

Careful not to rouse her, I slipped out from beneath the hospital white sheets and made my way across the floorboards, into the *en suite*. After running cold for a minute or two, the shower slowly began to steam up the room, until I could no longer see my face in the mirror. I stayed under the torrent for a long time, letting the pressure wash over my body, watching as the many rivulets converged on the cracked porcelain at my feet, before running off down the drain.

I shaved my face slowly, quietly, deliberately, enjoying the peace in the apartment as I drew the warm blade across my cheeks, my chin, my neck. I was in no rush. Not yet.

Afterwards, dressed in a collared shirt and comfortable, corduroy pants, I leaned over to kiss Evie on her forehead. The light was brighter now and it played on her hair, lending it a rich chestnut hue. I remembered her having lately remarked how thick and lustrous it had become.

"And my nails," she had added, impressed with the superhuman qualities of her own remarkably transformative vessel, "they're virtually unbreakable."

I looked at my forearm, summoning easily the feeling of excitement between us as she had pressed those same nails against my skin, the morning she first told me. Moments like this are still palpable and immediately recallable. Everything, it seemed then, felt within reach, writ large, existing in a kind of hyperrealism while, at the same time, appearing to be almost dreamlike in state and texture.

"This is really happening," one of us had said, had *affirmed*. That was only six months ago, but even in the moment it seemed like another conversation between other people in some other place. Not us. And not then. We had come so far since the beginning.

I felt her shape move, her form stretching under the crisp white sheets.

"Shhh. Go back to sleep."

My hand met Evie's in a shower-warm clasp on her stomach and I watched a faint smile form at the corners of her mouth. I held my hand against her near-translucent skin for a while longer, imagining the life inside her, until I felt her drift off again.

My mind found its way automatically back to its resting place, the date: Exactly two months from today.

* * *

Two friends tell you they're "trying" for a child, which is really to say they're going to stop trying not to have one; they're going to cease actively preventing life from happening, as it has a historically measurable tendency to do. But before the first exhilarating, tactile moment of non-prevention, before the agreement has been reached to begin "trying," even before the would-be parents exchanged a charged and furtive glance across that crowded room, there existed an unspoken idea, an inherent, universally understood proposition, something more than a mere hint of expectation.

In a strange but very real sense, life has a way of edging itself into the record of reality long before actual conception. Potential life is very much part of our present experience, even when it is only projected into the future, inked indelibly, unforgettably on the minds of those who hope to create and nurture it. More than merely contemplate it, we absolutely expect it. We understand that there will be a time after our own, that there exists some point beyond the visible horizon, in which our childrens' childrens' children (etc.) play and sing, their little voices stretching out across the infinite unknown. We go about our lives understanding that, even if our own family line comes to rest with us, someone, somewhere is going to get on with the busy business of life. We draw the line from our past to this moment with the explicit understanding that those dots extrapolating off into the distance have names and faces and personhoods.

Consider again the couple that is trying/not-preventing. From the moment the possibility becomes apparent to our hypothetical guardians, there exists a human-shaped canvas, painted with their collective hopes and dreams and narratives, a life to be mapped onto their own, a defined part of their own future existence. They begin to imagine all kinds of events and milestone moments, as yet far off and unrealized, but nonetheless as real and reliable as one's next birthday, the coming vacation, the very next meal. This future lives in, and greatly impacts, the minds of the present.

The morbid corollary, of course, occurs when, in some cases, that future potential dies. Who is going to tell a woman, who discovers after one too many heart-wrenching disappointments, one too many miscarriages, that her grief is not real, that the sudden non-child in her future is not to be felt, missed, mourned, even? Who is to tell the newly non-father, who processes this information as his crying wife delivers the news in sobs and convulsions on his own quivering shoulder, that the weekends he will spend not playing catch in the backyard, the road trips he will pass not proudly pointing out the national monuments from the front seat of the family wagon, the height markers he will not sketch on the bathroom door frame, that something, someone, hasn't really and truly died for him?

These are the kinds of mental meanderings that occur at regular and random intervals to expecting parents-to-be, especially as they contemplate the buzzing, decidedly lifelike world beneath their kitchen window while the coffee pot takes a lifetime to reach a boil. Such was the case on this particular morning, exactly two months from the date when my own role on the planet would irrevocably change from that of singular, carefree, egocentric, individual entity, to that of responsible, somewhat-adult-ish father. The life-not-yet-begun has a very real way of occupying a space in the life-at-present-lived. The future, as they say, is now.

But that was enough time travel for one morning. Glorious caffeine now coursing through my veins, I returned to my desk and tried to focus on the moment at hand. From across our light-filled apartment, I could hear that Evie was up and in the shower. I thought of those little rivulets, running between her fine toes with their hardened, unpainted nails. I thought of their confluence, their common destination. And I thought of the paths that had led us to this present, Evie and I, so pregnant with the future.

* * *

At the time, two months seemed both unbearably distant and frighteningly soon. There was so much to do, to prepare, to arrange. So many things that, to our naïve state of mind, appeared as imminently important, even critical. We could have had no idea, Evie and I, how wholly, utterly irrelevant these considerations would quickly become. In the moment, they simply stood there in front of us, demanding all our focus and attention and effort.

First, there was the non-trivial issue of where to live. We had just returned to the city after a long spell abroad, visiting family and friends back home and sharing in the exciting news. Now, the temporary rental contract was coming to an end and the desire for something more permanent grew daily. A frenzy of red circles and exclamation points on the fridge calendar announced a relay of apartment viewings and meetings with real estate agents. We had so far narrowed the choice to three possibilities, scattered across the city.

The first, a second-floor walk-up located in an older part of town, was cozy and quiet and set back off a sleepy, jacaranda-lined street. Although considerably smaller than the others, and not in one of the romantic, Belle Epoch-style buildings Evie and I so adored, it had the practical advantage of being both more affordable and available to move in to right away.

"It doesn't have to be forever," Evie had said, sensing intuitively my disappointment when the agent left us alone to "talk amongst ourselves" at the end of the tiny, dark hallway. "We can always get something bigger in a few years, something we can grow into when the time is right."

She rested one hand on her belly as she spoke, her smiling eyes all kindness and understanding and support. I looked at her then, her face full and glowing, her movements calm and unhurried, her breathing steady and measured. Next to my anxiety and confusion, she was the picture of patience. Yes, I said to myself, Evie was going to make a wonderful mother.

The second apartment, Evie's favorite of the three, was in a more familiar neighborhood, closer both to our friends and to the city's famous parks.

"They call them *los pulmones*," Evie explained to me with her finger on the map and a sweet, childlike excitement on her face. "They absorb all the smog and pollution from the air, just like giant lungs."

The place itself was a little shabby, with worn carpets in the bedrooms and a kitchen smothered in a shock of lava-orange tiles. Plus, it was "*contrafrente*," meaning it faced away from the street, looking instead toward the inner workings of the city block. Evie's enthusiasm was undeterred.

"It will be peaceful and quiet this way," she mused as she looked out over the kitchen sink and down to the little playground located on the building's ground level. "We can replace the carpets and…"

"And this?" I looked around at the magma-colored kitchen walls, sure that the hue was reflecting off my own face.

Evie just laughed. "What, you don't like living deep under the earth's crust? Maybe we could paint little dinosaur fossils on them. It could be educational, like a fun science project? No? Ok. Well, we could just get it retiled… or wait for volcano-chic to come back into fashion. Anyway, we're not in a rush, are we?"

Not then, no. But I was already thinking of my own favorite apartment, a short walk from our temporary rental, over near the iconic Recoleta cemetery. The building, Evie readily agreed, was more like what we had imagined all along, an example of the classic French style, built during the beginning of the 20th century, when "to be rich like an Argentine" was something people said with a straight face.

The ceilings, double overhead and framed by crown molding, felt impressive and grand. The space – three bedrooms and an office, as well as generous dining and living areas – all had polished floors in (the agent gushed) "imported Slovenian oak." It suddenly seemed to me that no other material could possibly do for a serious floor in a serious house, and I could not help but notice my excitement reflected in Evie's own cheerful countenance.

The windows were large and admitted plenty of natural light, even though the apartment was on one of the building's lower levels. Moreover, the tile work in the kitchen and bathrooms (including one *en suite*), did not lend itself to science projects of any sort.

Yet, these were merely the superior physical characteristics of the place. Along with the future, in which I could all too easily imagine our happy family, the building also had something of a distinguished past. Upon entering the lobby, the agent had pointed out a shiny brass plaque, which announced that the nation's finest writer, a blind man of towering literary achievement not since surpassed, had indeed lived and worked in one of the upper apartments.

It was, predictably enough, some way out of our budget and would, necessarily, require additional financing. At this prospect Evie had reservations, preferring to go for something modest and affordable with the goal of upgrading later down the road.

"We're not in a rush, are we?" I can still hear her playful words, so soft and innocent.

*   *   *

Pressing as the issue of where to live was at this, the seven-months-and-counting juncture, it stood squarely in the shade of a yet larger consideration: that of livelihood itself. A writer's income is always and forever subject to the whim of forces beyond his control; his agent; his publisher; the reading (or non-reading, as the case may be) public; the habitual and unpredictable truancy of his own fickle muse. That is to say nothing of the capricious Fates themselves, the *Moirai*, who, according to the Ancient Greeks, spun our inescapable destiny out for us well before we were even born.

I considered this mythological proto-triumvirate as I sat down to my own day's work, the future's blank page staring up at me. What had Klotho, she who spun the thread of life itself, in mind when my little family's number came up? And what of Lakhesis, she who measured the thread out, who allotted portions to we earthly beings; what fortune, vast or meager, did she see in our future? I almost dared not think of Atropos, whose unenviable task it was to cut the thread loose for us all...

We had discussed the idea of destiny and fate often, Evie and I, during times that seemed both favorable and unnerving. On one of our extended wanderings, a multi-month walkabout around Europe's eastern capitals, we had passed an unhurried lunch in Bratislava (or was it Budapest?), reckoning on the implications of determinism. Did such a view leave us entirely without free will, impotent to effect any meaningful change in our own, preset course? And if so, could such a trajectory rightfully be called 'our own' in the first – and last – place? Even the ancients didn't quite believe that much, holding instead that, although the Fates prescribed events in accordance with the laws of nature, they left room for both gods and men to steer their own ships.

This discussion traveled with us through the years and over the seas, as our lives seemed to lead us from one place to another. It followed us to unassuming Moroccan riads and down winding Chinese hutongs. We carried it to the Pacific Northwest where, deep in reverie, we had missed several streetcar stops somewhere in Seattle and thus were obliged to walk through an hour's worth of warm evening mist, all the way back to our B&B. It accompanied us, like a faithful companion, all the way to a quaint little town square in Savannah, Georgia, with picnic tables and a water fountain and live oaks weeping their Spanish moss into the cool afternoon breeze. We were coming to the end of a Summer-long road trip then, one that had begun in California, thousands of miles ago. As usual, the investigation resumed as if it had never been on pause, but was running in the background (or was it the foreground?) all along.

If man was permitted a certain degree of freedom to choose his own destiny, perhaps it was merely the consequences of his choices that were predetermined? But then, was the idea of freedom itself something binary? Could one have freedom up to a point any more than a prisoner could enjoy freedom up to the gate and, if so, was he really free in any useful sense of the word?

Sometimes, usually when things were going well, it seemed pleasant, even plausible, to imagine some grand celestial roundtable, high up on Mount Olympus, decreeing our paths to be just so. They would tinker a bit here, lavishing us with experiential riches, then fiddle the knobs a degree there, holding some achievement barely beyond our grasp.

I pondered our threads, Evie's and mine, as I sat at my workspace that morning. We were trying to put down roots at *el fin del mundo*, the "end of the world," as they sometimes call Argentina, attempting to create certainty out of chaos, to derive meaning from randomness. A decade ago, we had tied our singular threads together. Evie and I had become intertwined on this grand and unpredictable adventure. And now we were about to braid in a third strand, a tiny gossamer fibril that would grow and strengthen and bind us in a way that only the Fates themselves could undo.

"How's the writing going?" Evie felt warm in the room, as if she had carried the shower in with her. She kissed me on the forehead and bore her steam cloak off into the kitchenette, immediately adjacent to my desk.

"I'm on the thinking cup," I craned my neck around the corner, brandishing my half-finished coffee mug. "The second, actually."

"Why don't you go out to that little café on Ayacucho, where you saw the Kodama woman, Borges' wife, the other day. You liked that place."

"Well, I *am* working," I said to myself more than to Evie. "Thinking *is* part of the process, you know."

She cocked her head to the side and raised a single, runaway eyebrow. "I didn't suggest you weren't thinking, my Dear, only that said thinking might be clearer and more focused if you got out of this tiny apartment for an afternoon."

Evie rummaged in the fridge for (I guessed) the olives, while I thought of an excuse to remain indoors, close by her side. When a few moments later she returned with a fork in the jar, I had still not come up with anything I knew she wouldn't immediately see through.

"You don't need to babysit me," she placed her free hand encouragingly on my arm, as a mother might on a child who is about to undertake some new and potentially embarrassing task. "You're sweet to think so, but remember, there'll be plenty of time for all that later."

I looked at the clock behind Evie's shoulder.

"I'll be a couple of hours," I conceded. "And not a moment more. But please, I want you to take it easy, eh? Remember what the doctor…"

But Evie was already waving her hand, soft and white and unavailable to appeal. "Take your time, Love. We'll be right here when you get back."

* * *

Buenos Aires was Evelyn's idea. I had championed Opatija, in northern Croatia, an option Evie had since jokingly chided me for on many an occasion. She was right, of course. From the moment we arrived in the "Paris of the South," it was obvious that the city would become part of our story. The immense boulevards, lined with umbrageous jacarandas and weeping tipas, the grand plazas, replete with imposing monuments to revolutionary thinkers and artists and statesmen; this was a real capital, a place to be taken seriously (As opposed to a sleepy little seaside town in some far-flung enclave of the Adriatic…)

Evie felt immediately at home amongst both the *porteños* and the roll call of transient visitors, too, making quick inroads to the local "scene." A few young months into our stay, Evie hosted a rooftop *asado* for twenty or so artists, photographers, writers, poets, amateur filmmakers and assorted other rambling travelers. I remember wandering from group to group late that autumnal afternoon and, with more than a few Malbecs to my credit, trying to ascertain where on earth Evie had managed to collect such an eclectic group of characters. And when? We were with each other virtually every waking moment, working, as we did, at opposite ends of the same kitchen table. But that was Evie; full of surprises.

Our temporary accommodations at the time could not have hurt matters. Owing to the generosity of our common publisher, who was in need of a couple of reliable house-sitters, we were installed in a house of embarrassingly lavish proportions in one of the trendiest parts of Palermo, a "temporary" arrangement that ended up lasting for well over a year. Still, I got the feeling that Evie could have thrown an equally impressive soirée – and been just as enthusiastic in doing so – had we taken up residence in a phone booth. Indeed, I had watched Evie gather people about her with her genuine, direct conversation in the most unlikely of locales over the years. Once, while wandering around the Grand Bazaar in Istanbul, I returned from haggling with a cheerfully aggressive salesman over some bauble or another, only to find Evie surrounded by a dozen brightly-clothed women from the marketplace. At first, I worried that she might be in some danger, that the group might be cajoling her into a sunset cruise up the Bosporus, or in purchasing a carpet or a suitcase in which to carry one. I pushed through the multicolored gaggle, ready to rescue Evie from the swirling touts, only to discover that it was she who was regaling them with a description of the Norwegian Fjords, whence we had just come.

"… and it's just as sheer as you like, all the way down to the water far, far below. *Preikestolen*, it's called, which means 'Pulpit Rock.' It's like standing on the edge of the world, with that Nordic-fresh wind blowing in your face. It's both terrifying and inspiring and… ah, there you are my Dear!"

Twenty-four eyes, wide as spinning plates, followed Evie's outstretched hand to where it met my own in the crowd.

"And this one wouldn't let me go anywhere near the edge," she laughed. "Why, he was standing way back, behind where the rock splits, trembling like a leaf."

Some of the women let slip a furtive giggle. Most were the picture of confused fascination, a look Evie delighted in provoking wherever she went, be it in the Byzantine capital or down here, in Buenos Aires. I could recall a hundred stories just the same. Only the imagined setting need be changed.

Turning left onto Ayacucho, I followed Evie's directions toward the little café in which, as I had excitedly recounted to her, I once saw Borges' widow, María Kodama, taking an afternoon *cortado*. The graceful woman, now in her mid-seventies, had chosen a seat by the window, where she sat alone to stir her coffee in slow, counterclockwise circles. Gazing upon her gray-haired reflection in the smooth glass, I tried to imagine what it must be like to survive such a character as her husband, whose very essence seemed to challenge and even defy common conceptions of time itself.

"Time is the substance from which I am made," I remembered Borges' eternal words. "Time is a river, which carries me along, but I am the river; it is a tiger that devours me, but I am the tiger; it is a fire that consumes me, but I am the fire."

She stayed for only a few moments, Ms. Kodama, before stepping back into the vast pedestrian sweep outside. I watched her, carried off down the way, until she became one with the great body we called "society," disappearing beneath its undulating waves. After a minute – or maybe an hour – I returned to the sea of papers, notes and erratic marginalia laid out on the table before me. My head was swimming. I thought of eternity as a giant black hole, in which time appears to slow as it approaches the event horizon. And I imagined peering over the edge, a grand celestial Pulpit Rock, with all the time in the universe to survey the abyss.

It seemed to me at once terrifying and inspiring.

Entering the familiar café this particular afternoon, I took a place at Ms. Kodama's old table, opposite her empty chair, and ordered a *cortado* for myself. Outside, the pedestrian stream flowed on and my thoughts soon became lost again in the passing parade. It really is true that cafés are the eyes of a city. Peering out from behind their curious windows, one can readily observe a cross section of the population at large; stylish older men in their throwback tweed and fedora hats; young women returning from or heading to the gym, straining to appear effortless in head-to-toe Lycra; new parents, already a hundred years behind on sleep, propping each other up behind wailing strollers. It was all there, a high-definition cityscape screensaver in every bistrot, brasserie and beanery about town. Never mind the news or the daily soap operas, celluloid imitations of real and pulsing life. I once heard it said that owners who installed televisions in their establishments ought to be driven first out of business, then out of town. Could something be both harsh *and* fair?

Looking in, too, passersby were offered a careful snapshot of the city at rest, mid-break; couples canoodling over pre-date *aperitivos*; fashionistas nattering away about the hideous new designer bag they simply must own; and a gentleman with holes in his penny loafers and a heartily-thumbed copy of Balzac or Bellow or Bastiat in his tobacco-stained grip. He stores up notes in his head, this man, stockpiling quotes and rejoinders and off-tilt insights for his next intellectual encounter, with his friends and colleagues and, if he is lucky, his wife. First, he needs to be sure where he stands, to constantly test and retest the bedrock into which his ideas are driven. Then, and only then, he allows himself to be born into the world of conversation.

I was making slow headway on my own work around this time, a decidedly American novel told from a very non-American angle, an inside-out perspective on the state the world's only remaining superpower as it stood on the cusp of a new and tumultuous 21st century. I had notions about the "Idea of America" that I had not seen presented elsewhere, notions about freedom beyond the petty confines of imagined (*not* imaginary) political boundaries, about a kind of liberty that existed in the hearts of those who strove to achieve and safeguard it.

It was a grand ambition, I have to admit, but I was enjoying the challenge and, more importantly, Evie was beyond encouraging even before I put pen to paper.

"It seems to me your path is clear," she said to me when the motion was tabled the previous summer. I had been suffering my latest project, some lifestyle column or another, with a heavy heart, and doing a poor job of concealing my discontent besides.

"You're unhappy in what you're doing," Evie declared simply, matter-of-factly. "In a way, unhappiness is a kind of death, only in slow motion. That you choose it knowingly only makes matters worse. What's more, you understand exactly what it is you want to do, the thing that will bring you happiness and fulfillment. It's the last thing you think about, just before you fall asleep. That's what you need to follow. And you know it. So, why not start now, today?"

As usual, Evie had taken care to deploy her logic at just such a time, and in just such a place, as to render any hope of rebuttal positively ridiculous. We were, deep in that sunset amber hour, standing on our little Juliette balcony overlooking the Fonte Aretusa, in Syracuse's historic Isola di Ortigia. The fountain is said to be the place where the mythological sea nymph, Aretusa, resurfaced after escaping captivity in Arcadia. The wild papyrus that grows out of those naturally fresh waters, one of only two such places in all of Europe where it is to be found, inspired no less mighty a pen as Virgil's into action. Milton, too, had written of the fountain. And Pope. And Wordsworth. Who was I, then, to indulge in petty philistinism, a martyr to the merely material, willingly blind to art's brilliant light, refracted across time and tide?

Her back to the setting fire, in gold-rimmed silhouette, and knowing all-too well that I could see exactly the hand she had just played, Evie raised a glass and toasted, "So then, to you new novel, is it?"

I called my editor, who was headquartered in drab old Ireland, as it happened, and quit in less than twenty-five words. Finally, after years of penning advertising copy and reviewing weekend getaway destinations for inflight magazines, I would apply myself firmly and surely to my craft. I would read the greats, starting with Dickens and Austen and James, then build out French and Russian wings, in which Zola and Proust, Tolstoy and Dostoyevsky and Chekhov would seep into my subconscious rhythms. I would write something deserving of Evie's encouragement, something she would refer to with pride and confidence, something she would point to on our bookshelf, a novel of significance that could fairly stand next to her own work.

Later that evening, Evie and I dined in a little trattoria by the waterfront. The air was cool and still and a low light reflected off the lapping tide. A trio of musicians played Rossini classics for small change on the cobblestone promenade. We ate sundried tomatoes and baby octopus and thin slices of smoked *pescespada* served with fresh anchovies marinated in lemon juice. And we drank the local Grecanico wine, toasting to the gods and to the waiters and to our fellow diners and, when nobody else was left in the restaurant, to ourselves. Such were the unhurried nights with Evie. Life was always a celebration.

The novel itself came fairly quickly thereafter and covered plenty of ground philosophically, metaphysically, romantically and, of course, geographically. Most of the settings I had experienced in Evie's company, especially the scenes on the road, where the main character sets out from New York City, headed toward the vast Pacific Ocean in America's great Southwest. Part of the pleasure in writing came from reliving those moments with Evie. Part came from knowing that we would relive them together someday, through the eyes of our firstborn child.

It was somewhere between Pittsburgh and Indianapolis that I picked up the action in Ms. Kodama's café. I worked solidly for an hour or so before my thoughts again began to wander. There were perhaps half a dozen blocks between Evie and me. I counted them in my head, noting the names of each street as I mentally walked the distance. The due date was not for another two months, but already it had a way of sitting on my concentration, immovably, nonchalantly, like a chicken on an egg. No sooner had my mind returned to the tiny apartment that I decided to head there myself. I would dawdle a little, so as to stretch out the time. No need to alarm Evie, I told myself. Maybe I would pick up some flowers at that little store on the corner of Arenales. As long as I was making progress toward Evie, I thought, as long as the space between us was contracting...

The journey, which I half walked, half skipped, took less than ten minutes. That included two red lights and what seemed like a Socratic dialogue with the old lady at the flower store. Before I had the chance to realize how little time had actually lapsed, I found myself staring at the peephole in the door to our tiny apartment. The lift having been engaged on some other floor, I ran the five flights of stairs, ascending them two at a time. Taking a moment to catch my breath (again, no need to alarm Evie) I stood a moment on the threshold, imagining myself through the fisheye lens. When I finally took the handle in my grasp, I knew immediately that Evie held the other side. I let go and tried not to breathe too hard as she opened the door and, with her eyebrow knowingly cocked, welcomed me inside.

* * *

It was apparent that Evie had some news to tell, and that it was good. She could no more tell a lie, even of omission, than she could so much as conceive of an untruth. It simply didn't occur to her to be dishonest. She would not have seen the point in it. We were standing in the living room, her by the window and I at the desk-cum-dining table. I let the unspoken notice rest on the silence between us for a few thinly stretched seconds, knowing she would soon cave and spill her information. So she did.

"Dolores came by while you were out," she beamed, despite her obvious efforts to appear composed. "She spoke with her cousin. The owners of the Quintana place have agreed to negotiate. She thinks they might come down another ten percent. Maybe more."

Evie turned and looked out the window as she let the last two words fall into place. I imagined her rehearsing this delivery while I was at the café, reminding herself not to smile and give the game away.

"Evie, Sweetness, you know what this means…" I began, forgetting the flowers in my hand.

"I know, I know. I'm happy too, but we still have to think this through. It's a lot of money, even less than ten percent, if they do in fact drop it that much." She seemed tired, my Evie. Fatigued. Was there something else on her mind?

"I thought you said 'maybe more'? What, exactly, did Dolores say? Trust her to call by during the only two hours I'm out of the apartment."

"You call that two hours? Ha!" Evie's glance fell on her imaginary wristwatch. "You've barely been gone an hour and a quarter!"

"I'm sorry, I'm sorry," I muttered. My concern hardly seemed to matter now, now that I could see Evie and share in this news. "You know how I worry."

Evie took the flowers from my hand and, leaving a kiss on my cheek, disappeared behind the kitchen door. "You really shouldn't, though. These are lovely by the way. Arenales?"

"That old lady could talk the sand out of an hourglass," I replied.

"Aw, she's sweet. And her flowers really are the best. These calla lilies are gorgeous."

I could hear her inhaling the fragrance from behind the paper-thin door. Evie loved the tropical flora in the city during the spring months. Often we would take long afternoon walks together around the Japanese Garden or the Rosedale or along the ecological reserve on the Costanera Sur. I would clumsily piece together some new plot idea or character development I was working on and Evie would listen patiently, stopping every now and then to inspect a strange fern or tree or creeping vine.

"It's wonderful, darling," she would compliment, before honing my point with a subtle observation that I had overlooked, adding her own key insight so that everything else fell effortlessly into place.

"It's like this tree," she might continue, drawing from the world around her as if it were a theater full of props made available for her specific purpose, "here they call it the 'drunken tree,' but in Bolivia it's the 'tree of refuge.' Same tree, different understandings. Different experiences informing perspectives. Like you were saying. That's your primary point, I think. Your focus. I'd stick to that. Flesh it out some more, this idea of opposing vantage points and complementary knowledge. It's tempting to get carried away, but that's what needs to be underscored. Here, look at this flower. Kind of like a hibiscus, right? The hummingbirds can't resist the sweet nectar. See, there's one now..." and she would be off again, following her own thirst for knowledge right down the next path.

Evie returned from the kitchen with a vase in hand; a flush of pink and white. She lowered the vessel gently onto the coffee table, the only place they could really fit in the little room. I might have noticed a subtle wince as she rose to her feet, but I was already carried away by the news.

"Well, I think this calls for a celebration," I declared, wholly relieved that one piece of our chaotic life was finally drifting closer to some semblance of order. A place to live. A family home. A setting for our own little story.

"I'm going downstairs to buy some champagne," I called from the threshold, my feet already carrying me back down the stairs. Over my shoulder I sang back, "Why don't you call Dolores back around? Ask if she wants to drop by after work. Maybe see if some of the others are free, too."

Taking the stairs two and three at a time, I burst out of the lobby and into the honeyed afternoon light in a kind of breathless lurch. The city exuded an irrepressible vitality. I drank it in for a moment, there on the stoop; the churning sweep of humanity, all jumbled together in a hectic mixture of dentist appointments and lunchtime affairs and clotting traffic, of fresh produce and swirling dust and squealing car horns, of swinging briefcases and fanning newspapers and neckties stained with busily consumed *cortados*. At my feet a thousand rivulets converged, carving space and time between Recoleta's ornately molded concrete canyons. And five flights overhead, in my tiny, temporary apartment, two precious hearts beat on steadily above it all.

*   *   *

"*¡Ya está ella aquí!*" exclaimed Jorge, the unforgettable character who owned our local wine store, when he noticed the quiver of iconic orange bottles in my eager clasp.

I shook my head behind a nevertheless self-satisfied grin. "Not for another two months, amigo," I replied in my heavily accented Spanish. "Today, we celebrate another milestone: a place to live."

Jorge threw his hands over his enormous head, bald and red like a ripe tomato. "*¡Ah, Genial!* First the nest," he quipped, "*then* comes the family!"

I still remember Jorge's face, the very picture of genuine satisfaction radiating out from behind the counter. One could set a calendar by Jorge's wardrobe. That afternoon he wore his Monday tie, an olive green number, which he pinned down behind a navy blue cardigan. Tomorrow, it would be yellow; Wednesday, brown; Thursday, cream. Then rinse, and repeat. Like clockwork, old Jorge. Even now I cannot imagine him outside that familiar setting, framed by bottles and cigarettes and assorted snacks, his precious Gardel tracks scratching out from the old victrola he kept in the corner, over by the window.

"And your *señoritas*, they are doing well?" he lowered his voice ever so slightly, as if to duck beneath the warbled sound waves drifting over from the dusty instrument.

"Better than ever," I replied, almost automatically. "We visited the hospital on Friday, just to see the doctor and make sure everything was coming along."

I sensed a half-breath of apprehension escape Jorge's tremendous chest. Quickly, I sought to assuage any suspended doubt. "Evie's blood pressure was a bit high, that's all. Nothing urgent or anything. They did a few tests, routine stuff. The doctor says she's doing well... that *they're* doing well. A bit of stress is probably to be expected at this stage, he told us. She only has to rest and take it easy, that's all."

Jorge nodded along, as if affirming the doctor's prognosis, doing his part to nudge things in the right direction. He suddenly looked fatigued behind the desk, as if he had been standing there all his life. "Not too late tonight then, eh?" he motioned to the champagne in my arms, a bead of sweat forming on his brow. "She's a special one, Evie. And there's precious cargo aboard. Well..."

I thanked Jorge for his kind words, backing out of the store while he was still midway through a volley of "*ciaos*" and "*suertes*" and heartfelt well wishes to "*las señoritas.*"

Ambling home, I found it difficult to resurrect my previous sense of jubilation. Somehow, I could not convince myself of its verity, its permanence. I kept visualizing Jorge's ruddy countenance, hearing his deep and straining breath. Why had he paused like that, when I told him about our visit to the hospital on Friday? And what business of it was his, anyway? I only told him because he always seemed so genuinely interested in Evie. He would often chat with her while I was off choosing wine, and she did seem to enjoy his banter, even if it was a bit overplayed. But then, Evie enjoyed everyone's banter. Why was Jorge so special? And why should I care for his unsolicited advice? Of course I would see to it that Evie got her rest. What did he think, that I would keep her up all night with some raging festival? In the end, what did Jorge *really* even know of our situation? He was just some nosey, overweight guy who ran a wine store near our apartment, soon to be our *old* apartment.

By the time I had properly dispensed with Jorge's unhelpful meddling, I realized I had already passed my address. Turning homeward, I suddenly had the urge to dash across the street. Somewhere off in the distance, I heard a chorus of car horns bellowing in my direction, but I was already half way down the block. With a clang of bottles, I rounded the corner and practically dove through the entrance. Not waiting for the lift, I hurdled once more up the stairs, which seemed now to be unending. When our platform finally came into view, I saw Evie standing at the threshold. She looked pale; her widened eyes a mirror of exhaustion and fear.

"Darling, I feel a little... I feel," she leaned into me, her hands clammy and hot on my neck and shoulders, her breath warm on my face "I feel very light headed all of a sudden. But I wrote to her again, explaining everything. I'm sorry. I'm so sorry." She felt heavy, my Evie. "I said, 'daddy loves you and not to worry.' I said, 'daddy loves you and mommy loves you and everything will be ok.'"

Then I felt her weight pour into my arms, her double-time heart thundering against my own. The next moment we were in a taxi, a foreign city and the great, heaving sway of society hurtling by our window, nothing but a blur of colors and uncertainty and confusion ahead.

* * *

Chapter II

PRE-DAWN

Dear Little One,

We love you.

Before we set down another word, explore another thought, surrender to another impulse, let's begin this conversation there. It's very important.

Here it is again, slowly: We. Love. You.

Right. Now that's been set down, the first three words you ever inspired firmly, indelibly etched onto the historical record, perhaps a little explanation is in order...

First, we've only known about you for a few hours (mommy a little longer... she didn't want to wake daddy). So if this comes across as a little... scattered... it's because that's kind of how we feel. You're quite the rush of excitement, you see!

It's very early here ("here" being London... a city in England... which is a country in... well, there's much to tell, all in good time).

The sun is still asleep. So are the people. They're dozing in their big comfy beds, happily dreaming away. They're like you, sort of. Asleep. Waiting to be born again, into the new day.

Soon enough the sun will rise and the day will begin. The city will come to life with noise and activity. The whole grand narrative will continue.

Here, a little about that story... and your place in it.

Your parents (that's us!) have been thinking about you for a long time. In fact, we've carried an idea about you all around the world. (Having done a little mental math, we think you might have begun somewhere between Brindizi, Italy, and Patros, Greece.) We've been traveling, you see, adhering to mommy's life motto:

Explore. Experience. Express.

Your mommy has lots of wise thoughts and ideas bouncing around her head, as you'll come to discover when you meet her. (Daddy too, she adds.)

Well, it's a wonderful place, this world you are about to discover, full of adventure and potential and surprise. It's not always easy going. We shouldn't set up false expectations. Sometimes it can be very challenging. But with love and support, with understanding and compassion, with patience and honesty – to yourself and to others – you will find the experience ahead of you rich and rewarding.

There will be plenty more to unpack in the weeks and months ahead. Thoughts and feelings that right now haven't even occurred to us. For now, we just wanted to begin this correspondence, to say "Hi!" and to tell you those three very important words: We. Love. You.

We'll write to you again – both together and individually – along the journey. For now, daddy is heading down into the crisp morning air to grab some coffee and breakfast bagels (but two of life's many, many miracles that await you). And mommy has to rest. We're about to begin another big trip, you see. You'll have half of Europe covered before you know it!

So sleep tight in there, Little One. Enjoy your dreams and that pre-dawn peace and quiet. The sun is just now coming through the window here, slowly filling mommy and daddy's room. Your room. Our room. We can't wait to meet you, to hear your little voice, to hold your little hand, and to share with you this magical experience called life.

All our love,

Mommy and Daddy

London, England
September, 2014

P.S. Mommy here. Daddy's downstairs, "hunting and gathering food for the family," as he put it before forgetting first his keys, then his wallet, on the way out the door just now. (Let's hope he remembers the cream cheese!) Anyway, I wanted to write to you again, if only to add a few more words. Generally, I find writing helps me focus my thoughts, allows me to feel closer to whatever it is I'm trying to understand (though I'm not sure it's possible to feel closer to something that is literally growing inside of one's own body).

I must admit, it's an odd sensation, to know that I'm now sharing a body. Not that I mind. It's all very exciting, if a bit daunting. It's just that, I've only ever experienced my body as my own, so I expect this new arrangement will take some getting used to. (Hmm… maybe this would be the appropriate time to say, "welcome aboard!" and to offer advanced apologies for any unforeseen, in-flight turbulence.)

Perhaps it all seems a bit strange, writing to you before you can even read. I suppose at first, it'll be more an exercise for us, your parents-to-be, to help us process this new information, but I hope in time you'll find in these pages some clues as to the kind of people your parents are, we who would set out on this journey with you. For a start, we feel entirely fortunate to have come even this far. Many don't make it to the "fetus pen pal" stage. So, for that, we're mighty thankful. We're also very much in love, your daddy and I, which is not as common a state as you might think, or hope, in this world. We're healthy, too, as far as that goes. And young(ish). So, we've got lots on our side, to help our little family off to a good start.

Well, I'm not sure if it's my superheroine sense of smell (when does that kick in, anyway?), or the fact that I've been awake for hours now, full of nervous energy and without a bite to eat, but I feel like your daddy's due imminently with the spoils of his hunt. It seems odd to end on "goodbye" or "see you soon," since neither of those sentiments really work, so I'll just say, I love you ~ Mom

*   *   *

Chapter III

A JOURNEY BEGINS

Hilda Nilsen was not yet twenty-one years old when she stood on the platform of the Grand Forks train station in North Dakota one gusty September morning and wished her father a tearful goodbye. She had never before seen the man cry, not even when her mother passed away almost three years earlier. The tears seemed strangely out of place on his weathered skin, like raindrops on an ancient clay creek bed, long forgotten by the heavens. He was a tall, handsome man who had borne a lot of life's hardships. It didn't seem right to her that he should suffer so.

"You must keep well so you are living when I come back," said Hilda, with a solemnity that hung in the swirling air between them.

The father held his daughter's face in strong, familiar hands and drew her into his deep embrace. She listened to his breathing beneath his woolen coat, feeling the constrained sob welling up from deep inside his chest. He kissed the top of her golden blonde head and, without meeting her eye again, dug his hands deep into his jacket pockets and marched off along the platform. She watched him until he disappeared into the crowd and prayed to God that He might spare this gentle man until her return, seven years away.

Hilda's train sat idle on the tracks, but already the journey ahead rose up before her like a cresting tidal wave. To the west lay thousands of miles of unknown continent and an ocean so vast it seemed that, to reach the far edge of it would be to come to the end of the world itself. But even that distant, unimaginable point, flung clear over the receding horizon, would only signify the beginning of Hilda's passage. Beyond those foreign shores were hidden people and places of which she could form no firm perception in her mind. They were faces with strange names and expressions, with stories so peculiar, so distinct from her own, that she wondered, standing on the station platform in America's great Midwest, whether she would ever come to understand the nature of her mission, much less fulfill it.

Closing her eyes, Hilda felt the fall breeze at her back as it gusted over the cooling prairies, with their time-smoothed hills and rolling pastures, their familiar townships and Main Streets and tight-knit Sunday congregations. They sang the same hymns, these people, and Hilda knew them all by name. They were her people and her songs, too. From all over Scandinavia they came to settle the northern reaches of the New World, to build a life and to raise their families. They were disposed to the severe climes, against which they labored through season and sickness. They bore children with straw-colored hair and pale complexions and glacier blue eyes, built hearty for the howling winters. They saw their progeny thrive and, when they did not, which was sometimes just as often, they wrapped their tiny bodies in blankets and lowered them into the cold, unforgiving earth. Then they sang different songs, prayers that stitched communities together in grief and sorrow and that marked the years as they passed them by, like so many empty nights.

There were other people, too, who came with messages of their own from strange and distant lands. Hilda remembered the missionaries who had boarded with her family over the years, even when there did not seem to be food nor space enough to feed and house her own brothers and sisters. Sometimes they came for a few days or weeks. Often, they would stay on for many months at a time. One year, a group of young women arrived from Lebanon. They brought with them aromas of clove and cinnamon and strong coffee and they carried little sacks of dried dates and yogurt-covered cherries, which they would share with the children after meals. Their laughter, which came often and easily, filled the house like birdsong. Another year, on a rainy afternoon in late February, three Persian men came for a week and stayed through the whole of spring. They wore long, flowing garments of the most brilliant colors Hilda had ever seen, and their beards were dark and wooly like the fleece of a sheep's belly. On weekends they sometimes cooked dinner for the family. Their gurgling Farsi language swirled around the kitchen and mixed with puffs of steam and exotic spices in the warm, evening air.

Once, back in the earliest light of Hilda's memory, a man came to visit who had traveled all the way from a place called Madagascar. He sat, long-legged in the visitor's chair by the wood fireplace, speaking with her father. Hilda stopped still in the sunny doorway, her own shadow short on the long wooden boards. She had never seen a person with such dark skin before. He was blacker even than Mr. Samson, the man with the scar where his eye was supposed to be, who had helped her father to paint the church for the Easter service. Hilda felt small and shy, but when the man from Madagascar noticed her, he smiled such a great, gentle smile that it seemed to take up his whole face. Later that night, after her usual bedtime story, Hilda's father showed her the big Book of the World, which he kept on the shelf by mother's piano. It contained all the places known to man, he once told her, and some more that were as yet unknown.

"Here, Hilda. Look," father drew his forefinger, yellowed by till and tobacco, over the dust-covered page. "Our friend has come a long way to stay with us. All the way across the ocean, from down near the very bottom of the world."

"Will he stay with us a long time?" Hilda asked, her little voice heavy with sleep. Her father's casual shrug replied that he did not yet know. "I like his smile," she confessed. "It's like a gigantic, enormous piano."

"I like his smile, too," father agreed, brushing his hand through her curly blonde hair. "He will stay with us as long as he needs to."

"And then?"

"And then he will go along his journey, to wherever the Lord calls him."

Hilda thought for a moment. "Why does the Lord call people on journeys?" She looked at her father in earnest. He closed his eyes for a full breath, the way he sometimes did when he was thinking. "He calls them to teach," he replied at last, "but also to listen and to learn. Remember, Hilda, whenever we go out to meet the world, the world also comes out to meet us. There is a lot for us to learn in this life."

Standing on the Grand Forks platform, the wind rushing through her hair, Hilda remembered the Lebanese women's easy gaiety and the Persian men's scruffy beards and their spicy dinners. She remembered the man from Madagascar, too, with his shiny, blue-black skin and his kind eyes and his gigantic, enormous piano smile. She thought of her father and his slow, lonely ride back to the farm in Wisconsin. And she thought of all the men in the Old World, young men of all colors and creeds, who were at that very moment busy fighting each other in a war that was supposed to "end all wars." Hilda wondered whether, after all these years, people really had learned much of anything.

In the distance, she heard the rush of steam as her train groaned to life behind her. The stationmaster took to his whistle with gusto and the crowd began to shuffle alongside the great engine. Turning her pale young face to the west, her father's words in her ear, Hilda Nilsen prepared for her calling, to go out and meet the world.

*   *   *

"Pardon me, sir," Hilda inquired of the young ticket man as he strolled through her carriage, "I wonder if you could take a message to a Dr. Distad and his party."

The man glanced up from his notebook. He wore a weary expression that seemed to age his face beyond its boyish features.

"I'm to meet them on this very train," continued Hilda, filling the silence she had left for his response. "It's rather important, you see. We're to travel on to Shanghai together. Shanghai as in 'China,' you see…" she trailed off.

The man allowed himself a nod of bare minimal acknowledgement, then continued, unhurried, on his rounds.

"No rush," thought Hilda to herself as she tried to find a comfortable position in her window seat. "I have a view and an imagination and all the time in the world before me. Besides, it's not as though I could miss the good doctor and his family. We're on the very same tracks, perfectly parallel, physically *and* metaphysically speaking."

Thus satisfied, she turned her attention to the grassland, soon speeding by in undulating bands of pale green and yellow. Not a single cloud trespassed on the featureless blue sky overhead. Hilda thought again of her father and of her brothers and sisters. She imagined them running around the tamaracks and sycamore maples down by the lake and, afterwards, lying down in the long grass behind the churchyard to gossip and tell tall tales. She felt the dewy grass on her back and the warm sun on her face. Her youngest sister, Ruth, was telling the story about the boys from Old Jeb's farm. The others were giggling, their childish laughter carried away in the wind. From somewhere off in the distance, Hilda heard her mother calling for lunch.

"Hilda… Hilda… Miss Hilda Nilsen…"

Hilda woke with a start, her sweet childhood slipping away again over the horizon of her subconscious. In its place stood the young ticket man, who was tapping her mechanically on the shoulder. He motioned impatiently to a woman in her mid-forties, standing one careful pace behind him. Then he frowned at Hilda, bade the other woman a silent farewell and strode off stiffly down the aisle.

"Miss Nilsen." The woman had a soft, soothing voice, which Hilda was glad to receive. "I am Karen Distad, Doctor Distad's wife. May I?"

Hilda hastily cleared her weathered valise, which contained a few books and some personal items, from the adjacent chair. Bending her tall, slender frame beneath the overhead luggage compartments, she begged the woman to please join her.

"Mrs. Distad. Of course. I was just…" she began, collecting herself. "It's been a long journey already. Excuse me. It seems that I… I must have dozed off. Well, it's a pleasure, I'm sure."

The woman opposite smiled sweetly and, taking her seat, turned her focus out the window, where it became immediately lost among the passing fields. She was well dressed, Hilda noticed. Her fair hair was braided and pinned back tightly at the sides. Her hands she kept firmly in her lap. Her navy skirt fell beneath the knee over long, white stockings, automatically crossed at the ankles. She seemed both kind and severe, with a familiar, pious demeanor, known well to Hilda's own experience. No need for idle chit chat, she thought.

"I was saddened to learn that Miss Pilskog won't be joining us," ventured Hilda, after some silence, then added, "though I'm sure the Lord has His plans for her, too."

"It was not the Lord who stood in Miss Pilskog's way," returned Mrs. Distad. A stern look passed quickly over her countenance. She held Hilda's eye for a second longer than the younger woman found comfortable, then turned her tight, thin neck to the window once more. "Rather, it's something to do with her papers," she muttered, allowing the softness to re-enter her voice. "It is common during wartime, you know, for papers to be held up. The embassies and consulates are terribly busy. Terribly so."

Mrs. Distad shook her head absently and returned once more to the racing landscape, her mind evidently occupied elsewhere. Hilda began an observation, but quickly thought better of it. They sat in silence a long time, mile upon mile of untouched prairieland passing them by. Their reflections transposed themselves onto the racing landscape and Hilda studied them by contrast. She guessed Mrs. Distad to be perhaps twice her age. Their palettes were similar; blonde hair; pale skin; wintry blue eyes. Mrs. Distad showed signs of strain and time, of course, a few gray streaks at the temples, clusters of tiny red vessels bursting on the cheeks, a faint cloudiness in the irises. Both held the same sure posture, though Hilda's frame was somewhat sturdier. She sat taller in the seat by a good few inches.

At length, the older woman pinned her shoulders back and, taking a deep breath through her nose, began what she had now obviously come to say to her younger companion.

"The doctor has been taken ill, Hilda," she declared at last. The seriousness of the situation conveyed itself clearly in Mrs. Distad's measured, almost clinical voice. Hilda had the impression that a single fissure in the woman's composure might let forth a deluge of emotion. So, with some effort, she remained silent, fixed in her seat.

"He has been working almost non-stop these past weeks," Mrs. Distad went on with a hint of remonstrance in her timbre. "He treats his patients day and night. They are sick with influenza. It seems every man, woman and child in the Dakotas has a touch of it. Some of them are long past hope when they arrive, coughing and spluttering as they do, but he treats them anyway. I've never seen him turn a case away yet, miserable as they can sometimes be. And now," she drew another long, measured breath and patted her lap nervously, "well, now he is resting. In the morning we shall see."

The woman took one last look out the window. Hilda saw the creases around her eyes tighten for a second, then release. She seemed to have aged even during the time she sat there so that, when she rose to her feet, she appeared frail, as if bearing an enormous weight on her diminished form. Smiling, defiantly, she offered her outstretched glove.

"Try to get some sleep yourself, dear," she squeezed the younger woman's hand. A vague, distant kindliness had returned to her eyes. "The journey is long, but our time here is brief."

Hilda hardly slept that night. Her preoccupations simply would not permit a moment's reprieve. She tried reading, only to find her eyes running on for pages at a time, entirely detached from her concentration. She drank lemon tea from the lounge car, but had little appetite for the food. Nor did her Psalms give her rest. "The Lord sustains them on their sickbed," she recited from memory, "and restores them from their bed of illness." At a loss, she stared out into the blackness, the glass of the windowpane cold and hard against her forehead. Other passengers boarded, at places like Williston and Malta and Havre, but she hardly noticed them coming or going. They were merely shadows, silhouettes of life going about its distant business, a bleak rotation of hats and overcoats and cumbersome baggage. Life on the move, she thought to herself.

Sometime around Shelby or Cut Bank or Browning, she felt the train leaning into a slow, winding climb. The rhythmic click-clack, click-clack became labored, as if the whole lurching convoy might give up at any moment and simply stall out on the tracks. Hilda heard passengers coughing in the other carriages, their death-stained barks filling the common space around her. She felt a draft of icy mountain air swirl beneath her seat. It seemed to get in everywhere, the cold, from under the carriage doors and through the window seals.

"He sent His word and healed them," she whispered into the cold, "and delivered them from their destructions."

But it was of little use. She wished people would stop shuffling along the aisle, would stop opening the doors to her carriage, would cease coughing their vile pollution up and down the train. She wished she could think of something other than Mrs. Distad's aging features or the Doctor and his hoarse, croup-filled lungs. She wished Miss Pilskog had been able to get her papers in time, and that the stupid war had not contrived to cut short yet one more journey, before it even had a chance to begin. Most of all, she wished she could wade into a deep, dreamless sleep.

* * *

It was very early morning when the train slowed into Everett Station, a short ways north of Seattle; its final destination. Already passengers were gathering up their belongings, fumbling in the young light to reach cases and hat boxes in the overhead compartments. They whispered among themselves and hushed their bleary-eyed children, so as not to wake those still sleeping. In the next carriage, a baby could be heard crying.

Hilda closed her eyes again, listening to the human movement around her. She tried to remember when she had fallen asleep. "Libby... Spokane... Ephrata..." She recalled the conductor's announcements as they had punctuated the still night. Then she remembered the doctor and peeled her eyes open. She would have to see him, or Mrs. Distad, to arrange the next leg of their journey. They had two children with them, too, she recalled. Boys. Were they aware of their father's state? As she collected her thoughts, the service trolley approached her seat. Hilda accepted a hot black coffee and two plain biscuits from the young girl in attendance. She smiled and bade the girl to keep the small change.

The coffee was bitter, but Hilda welcomed the warmth as it spread through her chest. She had just returned to her thoughts when another man in uniform approached her seat.

"Miss Nilsen," he read her name from a folded piece of paper, "Dr. Distad and his wife will see you in their cabin when you are ready." He gave Hilda the cabin number and a stern, though not unkind, look. She thanked him and, when he did not move on, added with a hint of indignation that she would make her way there presently. Still he did not leave, but rather studied her with a quizzical expression. At last, and seemingly against his own intuition, he asked, "Have you plans for onward travel, Miss Nilsen?"

Hilda found herself suddenly flustered, even mildly annoyed by the man's nosiness. "Why, yes," she returned. "I am to continue with Dr. Distad and his family to," and here she hesitated, without quite knowing why, "to... to our final destination."

The man nodded his head and half made for a reply but, at the final moment, appeared to change his mind. "A pleasant journey to you, Miss Nilsen." He doffed his cap and left the young woman by herself.

Hilda finished her coffee and biscuits, shaking her head at the man's impertinence. Studying her reflection clear in the window, she fixed a loose pin in her hair and pinched a spot of color from her alabaster cheeks. She never used makeup, considering such small vanities to be a waste of time and effort. Ruth had once brought home some rouge, a gift from a friend, but their mother chided her trifling indulgence and made her return it the very next day. Hilda studied her reflection more closely and wondered what her mother might look like now. Before it had a chance to set in, she shook the image free from her mind, quickly as it came. Satisfied with her presentation, she buttoned a jacket over her plain white blouse and smoothed the fabric down over her form. No sense in keeping the doctor and his wife waiting, she told herself.

Passing through the train as it rocked gently beneath her gait, Hilda registered for the first time the faces of her fellow passengers. They were travel-worn and tired, most of them, the long miles weighing heavy on their expressions. Some appeared more alert than others, inspired to animation by either apprehension or excitement, or both. In one of the crowded carriages toward the rear, she noticed a family sleeping under the flickering shadows. Their faces were unclean and their clothes unkempt. The father sat slumped in the middle seat, his head cocked slightly to one side, as if he had only just nodded off. His wife, a mess of hair and scarves, leaned on his shoulder, snoring softly with a young, pretty-faced girl in her arms. Nestled against the man's other side was a brown-haired son, older, maybe six or seven years. His legs were curled up against the side paneling, one ankle bent against the window. In the father's arms slept yet another one, much smaller than her siblings, with a pacifier dangling from her drooling, half-open mouth. They looked like a pile of old books, Hilda thought, stacked against one another on some forgotten shelf. Pausing to observe them in the frail morning light, she noticed the boy's right sleeve was pinned at the elbow. A farming accident, she wondered, or perhaps an unfortunate birth deformity. She looked upon his sleeping face with a mixture of pity and sorrow. Then she turned again to the mother and father, bedraggled and unconscious, the mother still snoring faintly, her mouth open just like her daughter. Without knowing quite why, Hilda felt a strange kind of repulsion against them. She did not stop to dwell on the thought.

The doctor's cabin was in the next carriage, a sleeper car. She walked the length of it from end to end, stopping to check the names and numbers affixed to each of the doors. The doctor's name was not to be found. The aisle was empty, too, except for two young, fair-headed boys, no older than the little one with the missing arm in the adjoining carriage. They were arguing over a game of toy soldiers when, of a sudden, the smaller of the two began to cry. The carriage being otherwise silent, but for the click-clack, click-clack of the wheels on the tracks, his wails echoed down the hall. Hilda came to them and knelt at their feet.

"Now, now! Boys, please!" her tone was firm but not entirely without compassion. She had younger siblings of her own and knew well how to deal with such disputes. "What seems to be the matter here, then?"

The boys looked with apparent confusion into the stranger's face. The younger of the two appeared ready to let forth with another wail when their collective gaze was drawn off, somewhere beyond Hilda's presence.

"Nurse Clara!" they cried in unison, before the harmony deteriorated into a ruckus of teary accusations and defense pleas. Hilda turned to find a stout black woman of no more than five feet in height standing directly behind her, hands resting firmly on her barrel-shaped hips. Over her shoulder, a door, slightly ajar, revealed a figure lying on a cot under a heavy gray blanket. With a shake of her head, the burly nurse

Clara swept past Hilda and, apparently well known to the boys, ushered them off down the aisle and into a cabin at its far end. Hilda heard their frustrated cries as the door closed firmly behind them. Watching them disappear, she thought of the poor little maimed boy in the other carriage, sleeping soundly on his daddy's lap.

"My dear child," came a voice. Hilda turned to encounter a woman who looked like... no, who *was* Mrs. Distad. Her countenance had become pallid. Only her eyes were red. "The journey is over, dear Hilda. Over even before it was begun. Go home to your family." She held Hilda by the shoulders, closed her flooding eyes and shook her head slowly, despondently from side to side. Then she kissed her on the forehead and passed on silently down the aisle, towards her quarreling sons.

Hilda felt her stomach clench itself into a knot. Her breath seemed to escape her lungs. She turned toward the cabin door, through which Mrs. Distad had emerged. Inside, a man stood over the cot, examining the near-lifeless figure, hidden beneath the sea of gray. Hilda took a step toward the scene, trying to make out any movement, any rise and fall, any vitality left in the dormant body. Drawing closer, she glimpsed his fevered, blood red cheeks and lips, dried like fish scales. His eyes were half closed, so only the whites showed beneath the sheer, almost transparent lids. The room smelled of stale air and Lysol. And of old, familiar death.

"Ma'am," the figure by the bed was addressing her. "I'm afraid you can't be in here. Ma'am."

Hilda heard herself mumble something about her mission, about the doctor's wife and Shanghai and, for some reason, the little boy with the missing arm in the next carriage.

"Ah, you must be Hilda Nilsen," he muttered. The sound of her own name brought her around. She nodded in desperate, wide-eyed agreement, as if clinching to something known and solid might restore her strength.

"The fact is, Miss Nilsen, Doctor Distad is gravely ill. At this point, there is not a great deal we can do for him." The words sank into Hilda's chest, each one heavier than the last. "I'm afraid he will not see China," he pressed on. "Frankly, it will be a miracle if he sees another day. I don't know how he has managed to survive even this long. The Dakotas are full of this influenza they're calling the 'Spanish Flu' and the Doctor has seen his fill."

Hilda surveyed the poor doctor's face, at once flush with fever but drained of life. She recalled his wife's half-hearted admonition, that he had treated his patients until the last, labored against their disease, until it had become his own. How many lives had this one man saved, she wondered, before laying down his own.

"Look," said the man, a physician himself, Hilda now realized. "The doctor knew his time was drawing near days ago. He has made his peace, come what may." He examined the young woman's face before him, as if struggling to make a decision of his own. "Before we left Stanley, night before last, he gave me this message. He told me that, if a young woman with your name should ask after him, to give her this and to wish her fair passage."

Pressing the folded card into Hilda's palm, he held her trembling hand for a moment, and then returned, head hung low, to his patient's bedside.

Sometime later that morning, at a busy café in the Seattle train station, her few meager cases occupying the rest of her café booth, Hilda Nilsen summoned the courage to unfold the card. It contained a name and an address in downtown Seattle, beneath which was underlined the following:

In the Lord's name, go out and meet the world

Hilda looked at the clock on the wall; it was not yet 10 AM. With a heavy sigh, she ordered another coffee from the prim waitress, and asked if she might see their telephone directory.

* * *

Father Gornitska was a thin man of diminutive stature who moved in quick, nervous measures. His eagerness, which was kindly but uncertain, expressed itself in little twitches and ticks about his face and neck. He had narrow set eyes, always alert, and a long hawkish nose, on which sat a pince-nez, as was the fashion of the day among a certain, bookish type. A fastidiously trimmed mustache completed his look.

On the morning he entered the Seattle station café, ready to meet the young lady who had just telephoned his office in clear dismay, Father Gornitska was already arresting a kind of internal panic. His eyes shot around the room from behind his pince-nez, until they landed on a fair-headed woman sitting alone in a booth by the window. Not wishing to startle her, he approached the table with some hesitation, which had the direct result of scaring the young thing half witless.

"Oh giddy! Oh giddy me!" he spluttered his familiar phrase, shaking his head excitedly. "I didn't mean to alarm you, Miss Nilsen. I meant only to…" He was suddenly griped with a sense of looming embarrassment. "You are, Miss Nilsen, aren't you? Oh, giddy me."

Hilda found time during the strange little man's routine to compose herself. The poor fellow, she thought, he's worse for wear than I am! Immediately she set about calming his nerves. She made her introduction and gave what she considered an adequate, though not unnecessarily detailed account of her travels thus far. She told him of the journey on the train, gave an abridged version of Miss Pilskog's delayed papers and, with some delicacy, divulged Dr. Distad's unfortunate prognosis. Gornitska nodded along restlessly all the while.

"Oh yes, yes. Oh, giddy me. Poor Doctor Distad," he chimed in at last, his pince-nez shuffling up his rounded nose in a series of twitches and squints. "He called through a week ago, from just outside Fargo. He said his own doctor did not expect him to make it even that far, but that he was determined to complete the journey nonetheless. As an old friend of your father's, he wanted to make sure you arrived at port safely, and that there would be someone to secure your onward travels and to help in any way needed."

What composure Hilda had managed to bundle up was all of a sudden lost to confusion. "My father's friend?" she stammered. "You mean Dr. Distad? But I thought he was just another missionary, someone to…" her voice trailed off.

"Oh, oh giddy me," Gornitska blurted, "I thought you two might have had a chance to talk before he, well…" he struggled to bring his twitches under control, "before he was taken quite so ill. You met his wife, I suppose? Dearest thing. And the boys? Fine young lads they are. Such a pity for them, and at this tender age…"

But to Hilda's ears, his voice had already faded into the background rush of the lunch crowd, which had by now begun streaming into the little café. She thought immediately of her father, marching off down the platform at the Grand Forks station. Why didn't he tell her he knew Dr. Distad before? Did he already know of his friend's failing health, when he left his daughter in the family's care? Of course he did not, she affirmed in her own, swirling mind. How could he have? But what about the message on the card, the injunction, written in his own words, to "go out and meet the world?" It was all so terribly confusing. She felt alone, unsure of herself and her surroundings. She was a silly woman, she told herself, out of her depth before she had even embarked on her mission. How far from her old, familiar scenery she felt! Her confidence was plunged into crisis.

"I'm sorry, Father Gornitska," she felt a warmth flush in her cheeks, "this is simply all a bit much. I was supposed to travel to Shanghai, you see, with Miss Pilskog and the good doctor and his family and now… well, now I haven't anyone and I don't know where to go and I can't possibly, I just can't possibly see how I'm supposed to…" A surge of fatigue and frustration and helplessness welled up behind her eyes and, against every effort to constrain herself, Hilda began to weep right there in the booth, letting forth with a torrent of emotion and bewilderment.

Father Gornitska, for his part, was less than prepared for such spontaneous commotion. His face contorted into a series of rapid-fire jerks and twitches, his eyes shooting around the room in nervous apprehension. He sought to calm the tearful woman opposite him, but could only manage a quivering series of "Oh, giddy, Oh giddy me" outbursts of his own.

At length, Hilda peered up at this tick-tocking little man through her own cascade of tearful confusion and began, to her own surprise, to giggle, then to outright laugh. Gornitska continued his own private convulsing act, entirely unaware of the young woman's gaze, his head spinning like a top and his pince-nez threatening to fly right off his nose and into her coffee. At last, Hilda could barely take it. What began as a mere hiccup of involuntary glee had quickly escalated to unconstrained peels of mirth. Her eyes were watering more now than when she was crying, the tears flowing freely down her face. She struggled to catch her breath.

Finally, Gornitska cottoned on to her change of aspect. "Oh giddy," he uttered reflexively. His eyes grew as wide as they could. "You're good, yes? You're okay? We're laughing? Yes, yes! Laughing!" He too let off a shriek of his own, a self-conscious act that soon became a genuine, deep-belly cackle. Lost in his own zeal, he emitted a high-pitched little snort, which sent the pair into deeper peels of rolling hysterics. A few fellow diners looked on askance toward their booth, tut-tutting at the brazen scene held at such an hour.

"Zozzled already," declared one uppity woman, with ill-concealed disgust. "And not even midday. For shame!"

Hearing the admonishment, they only laughed harder, relieved to welcome some overdue levity into their midst. When they had collected themselves somewhat, Father Gornitska reached over the table and took Hilda's hands in his own. "There are many twists and turns along our road, Miss Nilsen," he said, nodding still. "Ours is to make the best of what the Lord deals us."

"I think I'm going to be okay, Father," Hilda smiled, wiping the tears from her cheeks with a paper napkin and adding, with a deep breath, "Now, somewhere near here is a ship bound for China, and I'm to be on that ship this very afternoon!"

"Yes, Miss Nilsen. Oh yes!" the jumpy little man agreed. "We'll get you on that ship and no doubt about it. Don't you worry. Just a couple of quick stops first."

* * *

With Hilda's cases tucked away in the trunk of his Ford motorcar, Father Gornitska climbed hastily into the driver's seat and, with a nod and a wink, or rather a twitch, set off down the hill. "Don't mind the bumps," he said as they bounced along, "I know the roads and ways well enough by now."

He need not have worried, however, as Hilda was entirely engrossed in her new surroundings. So preoccupied had she been with the recent changes to her situation, which begged a kind of blind faith enough as it was, she had neglected to do what she most promised herself before she set out: to keep her eyes open so as to record each passing moment. She had every intention of relaying, with as much color and context as possible, these precious details to her family, both through written correspondence and in person, upon her safe return. Often, in the hot summer nights counting down to her departure, she would lay awake, entertaining visions of herself as a woman of experience and worldliness, come home at last to the silver lake, regaling familiar faces with tales from afar. She could see them clearly, brother and sisters gathered around the hearth, father in his reading chair, held in thrall by the narrator's impossible, almost mythical yarns from lands unimaginable.

Her head grazing the roof courtesy of an unexpected pothole, Hilda craned her neck to better take in the rushing scenery. It was as far removed from home as she had yet seen. Grand structures of one description or another occupied every corner; buildings six, eight, ten stories in height and more. The whole city seemed to be reaching upwards, jostling, shoulder-to-concrete-shoulder, for the sun's scant rays. A light drizzle gave their façades a shimmering mirror effect. On the sidewalks below, meanwhile, a busy procession of men and women hurried along under a sea of black and gray umbrellas. They wore serious looks on their faces, as if they were all on some official business and could no more afford to dally than they could break into a spontaneous foxtrot.

"We'll drive by the Smith Tower a little further on," announced Father Gornitska with boyish pride. "She's a real beauty. Tallest building west of the Mississippi."

"Taller than…" Hilda motioned toward a towering triangular structure with enormous arches and windows, half way down the hill ahead of them.

"Oh giddy me, yes!" the man cried with excitement. "Thirty-eight stories she is, and no less!" He seemed rather pleased in his new role as guide and amateur historian.

Hilda could only shake her head in astonishment. What masterful feats man was capable of... and in the face of it all! The whole metropolis appeared to her a sort of affirmation of man's right as he saw it, wrought with a steely, cold-eyed determination. It seemed to declare that, if man was going to secure for himself a place in the future, he was first going to set about building that very future. No time to waste. No feat beyond his capacity for imagination, for aspiration. It was a different kind of mentality than Hilda was accustomed to, one she had not figured out just yet. There was something prideful in it; that much she could see. It held a defiant arrogance, a cocksureness that gave her an uneasy feeling in her stomach. Still, it was impressive, in its own sort of way. Instead of trying to moralize or rationalize it, she was content for the moment merely to take it all in. So she did, as Gornitska's shiny Ford knocked and rattled down the cresting hills, toward the distant bay.

"First we must go to the Japanese consulate," he declared, as if reading from a to-do list already typed out neatly somewhere in his head. "Your ship will make a short port call in Yokohama before continuing on to your final destination. That is to say, to Shanghai, in any case," he added.

Hilda sat in silent agreement, welcoming the new information as but one more happy absurdity heaped upon the last. The Lord had a plan for her, even if she did not quite understand it then. "Your knowledge of me is too deep," her inner voice found its way back to the Psalms, "it is beyond my understanding." She was beginning to find calm amid the chaos, to welcome it, even.

Gornitska, meanwhile, was chattering on, "Then we will make a quick stop at the Chinese consulate, to have your papers stamped and properly ordered. After that, it's down to the pier for your departure."

To Hilda, the early afternoon flew by in a series of unremarkable lines and registers, stamps and counters, papers and paper-shufflers alike. Gornitska seemed perfectly adept at such busy, detailed work, hustling and ferreting his way through crowds of huffy onlookers, talking at a rapid patter to uniformed gentlemen and typing secretaries, assuring them that a quick passage was, after all, a good passage. As if by sheer inertia, or force of nervous energy, he managed to usher his care through the bureaucratic labyrinth to have her standing on the dock, cases stowed and tickets punched, in time for the final roll call.

"I don't know how ever to thank you," Hilda looked at the odd little man before her, a true savior in her time of need. "I shall have to write, to tell you all about the journey, about," she motioned with a dramatic sweep of her arm across the deep, churning waters behind her, "about whatever it is that's over there."

The time had come to bid farewell. Gornitska looked up from his shoes, the green-gray sky reflecting in his pince-nez. "You take care now, Miss Hilda Nilsen," he bowed his head slightly, his features pinched as he squinted into the glare. "And may God speed you."

Then, with an awkward half-embrace, he turned up the pier and shuffled off into the misty Seattle dusk. Hilda looked up at the massive vessel before her. "*Fushima Maru*," she read the name aloud as it was marked across the giant, building-sized hull. With one last glance back at her old, familiar continent, she turned and, as she would recall some years later, walked up the gangplank alone, "humanly speaking, of course."

At long last, her voyage had begun.

*   *   *

Chapter IV

DAR A LUZ

T he emergency room looked like the one we had been in last Friday, but something was decidedly different about it this time around. It hung in the atmosphere; in the suddenly metallic smell of the place; in the way people seemed to be milling around without any real urgency, like mourners awaiting a funeral procession. What were they all doing here, anyway, these dreary-eyed men and women, when it was clearly not their turn? Had they nowhere else to be? I noticed a subtle change in the expressions of the nurses and the administrators, too, the great multitude of questioners and interrogators and human obstacles, an endless supply of non-doctors and non-specialists who could obviously be of no use whatsoever to Evie. And why was everyone being so impossibly slow and tedious, so irresponsibly, numbingly methodical? Biting my tongue, I answered their questions as politely and directly as I could which, in a second language and with Evie in the state she was, seemed to me no small feat.

"*Si, si, Señora. Yo estoy tranquilo, si. Entiendo,*" I replied to yet another face in the endless procession of matronly clipboard holders on rotation behind the small admissions desk window. "I *am* being calm, *Señora*. But you see, I've already filled out this form. Yes. Like I told you before, we were here last Friday. Dr. Kostas. Yes. You must remember us, surely. We sat right there."

As I was fielding a ceaseless barrage of questions, a dutiful looking nurse approached us from the side and took Evie by the arm. I watched out of the corner of my eye as they passed into the adjacent room, in which Evie had her blood pressure taken the previous Friday. The nurse was saying something to her as she wrapped the Velcro band around her upper arm. Evie nodded along calmly. She seemed composed, if a little vacant.

"*¡Señor! ¡Señor!*" the woman behind the little window commanded my attention once again. She was poking around under the glass with a pen, indicating places on a form for me to sign. "*Aca, y aca. Firma y aclaracion, por favor. Firma, y aclaracion.*"

I looked back to Evie's room. The door was closed now, but I could still see through the blinds. Evie was seated on the bed, nodding along to the nurse. At least, I supposed it was the nurse, for she was now out of view. There was just Evie's serene face against the white walls, looking up through doe-eyes in a kind of half-expectant, half-bewildered expression. She appeared tired. And swollen. Come to think of it, she looked very, very swollen. How had she gotten so... *big*? Was she like this a few moments ago, when we arrived at the emergency room?

I turned my attention back to the room. What on earth was taking so long? The other patients sat on a long metal bench against the far wall, under an oversized clock with a deafening *tick-tock*. They looked at me, or at Evie's door, but averted eye contact when I returned their gaze.

"*Firma y aclaracion, por favor!*" The directions were staccato now, the author's face determined. I took the clipboard and made some effort to glance over the fine print. There were pages of it. "This will take all afternoon to read," I thought to myself. And what's it all for, anyway? We were in and out of here last time in under half an hour. We just need a couple of quick, rudimentary tests. I looked back toward Evie's door. The shutters were drawn.

Tick-tock, came the taunting from the wall. Tick-tock... tick-tock.

I began to feel slightly faint myself. I sensed the sweat on my shirt-collar, suddenly turned cold against my blazing skin. Perhaps I should go in and sit with Evie for a while. Just to hold her hand, to reassure her that everything would be alright and that we'd be out of here soon enough. Now, where had the other nurse gone?

"*Firma y aclaracion, por favor. Y aca... y aca...*"

Perhaps it is best I finish these papers up later, I thought. No need to get to them right away. Why, we had months left to worry about forms and fine print. For now, we just needed someone to take Evie's blood pressure and give us the all clear. And maybe a glass of water, too. She must be hot in there, poor Evie, alone in that room. Had somebody turned off the air-conditioning? When had it become so hot and sticky?

"*Señor, uno mas aca, señor.*"

Tick-tock… tick tock…

The second hand sounded like a wrecking ball. Suddenly, the double-wide doors burst open and the afternoon light crashed in on a sound wave of city traffic. A group of doctors and nurses, all white gowns and stethoscopes and military gait, aimed their arrow-like formation in my direction. They were silhouetted, so that I couldn't see their faces until they were almost upon me. Abruptly, the leader of the peloton reached one firm hand out to shake my own. It was Dr. Kostas. He pulled me into a hurried embrace, while the rest of the white coats marched on through another set of doors behind us.

"Ready to meet your new baby." It was not a question. Taking me by the elbow, the stout little Greek man, in whose consultation room I had sat a dozen times during the last seven months, joking about sleepless nights to come and Evie's having eaten 'all the pies,' harried me through the swinging doors, into the long white hospital halls.

I began a protest, something about an obvious confusion. "Evie will be happy to see you, doctor," I mumbled. "She's feeling a little faint is all. They're just taking her blood pressure."

"That's all taken care of," Kostas interrupted. "What we've got to do now is get the baby out. You are ready."

Again, it was not a question. I tried to say something about needing some more time to read through all the forms, about Evie still having two months to go, about not having packed an overnight bag.

"Wait here just a moment. One of the nurses will get you scrubbed up and ready." He placed his hands on my shoulders. They felt very heavy. Or I felt very weak. I could not tell which. "Don't worry. You'll see Evie before we go in."

As he said these words, a nurse slid her grip inside my elbow and pivoted me into a small room off to the side. She handed me a set of scrubs and told me to use the pink disinfectant soap on the wall to wash my hands.

"*Dos veces, por favor,*" she made the universal hand washing motion, all the way up to the elbows. "*Dos veces. Muy, muy importante.*"

The door closed behind me and the tiny room began to spin violently. Suppressing the urge to be sick myself, I immediately did as the woman had instructed. "*Dos veces,*" I repeated to myself, rubbing my skin raw. "*Dos veces, dos veces…*"

When I could wash no more, I stood still for a moment, silent and alone. In the mirror was a man in blue-green scrubs, all fear and trembling beneath a ridiculous shower cap. Was this really about to happen? What about our plans? What about the date, carefully marked down on our fridge calendar, inked onto my brain? What about all the letters I still had to write, *we* had to write?

The nurse entered without knocking.

"*Listo, señor. Vamos a dar a luz.*"

* * *

I did not see Evie again before I went in. I did not visit her in a small, uncomfortable waiting room, where I could rub her shoulders and wipe her brow as she anxiously counted the shortening lapses between excruciating contractions. I did not hold and accept her hand as the pain passed in writhing waves through her precious, tender body. I did not follow alongside her gurney as a clamoring team of physicians in lab coats wheeled her frantically through the endless linoleum labyrinth. I did not hold her gaze, lovingly, reassuringly, as the flickering lights passed over her pale, frightened features.

I did not espy Evie again until I saw her strapped down on the operating table. Her feeble arms were pinned outstretched, crucifix-like, her swollen legs fastened in shiny metal stirrups. A pale green cloth was draped over her quivering form. I did not see her face until the nurse ushered me behind the curtain, a kind of drop sheet that fell on Evie's panting chest at the "head end" of the bed, like one of those miniature theaters one sees in the park of a summer weekend. The whole thing looked like a set up for some kind of gruesome magic trick. Only there would be no tricks here. No sleights of hand. No cheating the Gods. They would give and take according to their own whim. And what had they come for today? I expunged the very thought.

The room reeked of disinfectant and the air had a slightly metallic taste to it. Evie's body lay hidden behind the curtain, down the bed, where the doctors and nurses were readying their instruments and yanking her precious, helpless torso into place. She looked at me with panicked, upside-down eyes. Her hair was wet, as though she just got out of the shower. Her dilated pupils glistened under the fluorescent glare.

"Are you ready?"

It was her question; not mine. As in, *she* had asked it. Not me. Was *I* ready, she wanted to know. Was *I* okay?

Blinking back tears, I held her face in my hands and kissed her upside down on the forehead. Her skin was clammy and salty on my lips.

"I'm here, Evie," I managed at last. "Dr. Kostas is here, too. He says we're going to see our little girl soon."

"Yes, yes... our little girl." Her words came sharp and jerked, as if her vocal chords were being violently tugged. Behind the curtain, hands were working busily; clasping, clipping, cutting; squeezing, separating, cinching. "Our little girl," Evie mouthed the words again, her eyes widening with each sudden jolt downward. Her lips were trembling, their color almost completely drained. They were the white of teeth, of bone.

Presently, a new commotion began behind the curtain. The machines screeched in discordant urgency, as if vying for the nurse's attention. Streams of vital information pealed across the monitors in erratic, temporary flashes. I could hear Dr. Kostas' voice, severe and steely and direct, and the sound of metal instruments clanging into trays. They sounded sharp and hard and cold. There was a second of silence then, of a sudden, Evie's body was wrenched to one side, like she had taken the force of a dense, blunt object to her hip. Her eyes gaped open in their sockets, the whites flashing for an instant behind the flooding pupils before the abyss smothered the space. Again her body was shocked from the other side with a jolting, sickening thud.

She began to mouth something, struggling to grasp the words in her quivering lips.

"I'm… Love… Is this…" her breath gurgled back down her throat and disappeared into her heaving, sweating chest.

I pressed my cheek to her ear and whispered. "You're doing great, Love. You're perfect. You're perfect. I love you."

I felt the table jolt again under my head, under Evie's head. The machines were reaching fever pitch now. Instruments clanged in the metal trays, as if tossed from across the room. Evie groaned heavily, breathlessly in my ear, a deep, aching sound that began low down in her torso and coiled painfully upward. I felt a ripping shudder echo along her spine and wrap around her neck. Then another low, writhing wince stole her air. Again her shoulders were wrenched violently lower, as though she were being dragged away, inch by inch, behind the curtain. Again her eyes lolled back in her head and her neck arched with involuntary shock. I pressed my lips to her forehead and closed my eyes.

"My Evie… My Evie…" I repeated in a kind of desperate, deranged incantation. "My Evie…"

Suddenly, I felt her whole body seize up, as though shot through with a bolt of electricity. Evie exhaled in my ear with an exhausted groan. The curtain became still. The room fell silent. Only Evie's breathing punctuated the air, her neckline glistening with a cold sweat, rising and falling under my hand. A few precious seconds passed this way.

Then came another sound: a tiny voice, gasping for life.

*   *   *

We had planned all this, of course. Over many meals Evie and I had discussed everything from the welcome announcement to the likely order of congratulatory visitors, from the contents of the overnight bag to our exhausted but exalted replies. To claim I had not rehearsed a few of them myself would be well shy of the truth.

"We're both so happy, yes. Such a wonderful moment for our little family."

"Evie was incredible. They both were, really. I'm a very lucky man."

"Yes, isn't she just perfect. Her mother's eyes, you're right. And, yes! Her daddy's appetite!"

Among the many imagined blisses, we also counted those precious moments before the news would become known beyond our own private world, the peaceful sanctuary of familial togetherness, the feathered pocket in time in which we would bathe in a soft, powdered embrace, feeling out the sheer physicality of our new presence, the new shape of our "us," the beating, breathing rhythm of three hearts and six lungs, a chorus with a new pitch, a cosmic coordination with an unmapped dimension, a new dynamic with a fresh orientation and a heretofore unimaginable overflowing of love and warmth and tranquility.

Of course, the dirty diapers and the sleepless nights and the infant fevers would all follow. That was certain enough. So too would the stomping tantrums and stomach rashes and canceled dinner plans and the "I told you sos" from vindicated veterans of the grand parenting project. There would be bruised knees, too, and broken hearts and battered egos and all the rest. Those tests would arrive sure as day and, as a family, we would face them together and overcome them as best we could, in our own unique way. But that was all a long time off. That was a future that would take years to arrive. Or a couple of months, at least.

So it was with a deafening cosmic collision that the raw, unscripted present slammed full force into the academic, hypothetical, once-distant future. From behind the mysterious curtain appeared the being who marked that very point of intersection, where projected ideas and unfolding reality became an inseparable moment of pure, vital immediacy. I watched the precious life carriage transported to Evie's pulsing, sweating chest, the transparent protective membrane flushed red against her mother's pale whiteness. There she laid, curled silent, skin-to-skin, unmoving for a hundred million microseconds and every reverberating echo between. I watched them there, turned inside out, a life cell split from its host, cleaved from the animate flesh. Evie was whispering something, cooing, but mostly she was crying soft, exhausted tears. It seemed impossible that there could be energy left for her to give, that there was anything the ordeal had spared her, that she could afford even a single breath of her own. I watched her chest rise and fall with gentle sobs, but could sense no movement besides her own internal force.

Just then, the curtain came down and I could see Evie's body stretched out on the bed. A fresh, dark green sheet had been laid on top of her. One of the nurses pulled it up over her chest, up to her neck. Only her face showed above the sheet.

Without offering a word, one of the nurses reached out to me with both hands and I felt a fragile, weightless energy come into my arms. Somewhere down the hall, in another room, a tiny baby was crying, its vocal cords raw and straining against the world-heavy atmosphere. It took me a second to register that the tender movement was in my arms, a nearly imperceptible panting, a fluttering voice barely bumping atoms, only just forming into sound waves at all. Instantly, the beeping machines and the iron smell and the buzzing nurses became part of some other scene, of some other movie. As the rest of the world quietly departed, I looked upon my daughter for the first time in our life together. And in her presence, her realness, her sheer actuality, I began to realize that I, too, had been born anew.

*   *   *

This epiphany did not last long. In fact, it was over before I registered its brimming significance. No sooner had this life come into my arms she was spirited away by another of the nurses, a short, shuffling woman who motioned for me to follow her – *them* – into the adjacent room. I obliged, dumbly, feeling conspicuously helpless, like a man who has just bought a spaceship but realizes he has not the slightest understanding of ballistics or rocket science, much less the heavenly dance of the planets.

"Did you see what he's gone and done?" I could hear the other nurses' thoughts as they watched me, empty handed and trailing pathetically behind their honorable, veteran colleague. "Where do these guys get the idea? To think they'll know what to do, with a *life*! A precious *life*! Do they think it's some kind of game? That we'll be there to guide them through every little thing? Look at this one, the wide-eyed dolt. If only they would take the whole thing a little more seriously. Rocket science is a cinch by comparison!"

The head nurse was already busy running some kind of tests when I stepped into the room. She mumbled automatically to herself as she worked, expertly examining the puny figure before her as one might hold a glass of wine against a tablecloth to better study the contents. "Full body... strong legs... deep ruby color..." Gingerly, she applied the stethoscope to the tiny ribcage, first against where I imagined the bean-sized heart to be racing then, after a few seconds, all over the fragile lung and organ casing. The instrument was smaller than usual, that I could see, but even so it looked gargantuan when pressed against the miniscule frame, itself no larger than a soda can. The vigorous crying appeared not to bother the nurse, but I wondered if it was cold to the touch, this cruelly necessary instrument. One hand remaining on the squirming, blotchy red torso, and muttering all the while, the nurse made two notations on her clipboard. I had a sudden and irrepressible urge to know what she had written and exactly, precisely, in every possible detail, what it all meant. Before I could formulate the question, the nurse had moved on to some new part of the examination, which, to my immediate unease, involved yanking the precious baby bird limbs here and there, first with the wings, then the coiled little legs. Each time the spindly wishbones sprang back against the body, but still the nurse appeared unperturbed. Again she made her notation and, again, I fought the urge to lean over and interrogate the critical information. Next she began tapping the pads of the rosebud feet, so much so that the woman appeared to cause undeniable visual distress to their wailing new owner. At this, the nurse merely muttered to herself again and continued with her infernal notations. Finally, she hoisted the trembling autumn leaf onto a scale, at which point another nurse entered the room and assumed note-taking duties.

"¿Y que peso tiene?" the second nurse asked from behind her facemask.

"Un punto trescientos doce," replied the first in a clinical monotone, conspicuously devoid of emotional content. The newer nurse shot a look back at the attending superior, then down to the fresh life on the scale. She appeared to make a pointed effort not to notice me and, instead, cloaked her response in rapid-patter Spanish, the only word of which I caught for sure was: *oxígeno.*

I felt my own breath leave me. "Wait, I heard that!" I panted, eying the first nurse, who was now handing her patient, my little girl, off to her colleague. "*¡Escuche eso! ¡lo esuche! Tu dijiste 'oxígeno.'* What do you mean 'oxygen'? *Discuplame, Señora.* Excuse me, please. Nurse!"

Without raising her voice, the kindly woman motioned for me to put my facemask back on. I could see the ancient creases framing her patient, indigenous eyes. "*Por favor, señor. No se preocupe.*" She extended her hands toward me in a calming gesture when, behind her, two more nurses entered the room, wheeling an incubation unit. Sensing my instant panic, the old nurse continued with her lullaby routine. "*No se preocupe, señor,*" she soothed, "*La nena esta bien. Señor, por favor.*"

The other three had taken over now. A cradle of soft brown hands transferred the writhing life carriage into a swaddle of white blankets. One woman affixed a plastic green label around the bendy straw ankle. A yellow hat, the size of a doll's sock, was pulled over the miniature cranium, not quite down over the flickering eye slits. From somewhere else came a series of tiny tubes, two of which were pushed inside pinhole nostrils and taped over downy red cheeks with adhesive paper. My own heart thumped nervously inside my chest at the sight of such a precarious collection of vital organs and bodily processes, each so delicate and critical, each part of an intricate hierarchy of importance, from the curling toenails to the pulsing capillaries to the connective brain tissue that flashed with microscopic thunderstorms inside a floating, Plasticine skull. And what of her little emotions? Was she scared? Did she know what was happening to her? Could she even feel nervous or anxious or stressed? And shouldn't she be in her daddy's arms? I felt suddenly faint, as though my legs were filled with fast drying cement. Then I glimpsed a hair-width catheter needle piercing the dermal layer behind her little toy wrist. Vicarious pain shot through my system and her crepe-thin lungs let out a pathetic, defiant wince. A surge of nausea might have wrenched me asunder had not the first nurse steadied me by the arm. I translated her words as though my mind were a thousand leagues under water.

"Your daughter will be fine with us, *Señor*. But your wife, she needs you now."

*   *   *

Evie was gone. Absent. She was not there.

I peered through the still glass window, into the operating theater. The machines were silent. The screens were blank. The naked table on which my wife, my Evie, had writhed and jerked and sweated and cried and given her light only minutes earlier, was empty. The stirrups and arm straps held no struggling limbs. The curtain concealed no crimson procedure, shielded no violent mystery, protected no shuddering, palpitating viewer from life's essential rage against death. Even the green hospital sheets had been stripped from the bed. The room was full of absence, an icy indifference to events past and future.

For a moment, I considered the possibility, stark and looming, that none of this afternoon's drama had actually occurred. I might have simply walked in here by mistake, led astray by some honest confusion, misdirected by a mere language breakdown, a simple *derecho* instead of a *derecha*. Evie, of course, might now be relaxing in a waiting room off the main hall, her vitals casually confirming all was well while she flipped through a *Caras* or an *Hola!* magazine. Her nurse would return presently with a colorful Latina *"¡Todo bien!"* and we would be sent on our way, home to chill the champagne and to set out some *hors d'oeuvre* for tonight's guests. Won't they be excited, these dear friends, to hear that Evie and I have found a place, a home at last, a nest to welcome and nurture our little girl.

But Evie was not there. The room was empty. She was gone. The concrete surface of this reality brought me to rigid attention.

"*Piso cuatro.*" The nurse was shaking my arm. Her beady eyes told me I had been staring at the vacant room for some time. "Your wife, Señor. *Piso cuatro.* You must go, now."

I pinballed down the corridor, paddled on by a series of stout women in pastel nurses' scrubs. Arriving at the elevators, I was met by a grimacing swarm of impatient figures; pen-clicking physicians and arguing administrators; women in wheelchairs pushed by granite-faced caretakers; the occasional relative, grief-colored and exhaling desperation and confusion into the muttering pack. I noticed a "PISO 2" sign between the tag-teaming elevators and, realizing that I would miss the first few passenger loads anyway, opted instead for the emergency staircase. The very idea of labeling a staircase "emergency" in a hospital struck me as annoyingly redundant. This I pondered as I swung myself up the four flights, toward Evie's door.

Following a sign that read, coldly, formally, "*UNIDAD DE CUIDADOS INTENSIVOS*," I pushed through two metal doors into another empty room. Aside from a perforated buzzing sound coming from a defective fluorescent tube, which flickered somewhere in the distance, the space was silent. I stood in front of a vacant window, nervous, like a key witness waiting for a guilty suspect to enter an interrogation cell. On the other side of the glass was a small desk, on which sat a microphone and a keyboard. The little office was unlit, except for the light that fell in, or flickered in, from the main room. On the wall beside the glass was a single red button, above it a speaker. I pressed the button and heard nothing. Half a minute or so passed before an unhurried woman appeared in the frame. She was middle-aged and wore an expression that was once probably quite pretty. I watched her lips move but no sound came out. The buzzing from the light grew louder in its place. I shook my head and pointed to my ears. She fiddled with a chord on the microphone, then her voice cracked through the speaker.

"*¿Estás aquí por la mujer, no? ¿se llama… Evie?*"

"*Si, si. Evie…*" I replied in earnest, grateful simply to hear someone outside my own head annunciate those twin syllables. The nurse motioned for me to take a seat, then left the little office to our shared, flickering light.

There's a lot to think about in between things. In between rooms. In between floors. In between appointments. In between apartments and jobs and other people. So much of life passes by between things. This is the great dark matter of our existence, immeasurable except in relation to the certain undeniable events and moments of concerted animation that surround it. We glimpse it in the seconds preceding sleep, or following a destabilizing shock, when the mind is but a clod, washed away by the sea, unable to grasp even the idea that it used to belong to something else, something permanent and continuous, without holes and tears and stitches in time. We do not register these instances, of course, until after the fact, when we sew them into place, incorporate them into our history and use them to inform our expected future. Then the dark matter of our existence elapses, folds in on itself, and returns to the inaccessible unknown, like a dream you cannot quite recapture once you have stirred awake.

So I stood, in my own two shoes, between rooms and floors, between life and death, between wife and child. Overhead, the fluorescent tube buzzed away, photons bursting in and out of existence. Here... gone. Local... non-local. I thought of the cosmic impossibility of life, despite all the evidence. I thought of my impossible daughter, two floors down and two months ahead of time. I cradled her tiny form, whimpering in the dark, half-sized and squirming in that ghastly marvel of a capsule, that death-defying incubator with all its chords and wires and gauges. I imagined her helpless little body, the needles puncturing her transparent skin membrane and the oxygen tubes funneled into her desperate, frightened lungs. There she was, quivering in the in-between, in the liminal, suspended in the darkness between her mother's safety and that moment far off in the future, two months from today, when she was scheduled to arrive seamlessly, healthily, vitaly, into the present.

Of course, her mother had her own limbo, her own in-between to contend with. She had held her child, nuzzled her against her breast, but had she heard a heartbeat, felt a single momentous breath, registered an autonomous movement beyond the battle charge of her own exhausted panting? What, if anything, did Evie know of her baby's frail situation? What was Schrodinger whispering in her tired, mother cat's ear? Was she...or was she not?

I paced the room lengthwise under failing, intermittent electricity, the faint buzz providing a kind of white noise off in the distance. People had gone insane in this room, I realized with a cold and sudden terror. They had fallen into the space between life and death, never to find their way free. They had lost a wife, or a child, or both. They had lost hope. For this sad parade, the light had stopped flickering altogether, leaving nothing but darkness. Forever.

An abrasive metallic *click* cut the buzzing glass tube. I surveyed once more the in-between space, and then rushed through the open door to find my wife.

*   *   *

Chapter V

BORDERLINE

My Dear Jot,

Before you worry your little Jot head, let me set your mind at ease: You won't have to carry this name around with you forever. In fact, you've only had it for about a week. Before that you were "Mote," "Spot", "Speck," "Atom" and, for three whole days – if only to test your mother's infinite wellspring of patience – "Iota." (Actually, she liked that one the most!)

In short, we haven't yet come to that vast river of names, from which we shall lovingly draw your pail.

For starters, we don't even know if you're going to be a little girl or a little boy! At the moment, I guess you're both... or neither. In any case, we find that out (and we *are* going to find that out) at ten weeks, give or take.

Mommy says she doesn't mind either way, and I believe her. In fact, she seems entirely nonplussed as to why it would even be a topic of interest. Me, I go back and forth. Sometimes I imagine you as a little man, a rascal, no doubt, like your daddy was, breaking toys and generally rampaging around the house. That would suit your grandparents just fine, by the way. They have passed a lifetime waiting for the cosmos to repay the trouble I dealt them in my toddler years! (Your Nana, who is traveling with us at the moment, regales us with stories of daddy's antics almost daily, more than a few of which are on repeat.)

Other times I see you as a sweet little girl, looking out on the world from daddy's shoulders, seeing your mommy, with all her gifts and goals and ideas and theories, walking right alongside us.

Evie, (that's Evelyn, your mommy), is a perfect light to guide you on your journey. She loves without hesitation and has a natural, unpretentious laugh. She is generous to virtue and forgives easily and without agenda. She has character enough for the whole family (and more!) and takes pleasure in things most people never even register. (Barely a bird flies over her head that she doesn't notice, know and name, in that order.) The only time of day she grows anxious (and this she does reliably), is a quarter of an hour before sunset, when her mind fixes itself on determining the optimum place from which to enjoy the view and how we can most conveniently arrive there in due time, to witness – nay, *commemorate* – another earthly rotation. She revels in culture and ceremony of all kinds and, in nine years, I have yet to see her pass an opportunity to commemorate a moment worthy of a raised glass. Her favorite drink is rose champagne, her favorite color rose gold, her favorite flower... orchids. She travels relentlessly (we are in Kraków as I write this note, but bound for Budapest in the morning) and her mind is as fierce as her heart is open. Oh, and she loves your daddy. Lucky, lucky me!

Whether you are a little girl or a little boy, that's one of the things I most look forward to sharing with you; your mother's love. I've traveled quite a bit myself in this world and I can say honestly and with unwavering confidence, there are precious few things in this life quite as whole and as pure and as all consuming as the love your mother gives. As I write to you this moment, she is asleep on the bed beside me. It's strange to think of you two together already, learning each other's bodies and growing together. I can almost see you in her eyes when she looks at me and hear you in her voice when she sings. You are beautiful like her, and already I love you with everything I have.

Well, I'll leave it there before I get all teary (your Nana teases me enough for being "quick to emotion," but I don't mind). Besides, I have bags to pack before tomorrow morning's train ride.

Sleep tight in there, Dear Jotski!

Love always,

Daddy

Kraków, Poland
October, 2014

*   *   *

Dearest Love,

Last night I saw you in my dreams. You were standing on a hill, the grass blowing gently at your knees. It was sunset and you were looking over the crest, off toward something in the distance. I called to you from down the slope, but you were lost in your own thoughts. You looked so peaceful standing there. So strong. So determined. My heart filled with pride until I wept. When I woke, I found my pillow damp with tears. Already you are filling my world with joy. Thank you.

It's been quite a month, my Little Love. And already you've journeyed so far! We've been traveling with your Nana, you see, daddy's mommy. (Mommy's mommy, that's Grandma Margaret, we'll meet in due course.) This journey we started in London, where we met Nana with news of your coming arrival. She guessed it, actually, when I declined to raise a glass of rose champagne – Perrier-Jouët, my *favorite!* – on three consecutive occasions. Of course, I was happy to share the news, even if it was a tad premature. After a week we crossed the Chunnel to Paris, where we spent too short a time in the Musée d'Orsay, acquainting you with Manet, Monet and Maisiat, among the rest, and wandering around the Jardin de Luxembourg. I won't pretend it was easy turning away *fins de clair* oysters and steak tartare (to say nothing of the Seine-side pichets that have colored so many flâneuring jaunts through the *Ville de Lumière* in years past), but to watch your daddy enjoying them with his own mommy was more than enough satisfaction for me. He really is relishing this time in our lives, this transition period.

That's something I'm looking forward to sharing with you, Little Love, your daddy's sense of enthusiasm. As you'll see, it's a happy, contagious kind of enthusiasm, one that gets everyone around him involved. From the moment I told him about you, that morning back in London, he's been just bursting with excitement. He talks about you constantly and devises new nicknames for you every few days (I can hardly keep track). It's sweet, really, how eager he is, how inspired. He's a charming man, your daddy. A loving, dedicated man. I just know you two are going to enjoy a very special relationship.

As it so happens, I'm looking at him right now, asleep against the train window. He was up late last night packing our bags (you and I went to bed directly after dinner). I'll let him rest a little longer, while you and I chat a bit more. There are just so many things I want to show you!

Outside the window, behind daddy's sleepy head, the Polish countryside whizzes by. It's glorious to travel Europe by train. The only way, really, if I do say so myself. We stop in little towns and villages once in a while – Katowice... Opole Glówne... Bohumín... – and I imagine all the people living there, going about their days, seeing to their affairs, raising their families. I try to picture their lives, to imagine what moves and motivates them. One man spends his days tending his father's hardware store, but really he wants to be a pilot, to escape into the blue yonder, to discover what's over the horizon, where the ocean ends. Another woman works at the jewelry store, selling wedding rings to happy couples, but nobody asks for her hand. And here is another man, who just got fired from his job. He doesn't know it yet, but this is the best thing to ever happen to him. Now he will finally paint his masterpiece! Every place has a story, you see, a tale of love and heartbreak, triumph and loss. These are Sisley's tiny dots on the great canvas of life. And between them the late fall light shines through. There's a kind of sweet melancholy to it all, really.

Well, we will be in Slovakia soon, heading down towards the capital, Bratislava, before pushing on to Budapest. You come from a long line of adventurers, my Little Love. I'll have to tell you all about them in another letter. For now, I think I might join your father in the land of sleep. If you want to visit me again in my dreams, I'll be waiting for you with open arms.

All my love, always,

Mommy

Somewhere on the border, Polska/ Česko

October, 2014

*   *   *

Chapter VI

A CROSSING TO
BEAR

Hilda had not yet reached her berth when news of death reached her. A young man, himself full of vim and the vigor of youth, waylaid her in the passageway. "I chased you all the way up the gangplank," he panted, "but you move so quickly. Then, I guess you're quite tall for a woman, and well… What I meant to say…" a look of embarrassment colored his hapless expression. He straightened to say, "Here, a telegram for you, Miss Nilsen," then handed her the envelope, doffed his cap and retreated under her fixed stare.

Worried that the message might portend yet another unexpected change to her itinerary, Miss Hilda Nilsen opened it there and then, right where she stood. The following words she read with a sinking heart:

My Dear Hilda,

It is with the deepest regret that I write to inform you of my husband's passing. As it happens, you were one of the last people to see him alive, such as he was during those final, most difficult hours. Despite our prayers and the sustained efforts of his own physician, Doctor Distad's condition worsened terribly during the last night on the train and, when morning broke, he was already in God's hands. All that remained was for the final pronouncement, which his dear friend and colleague rendered at 6:45am; dawn break of the first new day he would not live to see.

While it is indeed a merciful relief to see his suffering abated (for almost two weeks he was in immense pain and with fever), I cannot help but to think selfishly of the children, his boys. Though I pray for strength, I remain beyond grief, able only to write these words to you because, for the moment, shock spares me the worst of what is surely to come.

I am sorry to further burden your journey, heavy as it must already be, but I felt I needed to send you this news before your departure. Though I do not pretend to know His mind or His ways, the Lord has chosen you to carry forth my husband's mission, one he met with courage and compassion to the last. You will do his memory proud and, by extension, lighten the cross I am now to bear, should you apply yourself equally to the task at hand.

Go in peace, Miss Hilda Nilsen. Go in His service.

Yours faithfully,

Karen Distad

Hilda read the letter twice more in the passageway, then over and again for the rest of the afternoon as she lay in her upper berth, staring in gloomy silence at the ceiling. She thought of the little blonde boys and the difficult path now set out before them. Their spirits would be tested to breaking point, and at such a tender age. She thought of Mrs. Distad, too, and the sense of duty that must have compelled her to compose her telegram while in the throes of such agony and despair. She envisioned her countenance, grown older overnight. And she thought of poor Dr. Distad, he who had dedicated his life to aiding the sick, to comforting the stricken, to walking with the dying through the valley of death, seeing them with grace and care into the Lord's waiting arms.

Like Mrs. Distad, Hilda found some comfort in the knowledge that the doctor no longer suffered, that he must now be delivered into the Heavenly Father's infinite love and purifying forgiveness. And yet, somehow, it did not seem enough, commensurate to the immeasurable suffering Karen and her children would endure now and for the rest of their widowed, semi-orphaned lives. The tears they would shed, the questions left to plague their broken hearts, the empty nights and long years stretched out before them in bottomless, unyielding bereavement. She tried to repress the feeling of injustice that pitted itself in her stomach, as well as the guilt she felt for allowing her mind to question the will of God who, after all, had a plan for us all and was hardly answerable to our petty, ignorant confusions. Who was she, Hilda Nilsen, one woman adrift at sea, to weigh such universal questions as that of life and death when He, with the merest intentions, could whip the fathomless ocean into a frenzy, could wrench the whole world asunder in the blink of an eye, could destroy all within His domain as quickly as He created it! And why should He not, if that were His whim? What did He owe to us, tiny, wretched race, when everything we claim as our own came through His divine providence? Was it not His prerogative, to sweep away His ungrateful creation like so many scuttled toy soldiers?

But still her mind returned to the boys and to Karen and to Dr. Distad's own frail, pathetic body, abandoned to the very illness he cured in others. Why grant these wretched souls the gift of life if they are doomed to end in such pain and suffering? After all, what had this kindly doctor done but to serve at the feet of God, tending to the anguish and misery of His own dear children, afflicted with a disease of His own making? She thought of all His other servants, too, the Red Cross workers on the frontlines of a Europe plunged into war, the howling agony they must endure, the hopeless screams filling long and lonely nights. That there was evil in the world there could be no doubt. The war itself was high testament to that sad fact. But why punish those who sought only to alleviate the attendant suffering, who afforded comfort and succor to the very victims of such persistent, everyday violence? There were plenty of men in positions of power, who leveraged their God-given capacity of free will to visit torture and destruction on their fellow man. Why were they, so often and so overwhelmingly, spared His righteous wrath? What of these Kaisers and emperors and phony messiahs, marching their people to shallow graves by the millions? Modern day Herods the lot of them! Why were they spared from earthly judgment, in the here and now? And if some heavenly fulcrum was to weigh their sins, why wait until they had cost the world so many virtuous men in the meantime? If God really could dash away His world in an instant, why not start with the puppeteers of this hideous, blood-soaked theater? Why must He allow such waste, such pitiable, miserable circumstances to persist?

Not for the last time, Hilda turned to her Psalms for guidance in the darkness. "Those who sow in tears shall reap with shouts of joy!" she recited by heart. "He who goes out weeping, bearing the seed for sowing, shall come home with shouts of joy, bringing his sheaves with him."

The Word flowed through her but, as the vessel found deeper and deeper waters, the Light sank beneath the waves and Miss Hilda Nilsen found herself increasingly alone.

* * *

It was already past dinner when the young missionary woke. She felt a gnawing at her empty stomach and remembered that she had not taken a bite since the station café earlier that morning, when Father Gornitska had insisted on buying her a late breakfast.

"If one is to travel far, one must travel full," he had quipped, with a cheerful twitch of his funny little mustache. She was indeed glad for his company, his counsel. But how distant Father Gornistka seemed to her now. Even his over-animated face, which was not yet a day old to her, was already fading into Seattle's twilight mist. The world at her back had taken on a dull, grayish hue. She remembered with dread the message from Mrs. Distad. Instinctively, she felt for the telegram in her coat pocket. Her mind ran over the lines once more, so dutifully, if despondently composed. The words loomed again, but the emptiness of her stomach scattered them to the wind.

"For the better," she affirmed as she roused herself from a daze. "It is a tragedy, to be sure. But no good can come of dwelling on what has already passed. One must carry on, bear one's cross." Climbing down from the upper berth, no easy feat for a "quite tall" woman, she wondered if the young message boy would know where she might find some supper. She straightened her blouse, pinched the color from her pale cheeks and set off down the passageway to find out.

Being late in the year, the *Fushima Maru* was bound to take the northern route, so that she might avoid the seasonal typhoons. The voyage would last near on a month, weather permitting, with a scheduled port call in Japan for a change of crew and any maintenance that might be necessary. Coming onto the lower deck and glimpsing the ink black water for the first time, Hilda considered the sheer enormity of the distance before her. Barely had the ship put out, it seemed to her, and already the lights of Seattle were lost to cloud and to night. With some trepidation, she allowed herself to lean over the handrail, far below which she caught the wake glistening and frothing against the great ship's hull. Although she had no marker by which to judge their speed, not even the stars overhead, which the evening fog had gently veiled, Hilda sensed that the enormous vessel was already parting the seas at a powerful clip. She watched the waves peel off the hulking iron and counted five… ten… thirty seconds. Then a minute. Two. Three. How vast the ocean must be, to swallow something so colossal, moving at such speed, for an entire month!

The cool evening breeze swept the empty deck. Besides the churning wake and the low rumble of the furnaces, not a sound was to be heard. Alone in the world, the young woman offered a silent prayer for poor Dr. Distad and Karen and the two fair-headed boys, allowing the passing breeze to carry her words off into the cooling atmosphere and her simple, solitary tears to fall into the bottomless ocean below. The unanswering fog gave the distance an immeasurable aspect, at once infinite and immediate. Hilda felt small, but not insignificant, not without a firm place in the universe. Her heartfelt invocations steeled her sense of purpose. Against the wispy ether, she once more became solid and real, body and flesh. She felt as though she were riding atop a great iron steed, carried forth into the endless night sky, toward her chosen destiny.

Lifting her head from this quiet entreaty, Hilda was surprised to discover that some of her fellow passengers had sauntered out onto the deck. Until now, it had seemed the ship was hers alone. She heard the party even before they came into view, the conversation drifting down with the wind in equal parts familiar, muffled chatter punctuated by occasional laughter. The mood she judged as buoyant, even excited. As the figures traipsed leisurely toward her, shedding a cloak of fog in their languid steps, she made out two distinct groups. The nearer to her consisted of four or five women, whose movements swayed in time with the ship's gentle pitch and whose flighty mirth carried more easily in the evening air. Behind them, by a dozen or so paces and in no apparent rush to close the gap, a huddle of as many men bent over a flickering light. A moment later, the salty mist became suffused with the rich aroma of fresh-cut cigars. For a second that immediately escaped into the breeze, Hilda was reminded of the visiting Persian missionaries, whose scent filled so many childhood nights.

As the ladies drew nearer, the solitary woman observed that it was not the sway of the giant vessel that moved their gait just so; or at least not that alone. Their laughter, she noticed, was laced with the unmistakable abandon that accompanies inhibitions out the door, just as their owners happily surrender themselves to the warm, enveloping glow of wine and liquor. If not quite drunk, the ladies were in high spirits indeed. The gentlemen, their stogies now ablaze and dancing like fireflies in the fog, stopped to exhale their smoke into the surrounding mist. Promptly they fell into a muffled conversation about something so important as to command all their available attention. The ladies, swimming in the haze, veered toward the handrail. They wore fashionable dresses having, no doubt, just come from the dining room or the bar. On their wrists and necks glistened colored jewels.

Hilda subdued the impulse to discretion and, instead, allowed her ears to catch the snippets of conversation that perchance fell her way.

"I hear even the commonest Chinese woman is kept like a queen and dresses only in the finest silks," declared one flakey voice, before adding, "nothing like our own unwashed masses, mind you, who wouldn't know a sable stole from a corn farmer's hat."

"What utter rot, Beatty," retorted another, sterner intonation. "The average Chinese woman is lucky to get one warm bath a month. They're a positively filthy lot, nothing at all like we Americans. As for your priceless furs, we have a saying on the South Shore: 'Chinks don't wear Minks.'"

"Oh, that's positively awful!" said someone, and the gaggle let forth with a collective, involuntary gasp, which they shortly followed with peels of unsuppressed laughter.

"Why it's true," the second woman sallied forth in still louder tones. That her chide found such an agreeable reception had evidently emboldened her. "The American woman is the envy of the world, I can assure you. The envy of the world. What we take for granted in Chicago and New York is considered the finest luxury to the Asian woman. And I haven't even mentioned the greatest poverty those poor wretches must suffer. Their menfolk are not only wanting in vertical stature, you see, but… "

What reached the young missionary's ears next almost caused her to topple overboard in a fit of shock and embarrassment. As it was, her reflexive startle was enough to betray her presence, which had heretofore enjoyed the cover of night and fog. The ladies checked their laughter in order to inspect their newfound interloper. Caught wide-eyed in their collective gaze, Hilda was glad enough that the gentlemen were not stirred from their own debate which, meanwhile, had grown somewhat heated.

"I beg your forgiveness, ladies," she managed. "I was just… looking for the dining room, actually. It seems I slept through dinner, you see…" her voice trailed off.

"Well, you'll be lucky to find a hot meal now," the self-styled comedian led off, adding, after a long look up and down her nose, "I suppose you might find something in the bar, though I doubt that's much your scene."

"Come now, Darce," rejoined the woman named Beatty. "No need to be abrupt. The young lady is simply in need of some direction." Darce muttered something beyond Hilda's earshot, which caused the others to repress a snigger. Beatty went on, "You'll find the kitchen serving late fare in the brasserie until 10pm, my dear. That gives yooou…" she glanced at a gleaming timepiece, "just enough time, if you hurry along."

"Thank you so very kindly." Hilda had a sudden urge to curtsy, but stiffened her back defiantly at the very thought. "I wish you ladies a pleasant evening. And good night."

As she turned to make off, Hilda registered one of the men, who had broken conspicuously free from the growing squabble behind him and was watching her with ill-concealed interest. His frame was slightly stooped, his movements somewhat labored. Through the parting brume, she saw his glacier blue eyes following her, as if they recognized her from somewhere. She met his stare for a moment then, unsure quite what to make of it, hurried off to fetch her supper.

*   *   *

As the voyage began to stretch itself over the vast ocean, Hilda found herself content to pass the time in the comfort of her own mind. The days she traversed without appointments, untethered to chores or pressing duties, free to indulge in the kind of deep contemplation that accompanies long periods in which one's inner voice is left to soliloquize in blissful silence. In the mornings she would sometimes saunter along the ship's many decks, pacing the smoothed wooden lengths with hands dug deep into her pockets, her mind wandering absently over the horizon. Gradually, the weather turned colder as the great ship fought its way into the brisk northern wind, and the young missionary regularly found her deck strolls uninterrupted by a single other human presence. She relished her steady solitude, which she filled with Psalms and thoughts of home and her own spontaneous, private reflection. Other mornings she slept late, or simply laid awake in her berth, waiting for the other passengers to depart for breakfast, before rising alone to savor the unbroken peace.

At mealtimes she ate alongside but quite apart from her fellow passengers, the quotidian mess schedule only faintly transposed onto her otherwise anchorless day. Occasionally, during the dinner service, she espied the flighty gaggle she had met on the first night, Darce and Beatty and the others. She dared not acknowledge, much less approach them. For one thing, she had precious little appetite for their inane chatter and, in any case, she was sure their brief encounter remained lost to the women, drowned as it must surely be beneath the leagues of vermouth they seemed always to be consuming. As for the gentlemen with the stogies, they were a constant feature on the deck of an evening, their fireflies dancing tirelessly under the starry skies. Not without curiosity, Hilda noticed that the man with the glacier blue eyes was rarely to be seen among them or, indeed, anywhere else on board. She sometimes wondered why this was and, still more, why his absence inspired in her a feeling vaguely approaching that of loss or regret. Then, as quickly as the feeling emerged, some other flight would take her mental fancy, and she would forget all about him.

The one true constant in her day, indeed her precious remaining hold on the passage of time itself, was the span during which the sun broke below the green-gray clouds and sank into the waiting ocean. To Hilda's increasingly abstracted mind, it found its place like a bead on an abacus, counting one by one the days both fading behind and stretching out before her. Wherever she was on the ship, whether in her berth or at tea or traipsing the decks, the young Miss Nilsen would register, as though by some internal clockwork, the approaching dusk. She would then hurry, abandoning whatever temporary distraction had occupied her, to the starboard quarter in order to witness the grand celestial event.

It was on one such evening, as Apollo's chariot drew its cosmic train beyond the horizon, that Hilda met again the man whose gaze had earlier arrested her own. As had happened the first time, she heard him before he appeared in her view.

"A truly heavenly show," he remarked in a gravelly voice as he approached the younger woman. From the corner of her eye, Hilda saw his hands, wrinkled and weathered, fall casually upon the railing beside hers. A moment stretched out across the whitecaps, and then quietly disappeared beneath the surface. The sunset was particularly spectacular this afternoon, full of contrast as the warm orange hues burst out from behind the thick band of low hanging clouds. They were alone for hundreds, even thousands of miles in every direction.

It was Hilda who spoke at last. "Heavenly indeed. Yet here, in the middle of the ocean, we find the front row is very nearly empty."

"But you are here," the man replied. "You are here everyday."

"I am… in awe."

"Of the grandeur?" His tone was calm, assured. "Or by the fact that no one else joins you to appreciate it?"

"I hardly notice the others," Hilda half-lied. "Whether they are here or not is none of my concern. Nor yours, I should think."

In the silence that followed, she reproached herself for her haughty demeanor. Long another moment lingered. The sun was in the water now. Overhead, the blood orange sky was beginning to cool into soft pinks and violets. The spectators craned their necks, imbibing the full majesty of the event. "Heaven is for all to see," she offered as penance for her last remark, "if only they should choose to observe it."

They stood a while longer, quiet in reverence, until the flaming crown finally disappeared, its residual light thrown across the sky like a divine net cast wide to catch the falling stars.

"And what about your friends?" She thought of 'Darce' and 'Beatty,' and the others.

"You mean the passengers from the other night? I wouldn't say they were friends. Acquaintances, rather."

For reasons Hilda could not have explained, she felt a certain sense of relief, as though, now, they could converse more freely, more openly.

"I met them here, on board. They are men of industry and," he paused for a moment, "women of men of industry. Their paths are different from my own, so do our opinions on certain matters diverge."

Hilda felt embarrassed at having intruded on this man's private affairs, though he was open and frank and gave her no cause for retreat.

"You are traveling by yourself," he observed after a while.

"I have nobody aboard with me, if that is what you mean to say."

"Yet you are not alone, I can see. You walk with the Lord."

Hilda turned to the man at last. He was much older than she remembered, and carried a certain world-weary expression. His eyes, she saw now, were not severe and watchful, but deep and longing.

"How did you know?" She watched him closely.

He turned his attention to the endless waters, as if they had heard his story many times before. "This is not my first mission. Nor, God willing, shall it be my last. I have been to the Far East many times, in fact, as a delegate of so many righteous organizations. Their origins are not of particular importance, save for the uniting fact that they all fall under His watchful eye. Well, I've been all around China. And elsewhere, too. Hawaii, the Philippines. Even as far as the Middle East. One's path is rarely known to him in advance."

To her own surprise, Hilda felt relieved to discover in this strange sounding man a sort of kindred spirit. Familiar though he seemed, she hardly thought to ask his name, then or later.

Over the ensuing days, the pair met spontaneously on the starboard quarter for the grand twilight show. They spoke of far away events, which was easy enough to do from the middle of the Pacific Ocean. The older mind, as is common for those wading into the crepuscular years, reflected primarily on the unanswered questions of the past. The younger attention, meanwhile, focused itself on the unseen future with sustained and unsatisfied intensity, willing the mystical forms to take their shape. Back to back in this way, they talked of God at peace in heaven and of man at war on earth, and of their own peculiar place somewhere in between. The Old Man peered over the lip of the century behind him, marveling at the industrialization of the planet, the mechanization of nature, the receding European tide and the staggering growth of the American engine. Hilda, meanwhile, stood trembling on the cusp of the eschaton, tracing the ship's trajectory off into space, mapping an ocean into the starry night sky.

One afternoon, as a violet sky boiled away furiously on the horizon and the audience of two assumed their regular places, the Old Man veered away from the safety of generality and abstraction to inquire of this younger companion's personal situation. It was not easy for him, and he proceeded with some caution.

"I have seen many able disciples throughout the years, dedicated in their own way to carrying forth His Word. They come from all over the world, not only America. And they journey to wherever they are called. Poor or of means, old or in youth, it matters not. Each has his own calling. Still, it is uncommon to see a young lady, such as yourself, traveling so far unaccompanied," he took a deep breath and considered the woman before him. "I mean not to pry, mind, only to inquire whether you have plans for your arrival, someone to help with your onward journey. I've seen you on this ship, more or less content to keep to your own company, save for these little afternoon shows. Certainly I can respect that. But when the ship puts in, you will begin to see the world that awaits us. Your future will begin to take shape, and quickly. The road is not without peril, dear child, even when one walks in the footsteps of God."

Hilda recalled the man on the train on the morning they reached Seattle; he had asked after her "onward journey" in similar fashion. Did she look so scared, she wondered, so obviously lost? A poor little lamb, strayed from the flock? She surveyed the Old Man again and decided he was worth trusting.

"The family with whom I was to travel," she began, hearing the story out loud for the first time herself, "they suffered a great loss along the way. The father, a good doctor, was taken ill with the flu. He died the morning we reached Seattle. His wife and two boys remain there still, in America. I'm not sure what lies ahead for them. Fortunately, by His grace, I found help in a kindly Father from the Lutheran Church, my own branch. He saw to it that I boarded safely. He was a good friend in my time of need."

The Old Man nodded in the way one does when they have seen plenty of this world. "And now?" his silence seemed to inquire. With some hesitation, Hilda reached into her coat pocket and produced a folded slip of paper, on which was typed a letter from her mission secretary.

"I have only this address," she surrendered the slip, hoping the Old Man would find relief knowing that she was to be received into good Christian arms. "I am to stay at this hotel in Shanghai, until a river boat is available to take me to Hankow. From there, I will travel to Sinyang, and then…"

"Oh… no, no, no. You cannot possibly go there! No, no, no…" the Old Man interrupted. He read on, shaking his head in confusion, then finally declared. "Why, that hotel is the most wretched brothel in the whole of Shanghai!"

* * *

"I'm afraid I haven't any friends in town there who might help you." Hilda heard the Old Man's words with confused but growing alarm. "Those I used to know have long since moved on to other parts."

The pair had retreated to the brasserie to discuss the young woman's sudden predicament. Passengers crowded the space, their sparkling clothes and liquor breath and jolly conversation filling the background with a cheerful revelry. The air was warm and inviting, with plush red carpets on the floors and framed pictures of handsome people adorning the walls. Behind the bar were perched hundreds of brightly colored liquor bottles, which reflected the light off the multi-angled mirrors. Outside a deep, unbroken darkness had overtaken the sky and a soft rain began to fall.

"But I don't understand," Hilda tried to bridle her racing thoughts. "Why would the mission send me to such a sinful place? Surely it is a mistake?"

"Most certainly, yes," Old Man replied. "Perhaps it was once a perfectly reputable hotel, but that must have been a long time ago. The Americans assume nothing ever changes in China, that the Middle Kingdom remains idle, in a perpetual state of long and gradual, not to mention *inexorable*, decay. They assume this morally as well as societally, by the way. They see that the only salvation for the 'yellow man' is for America to rebuild his backward civilization for him, and to do so in America's great image, of course. But this way of thinking is very much mistaken. The world turns, even as we walk upon it. This is true in China as it is everywhere else. Change is the only constant, so the ancients say. Man himself modifies his surroundings in the most extraordinary ways, though not always for the better." He ran his hands through his thin hair and turned to the window. The rain was coming in harder now, lashing the decks. The immense vessel began to pitch and sway, gently at first, then with long, painful groans. In the distant sky a flash of light exposed the heavens for an instant, then left them to darkness once more.

The Old Man surveyed the young lady through calm blue eyes. "Don't worry too much about Shanghai," he assured her. "We will ask the ship's officers for a newspaper when we get to Yokohama. It will have the schedule for all ongoing vessels from Shanghai. You may well find one departing for Hankow the very day you arrive."

And if there was no such boat? No ongoing vessel? Hilda was about to inquire as to a contingency plan, but something about the Old Man's countenance told her that now was not the moment to question faith.

Another flash lit up the sky, this time much closer. The rain swept the decks in fearsome pelts. "What you said just now, about man remaking his world, 'modifying his surroundings,' I think you put it, I noticed that some in Seattle. Well, it's certainly an impressive city and all. Mightily so, in fact. But I had a strange feeling about it just the same. As if, somehow, all this striving for higher and higher buildings, for bigger cities and faster trains and, and these enormous ships…" she broke off, mid reverie, unable to quite formulate her thoughts. Just then, the ship pitched forth again. Small in her own seat, Hilda tried to imagine the size of the waves beneath them, the sheer force required to disturb a construction so massive as the *Fushima Maru*. Her mind reeled. Across the table, the Old Man remained still, patiently waiting for the young woman to find her own words.

At length, she continued. "I keep thinking of pride. As a sin, I mean. There seems to be something defiant in man's work, don't you think? In his zeal to constantly drive himself forward. Now, I haven't seen a great deal of the world, not so much as you, to be sure. But I do wonder at the pursuit of man, his obsession to remake the world in his own image. I guess what I wonder most is, if he continues to build such monuments, grandiose testaments to his own capabilities, will there still be a place for God in his life? It is said that 'The wicked are too proud to seek God…'"

"…'They seem to think that God is dead,'" the Old Man completed her recitation. "Psalm 10:4. But let us forget about what it says in the Bible for a moment. I want to hear what you think."

Hilda pondered this for a long while. It was strange, to be asked what one thinks, rather than what one knows or, at least, what one takes for granted. As usual, the Old Man gave her no cause to rush. Outside, meanwhile, the storm had grown into a tremendous squall, the wind whipping rain and spray against the glass, the metal frames creaking as the ship swayed and rocked. Somewhere across the room a cocktail glass slid off a table and smashed underfoot. The sound went largely unheard.

"On the one hand," Hilda pressed, her own thoughts tossing about inside her head, "it seems perfectly natural that man should use his faculties to further his lot. His talents and his abilities are God-given, after all. If the good Lord had wished him to remain on his belly, like a serpent, or fastened to a plow, as a mere beast, He would have denied him the powers of reason and the mode by which to communicate it. Certainly He would have held free will beyond his grasp, like for so many animals. And yet, there is a certain arrogance in a building that dares reach to the sky, a bridge that undermines a canyon, a tunnel that makes a mockery of an ageless mountain. It's… it's a presumption of power. A ghastly conceit. What I mean to say is: why should man be so important as to determine the shape of His universe, to bypass the work of God, undercutting His divine laws one by one?'

"Barely are we into the present century and already we are traversing the immense Pacific Ocean in a ship made of glass and steel. It all just seems so sudden, what they call 'progress,' so utterly unstoppable. One can hardly imagine what the next decade will bring, much less the next century, if we even get that far! Why, we're all so busy remaking the world, blowing things apart, only to put them together anew. And to what end? What constitutes 'enough?' Will there come a time when man looks to the skies overhead and, thinking the heavens empty, sets his sights on conquering the moon, the stars, the sun?"

The more Hilda tried to concentrate, the more her thoughts seemed turned about. Every time an idea began to form, another flooded in to contradict it, to smother and drown it. She felt the Old Man's calmness in opposition to her own, growing agitation. Her head was a whirlpool. Outside, too, the weather worsened. The lightning flashed much nearer now.

Determined to get a hold of her own position, to corral her subject and bring it to heel, she pressed on.

"When man walks in the footsteps of God, when he supplicates himself to His will and applies himself to His purpose, he commits to a life of worship. Honorable and simple. And in this way he may earn his reward in Heaven, just as Jesus said. 'Blessed are the meek, for they shall inherit the earth.' But when he strays from this humble path, he is tempted to see himself and his own creations as worthy of praise and adulation. In this way, he becomes not only a part of his own system, but its very centerpiece. He turns away from God and towards his machines and equations, toward his own explanations for the divine. He thinks in terms of material, rather than trusting in the Holy Spirit. He holds his truths in money and politics, yet scorns faith in the Almighty. And where does all this get him? Look at what is happening in Europe, where man-made ideas of morality fight for dominance. They say men of God lead the great armies there, but they march as if they were under empty skies and promise to stop at nothing for earthly power in the here and now. For how many years have they been fighting, killing one and other in spite of the Lord's plain commandment? Will this 'Great War' never end? I fear man has lost his way, that he has strayed from the path set for him by God, that he has shunned His Light and…"

A sudden clap of thunder severed Hilda's thread and drowned out the clamor of voices around them. The room fell silent, until a tray of glasses crashed to the floor and roused the crowd once more. Amidst the resumed chatter, a nervous tension was building in the atmosphere. Over by the bar, Hilda recognized one of the women from the first night (was it Beatty… or Darce?) As the floor tilted under her pretty shoes, she began to lose what little balance she had. Lamely, she reached for a handrail, only to miss and fall directly onto the sodden carpet. A nearby gentleman bent to assist her and, as the ship pitched forward violently once more, ended by spilling his martini all over himself and the fallen woman both.

Just then, an announcement came over the ship's main speakers, bidding the passengers return to their berths. According to the information, which came through between claps of thunder and shouts from the crowd, a typhoon had blown further north than forecast and, although the captain and his crew had taken all the necessary precautions, even rougher seas were expected ahead.

Hilda and the Old Man rose gingerly to their feet, holding tight to their table as the monstrous swells tossed the ship back and forth. It suddenly appeared that the vessel was not so enormous after all, that it might be sunk by a single rogue wave. The young Miss Nilsen turned to bid her patient companion well when, in another fierce pitch, she was drawn into the surging crowd and harried on through the passageways, down into the ship's groaning belly.

* * *

For four days and four nights, the *Fushima Maru* was buffeted by wind and rain. She pitched and yawed across the ink black ocean, her iron hull breaching the surface like a great leviathan before crashing beneath the waves once more. At times, it seemed as though she were destined for the depths, and that no feat of stewardship or act of prayer could save her from her fate. On board, the passengers dared not leave the safety of their cabins, rocked as they were to and fro. Many men and women were brought low by seasickness, unable to hold down so much as a glass of water.

Hilda recalled her father's advice against just such impairment, "Confine yourself to fare to which you are accustomed; no exotic dishes. Only drink water you know has been boiled. And to keep your legs, be sure to walk, walk, walk!"

So she did and, in this way, was spared the sickness herself. Even as the great ship was dashed against the mountainous waves like a peanut shell, Hilda marched the passageways alone, hands clutching the railings, for what seemed like hours on end. Heavy metal covers secured the doors and portholes against the crashing waves, so that all outside light was blotted out. Still the water crept in and sloshed in dirty pools up and down the passageways. Days and nights passed this way, in filthy dankness, without the sun to keep time. Inside, only the flickering of the passageway bulbs kept the ship from total darkness. From inside the cabins, Hilda heard the retching and heaving of those brought low. The smell hung stale and terrible in the poorly ventilated space. She imagined the medieval lunatic asylums she had once read about, where tortured souls were locked in cages, left to writhe and suffer amidst their own hellish torments. The passengers moaned and wailed as the ship swayed and rolled, their insides left hollow and their minds confined to counting the endless pendulum motions of the vessel. Up and down, back and forth. Sisyphus and his giant, rolling rock. Even the thought of calm waters, of flatness itself, seemed an absurd impossibility, a cruel joke. The sick yearned for land or for the bottom of the sea, whatever would bring sooner relief to the ceaseless swaying inside and out.

Early on the fourth day, the waters began to calm and the howling winds subsided. Slowly, almost imperceptibly at first, the great ship steadied on her hull. Emerging from the putrid air below, Hilda made her way out of the ship's darkness. On her way to the decks, she passed by the brasserie, where she saw the lovely red carpets sodden and spoiled, the furniture strewn around the room in a terrible mess. The colorful bottles from behind the bar were all smashed against the mirrors, their contents spilled into the brown water underfoot, their shards joined in with the swill. Outside, the potted palms that were bolted to the railings had broken loose. Their plants were upended, the soil mixed in with the water to form great mud puddles that ran the decks and seeped into the brasserie and sullied the carpets. Hilda climbed the stairs to the upper deck, where she saw a few of the metal railings had been twisted like hair curlers. She opened a door and proceeded carefully onto the open deck. Overhead, the menacing purplish clouds were receding over the rearward horizon, yielding the skies to an unusually clear blue. She stared at the wooden decks until the sunshine crept over her shoes. Somehow, miraculously, the *Fushima Maru* was afloat. It had been ravaged, tossed about and thrashed in the wild seas. But it was afloat. Hilda considered the mighty hull, beaten but steadied, tested but triumphant. She thought of the Great Flood and of Noah's Ark, of God's wrath and Man's epic struggle. Then she looked to the parting heavens and prayed that such a machine would never be pressed into the service of evil, made slave to man's hunger for power and his naked pride. Far below, the waves surged and settled into the deep.

"I thought I might find you here." The Old Man's voice was calm, as if there had been no storm at all, no terrifying typhoon that had threatened to submerge them, to drag them down beyond the farthest reach of light. How had they survived such an event? "A truly heavenly show, wouldn't you say?" he said at last.

"I am… in awe," she repeated herself.

"Of God?" he replied, plumbing her deepest thoughts. "Or Man?"

Just then, a crowd of passengers burst out onto the sundrenched deck. They were cheering and singing. Some embraced, locked in the throes of passion and excitement. Among the celebratory throb, Hilda espied Darce and Beatty, dancing toward the twisted railings, arm in sleeveless arm. One of them (she couldn't recall which) caught the young woman's confused glance.

"Why, whatever's the matter?" she squealed in delight, "Haven't you even a smile, my Dear? The war is over! Didn't anybody tell you? The war is over!!"

The women stumbled off, carried along by the jubilant crowd. They swayed and splashed to the very edge of the deck, where their men met them with champagne flutes and fireflies. Behind the retreating horizon the menacing clouds fell, and the great *Fushima Maru* steamed headlong toward the waiting Japanese waters.

* * *

Chapter VII

Lightning Strikes

S o I went to find Evie. Through the corridors and labyrinthine halls, under the flickering fluorescent tubes and past rooms full of empty beds and beeping machines, I went to find my Evie.

I went deliberately, knowingly, full of purpose and conviction and expectation. And, in light of the circumstances, not a small dose of humility, too. I went to see the woman I loved and my best friend and now, incredibly, *suddenly*, the mother of my child. I went to hear her easy laugh, to touch her hair, to kiss her face. I went to feel her warm breath on my cheek. I went to learn her perspective and to share with her my own, to process the day's events and understand them together. I went to see her familiar form, resting on white sheets, her skin flushed a vital pink. I went to find her presence, inseparable from my own, reliable and comfortable, and ready for interaction. I went with a clear picture in my head and a conversation already forming on my lips. I went to meet Evie, in other words, as a husband goes to meet his wife. In these ways, and others I could not have known in that moment, this was nothing at all like the first time we met.

* * *

I first saw Evie at the end of a long American Summer, though the place and the season hardly mattered. I did not expect to meet her, the night that I did. Then again, nobody ever expects to meet an Evie. People anticipate the already-known. They predict the previously-encountered, drawing straight lines from the trodden past off into the untraced future. But Evie was nothing like that. She was newness everywhere she went. Certainly, I had never come across anyone like her before. Nor have I since.

Our courses first crossed at a student ball, held at a college I was not attending, and from which Evie would soon be departing. That we were there coincidentally, she from her world and I from mine, hemispheres apart, on the same hour of the same day of the same year is, without exaggeration, one of the happiest statistical improbabilities to have impacted my life to this very second. The others I will deal with here, in good time. (It is also the reason I harbor a niggling, otherwise irrational suspicion that this may all be just a giant simulation. Either way: lucky me.)

As I say, it was early in the American school year, September, I think. To say it was "love at first sight" would not only be banal, but also an error in chronology. When I saw Evie enter the room (a cramped auditorium of some sort which, in any case, immediately became irrelevant) I knew I had loved her even before having set eyes upon her. This was a love at pre-sight, sight unseen, long before "that moment" arrived. It was easy enough to explain all this after the fact, of course. That I had always been enamored with this woman, had searched her out before I knew she existed, had felt for her in the future haze, wondering what my unrealized hopes might actually be like in a real and palpable sense, rendered true in a present tense. That was all simple enough. Infinitely harder was deciding what to say now that the young woman was approaching. Catching the hint of an accent as she drew near, I was poised to spoil the moment, as young men are wont to do.

The line I was rescued from spilling:

"Where are you from?"

Of the myriad questions that might have captured Evie's wide-ranging interest, this four word conversational cul-de-sac was nowhere to be found among them. To her naturally inquiring mind, it ranked right alongside the weather forecast (not to be confused with climatology, which she found deeply fascinating), popular sports (as quite apart from the thrill of the ancient games) and celebrity gossip (save for that concerning the Norwegian royal family about which, it must be said, she was unashamedly well read).

To Evie, no salutation could be duller than asking after one's accidental place of birth. It was not so much that the question itself foreshadowed a kind of intellectual laziness, a tendency to pigeonhole, but that it came at a considerable opportunity cost, leaving unturned so many closely related subjects that, to Evie, brimmed with untapped promise. Genealogy, anthropology, ancestral trees, native history, immigration, cultural norms and heuristics and traditions; all these fields and more she plumbed with unfaltering energy and vim.

But "Where are you from?"

And right at the outset of an encounter?

No. Not when the page was so blank, the potential so vital, the whole universe opening up in every direction all at once. Not only did it trespass overtly on the merely bromidic, the inane but, to Evie, it at times flirted with the aggressive, especially when an answer was not readily forthcoming. All of which is not to say Evie was easily ruffled; on the contrary. Nothing drew forth the sharpness of her wit more readily than an invitation to the controversial, taboo's door left ajar, the irresistible opportunity to unpack a poorly constructed axiom and turn it on its head. Get her going on church/sect typology, for example, or the inherent contradictions of whatever political party happened at the time to hold sway, and she could be relied upon to excite and flummox each and every unexamined point-of-view in the room. She reveled in doing so, in fact, and could playfully argue for one side just as easily as the other. It was part of her ongoing quest to "explore, experience, express," as she put it.

Nor was the issue bound up in some sacred idea of "personal space," a trendy term she also considered with ample skepticism (along with "offended," "alternative" and "post-modern.") Evie would happily wade into topics of race, sex and metaphysics long before handing her incurious interlocutor the bucket and brush with which to paint her into a merely geographical corner. Worldliness, to Evie, was more than a single data point stapled to a flimsy second in time. ("And what about time, as a Borgesian concept?") She considered herself international in the way that Socrates considered himself beyond borders. "I am not Athenian or Greek," she would sometimes quote the man who claimed nothing he did not know, "but a citizen of the world."

So it was with a small pang of regret that I watched whenever the dreary Hemlock Opener was put to my dear, otherwise loquacious Evie. She seldom let on to her hopeful questioner the disappointment she felt, but I could see it in her eyes, the imminent death of dialectic. Still, she would go through the motions, the depth of her answer depending on the context of the given social situation. A polite deflection, perhaps. A delicate demure. Or, if really pressed, a pithy prologue, followed by a keen pivot to the present.

"I was born in Norway, but my parents left when I was too young to recall," she would recite, slightly embarrassed that such mundane details should be given center stage. "After that I kind of grew up all over the place. England and the U.S., mostly… summers in Kazakhstan… a year or two in Russia… here and there, really. Anyway, tell me more about this delicious recipe/the book you were discussing just now/that show you saw last night?"

All this I learned much later, of course, during countless cocktail hours and late night kebab lines and shared train cabins and awkward family introductions, when I saw her field the one question I knew she dreaded more than any other. It is to my everlasting gratitude, therefore, that I recall the very first words exchanged between us. As Lady Fortuna would have it, they were hers, to me.

Leaning in, with widened eyes, she asked the question simply, naturally.

"Where do you want to go?"

*   *   *

Sarajevo… Sevastople… Suzuka… I continued answering Evie's Genesis Question (as we called it, "the point from which the dream begins") on my way to meet her in the hospital room, on her clean white sheets. We would often play that game when falling asleep, as an antidote to jetlag, to combat insomnia, or simply to follow each other's imagination around the world, a dream before dreamland.

"My turn to choose a letter," she voiced to me across the pillow one spring evening in Cape Town. We were nearing the end of our honeymoon, an ambitious odyssey that began six months earlier in Copenhagen. "Alliterative ambling," she had introduced the itinerary to me, sometime in the after-wedding glow. Ah, Evie. Always with the word games.

"I chose last time," I fibbed, hoping to proffer "U" so I could stump her with an unbeatable Ulm (Germany), Uruapan (Mexico), Ubá (Brazil) combo, right after we had picked through all the low hanging fruit.

"Okay then. How about U?" she suggested. Really, the frequency with which Evie read my mind did little to assuage me of my Simulation Theory problem.

That had been a fun trip, a brainchild Evie dreamed into our future even before we had wished the last reception straggler goodbye, before we had closed the final *ocho* in our brave, first dance tango (also Evie's design). Maybe it had even formed before then, who knows? Evie always had ideas like that, appearing on the surface of her consciousness, already fully formed. It was almost as if her subconscious mind was in such a hurry, it simply decided to perform all the concept assembly first, to present her present with an offer that was simply too good to refuse. Then there was no turning back. No undoing. Just a matter of figuring out the logistics. A half-year honeymoon that would spirit us across two continents and a dozen countries, from Andersen's sea nymph to Nobel Square, eight-thousand miles apart?

"Why on earth not? After all," she winked, "they do begin with the same letter. There's a certain symmetry to it all, don't you think? And anyway, who doesn't want to go to Dar es Salaam? It's right on the way!"

"So is half the world, Evie."

"Exactly!"

"What about work, about money?" I heard my pre-defeated protest, even as the words tumbled from my lips. We'll take our work on the road, she would respond. The travel would inspire us, pull us along in its majestic wake, open our eyes to the unknown, the unimaginable. All the great artists and scientists and poets had an urge to travel. It was called "curiosity." How far would evolution have gotten if Darwin remained a stubborn homebody? What Truth and Beauty might Keats have uncovered in miserable Moorgate? And Gauguin without Tahiti? It was unthinkable. A hypothetical blight on a more perfect past. Besides, what was the use of having geographically independent vocations if we were going to act like potted plants? Think of all the people forced to exist in an office every day, to suffer a commute, to feign camaraderie with coworkers they secretly despised. And here, I knew, would come the decisive point...

"Many are those who have done far more on far less," she would say, skipping down the tricolon. "On horseback and steam ship, without maps or guidebooks, to unknown lands half the world away. Imagine what they would have done now, in the era of jet engines and budget travel, what these curious souls would have seen of the world in the age of the World Wide Web. It would be ungracious of us, in the least, to squander such riches of opportunity."

Then the hammer: "Besides, now's the time for us to explore, while it's just the two of us. How are we going to give our children the world if we haven't even seen it for ourselves?"

So we began to plan it out, mostly in the form of meandering conversations conducted over unhurried lunches around Buenos Aires. At La Dorita, the one over in Palermo Hollywood, we plotted for the Austro-Hungarian chapter.

"The key will be Budapest," declared my lady general, "and Bratislava, to a lesser extent. By spending more time there, we'll be able to offset the cost of Vienna, which will be steep. Not to say that the Marriage of Figaro at the Burgtheater won't be worth the price of admission, of course, but some cheap lángos on the Danube will help rebalance the budget, if that's what you're worried about."

"Who said 'worried?'"

"Your brow, my Dear Man, the way it stitches like that when you're running into resistance. So cute. Now, back to 'Pest. Andrássy Street (Ut) intersects with Franz Liszt, where all the cafés and restaurants are…"

The expedition gained speed over at Lo de Jesus, a little *parilla* on the corner of Gurruchaga and Cabrera, where we stuck pins in mental maps around the Balkans.

"We'll rent a car here, in Dubrovnik, " she pointed to the ballpoint terrain, sketched out on the paper tablecloth, "From there we'll hug the coast all the way to Sveti Stefan. It used to be the summer residence of a Serbian Queen. Marija-something. Imagine, a whole *tombolo* to yourself because, why not, right? I was reading all about this somewhere just the other day."

Of course you were, Evie. You were always "reading about something, somewhere."

"And you know Adriatic sunsets are my favorite. Remember Rijeka, the little balcony off that crumbling old hotel room? We did it then, and on a shoestring. We don't need much, you and I. Anyway, it makes perfect sense, if we want to fit in Ksamil."

"...Albania?"

"No, silly... the *other* Ksamil," she rolled her eyes playfully, as if everyone outside of this tiny town on the Greek border was intimately familiar with its local affairs and plaza side gossip. "Of course, Albania! And it's right by Buthrōtum. Can you imagine? Walking in Aeneas' footsteps? Why, I was just reading..."

And then, a few weeks later at Don Julio's, two blocks down from Plaza Armenia, we floated over the Serengeti.

"It will be the perfect time for it," she enthused, and I knew her feet were hovering off the ground, right there under the table, "during the great migration. Picture the wildebeest, the gazelles, the towers of giraffes, protecting their young..."

"...no time for lazy browsing." I knew she would appreciate a correctly deployed verb.

"No lazy browsing, exactly. And from there we can go right on to Dar!"

"So we're already calling it 'Dar', are we? We haven't even been yet."

"You're only making my case for me, you know."

So we sallied forth, traversing the planet on Evie's imagination, even before the trip became reality. Thessaloniki (just off Aristotle Square) from Birkin Cafe; Maun's dusty airport from Coco Bistro; ancient green turtles and Freddie Mercury's birthplace in Stone Town from good old Rodi Bar, right by the Las Heras apartment.

"And if we have any spare time, we can sip a cup in Stellenbosch," Evie went on, piling city on top of city, "and the other one, Franz Something-or-Other."

"Liszt to 'schhoek...'"

"That's the spirit!"

So we stitched together the plan, Evie's plan, which culminated in Cape Town and the letter "U" and Evie's umpteenth victory.

"Uzhhorod," she whispered softly across the pillow, "previously known as Ungvár..." I heard the words (and registered the double-score), but by then I had already surrendered to my Evie and all her sweet dreams.

*   *   *

My mind was somewhere around Samara, Russia (or was it Samarra, Iraq?) when I entered Evie's Lennon-white room. Nothing rushes you back to the present quite like hospital air, an express ride to reality. The tubes and instruments, the cold steel and dials, the distinct smell of the pickled membrane separating life from the other. The machines beeped and I was right there, in the Intensive Care Unit, in Buenos Aires, by Evie's side. She looked drained. Damp hair, pink cheeks, raw and vital and urgent all at once. A commotion of feeling and instinct simultaneously vying for position, struggling to the front of the conversation.

"She's perfect," I answered the question in her eyes before she asked it. They immediately came alive with the news.

"And..."

"Her APGAR score was good, already revised upward."

Evie let go a deep sigh, undoubtedly the first full exhale since her surgery.

"She's perfect, Love. Perfect." I squeezed her shaking hand in mine. "But how are you feeling? You're trembling."

"I'm fine. I'm fine. It's the drugs. The doctor said... wait, what does her skin feel like? I only barely got to touch her." Tears filled her eyes.

"She feels..." I recalled the first touch on my own fingertips, her Saran wrap skin, translucent and covered in gossamer down. "She's, she's so small." I looked at Evie's own beaten body, at her midsection rising and falling under the clean white sheets, suddenly empty. *Emptied.* "Can you even believe this? Can you understand what's happening? That she's actually here?"

"And then they were three."

"Naturally, three."

Evie wiped a tear from my cheek. I had not realized I, too, was crying.

"This is us from now on," her voice was weak but confident. And hopeful. "This is our story. Our little family."

"Hey, you're a mom."

She smiled her first mom-smile and replied in kind, "Hey, you're a dad." I wondered what mine looked like.

"I guess we'll be a 'ma ma' and a 'da da' first.'"

We meditated silently on this sweet moment, until a nurse's footsteps broke the shared reverie. Immediately, Evie shot her an expectant, almost desperate look, like someone waving down a taxi in the pouring rain. But she was gone; her penny-loafer footsteps carried off down the corridor.

"I'm waiting for them to let me go down and hold her. They say I have to wait, but they won't tell me for how long. I know we're only two floors apart but, Zeus Almighty, it feels like a million miles!"

"She's resting, Love. She's comfortable."

"I know, I know. But she should be resting here, on me." She made an empty cradle with her arms. "Anyway, go on. Tell me more. What's she like? Her face? Her toes? Does she have your ears? Please tell me she has your ears. Attached lobes and all."

"Your ears are perfect for a little girl, Love. As they are for a perfect woman. But anyway, you know how I am with all that. Facial recognition and what-not. I barely notice identical twins. Remember the Bourdain brothers?"

Evie laughed out loud, showing all her Norwegian-American teeth. I always thought she looked her best without make-up, right out of the shower, flushed red from the scalding water.

"You don't have to have it so hot," I would remark as she felt around for her glasses in the steam. "Or be in there for so long."

"I just lose the time," she would vaguely reply. "I honestly don't know where it goes."

Just then I heard footsteps behind me and, with no small effort, Evie raised her tired arm again and flagged down a passing nurse. *"¡Perdon, perdon! Disculpame señora. Sabes cuándo podré ver mi bebe?"*

The woman smiled a kindly smile, but told us they were still waiting on some additional tests. It was not possible *"en este momento,"* she repeated to the new mother's protest. Doctor Kostas would be along shortly with more details. Oh, the expression on poor Evie's face! Two floors might as well have been parallel universes, "shortly" a bottomless eternity. She turned her pleading eyes to me, helpless me.

"I'll go down soon," I gave her hand an assuring squeeze. "We'll all be together again soon. I just wanted to come and see you first, to know that you're okay."

"I'm fine, Love. Fine. Only I feel like there's a part of me right here in this building that I can't reach. Can't touch. It's strange, to be separated like this. I mean, what tests are they waiting on? What's so important that I can't go down two floors and see my baby?"

"I know, Love," I tried to soothe her. "I know."

But I did not know. I did not know anything, helpless me. I did not know anything when I kissed my Evie on the forehead and squeezed her frail, shaking hand in mine. I did not know anything when I raced out of the room, leaving her on the clean white sheets, all alone with her machines and tubes and monitors. I did not know anything when I strode past the elevators and slid the stairs down two flights, passing by the third floor and whatever non-child, non-wife activity went on behind those mysterious doors. And when I arrived at the desk marked *Unidad de Cuidado Intensivo Neonatal* to inquire after my premature baby, I had no idea what was going on two floors above me, inside my wife's body, in her blood cells and her enzymes and her thrombocytes. I did not know of the storm and the lightning, (*the lightning!*) that was brewing, nor what would happen when it struck.

*   *   *

APGAR: a backronym made to fit Virginia Apgar, the bespectacled anesthesiologist who worked her miracles at the New York–Presbyterian Hospital in the forties and fifties. **A**ppearance, **P**ulse, **G**rimace, **A**ctivity, **R**espiration. Five criteria used to quantify the effects of obstetric anesthesia and assess the vitality of wriggly little lives, weeks, days or precious seconds new. I remembered now, at that NICU desk, Evie reading aloud something about this from one of her "What to Expect…" books, gifts from well-meaning sisters-in-law that she would occasionally flip through before returning to her own set reading list (mostly focused around childhood anthropology, Montessori vs. Waldorf vs. Reggio educational methodology and, as always, some dog-eared Loeb editions she wanted to revisit.) The conversation soon veered from Dr. Apgar's measurable contributions to more esoteric musings.

"Just imagine," went Evie's reliable point of departure, "an eternity without classification and, then, boom! Life with a capital "L" comes on, all thick and fast, with its assessing and measuring, weighing and cataloging, grouping and plotting, acronyms and backronyms and all the rest. Aristotelian classification. Sixty, eighty, one hundred years of quantitative analysis and bell curves and growth charts and then…"

"Then nothingness again. Into the void."

"It's astounding to consider, isn't it? This fleeting moment. This life. They had it right, the ancients, Lucretius and Epicurus especially."

"*Death is nothing to us, since when we are, death has not come, and when death has come, we are not.*"

Evie smiled and rubbed her swollen tummy. "It's unusual, isn't it? Unusual and precious. The sheer brevity of personal existence, that we're surrounded by this eternal nothingness, fjords of zero dropping off to either side. Simply to coexist at all is statistical madness. As for the three of us together, beating, breathing, thinking simultaneously? It's just preposterous."

Unusual and precious. Unusually precious. Unusually unusual. Evie's words played in my mind, until a straight-backed young woman with angular, indigenous cheekbones (nametag: Laura) stole me back to the present with a clipboard and the following instructions:

"You'll go through these doors and wash your hands thoroughly in the sinks on the right." She directed me in American-accented English. "Use the pink soap and wash thoroughly up to your forearms. Do this twice. And be sure to keep your scrubs on at all times. Especially your facemask. The quarantine environment is critical. Some of the babies in there are very, very small." Her countenance was grave, but not unkind. I nodded in earnest. "Doctor Maro will meet you on the other side of the doors and guide you to your baby."

I pushed through the doors, thinking how unfitting, how unfair it seemed for a brand new life to already be considered a "patient." An eternity waiting in the darkness, then Life, all "thick and fast." I followed Laura's instructions and then sat, prophylactic and impatient, on the green plastic bench seat in the intermediate zone. The room was bare, except for a creeping clock and, underneath it, a corkboard feathered with photos. Dozens and dozens of photos. I drifted toward them, a hundred or so children peering back at me from their phellem bark perch, their gaze fixed somewhere beyond the camera. They were two and three and four years old. Returning alumni, come to visit their old alma mater, to encourage hopeful future graduates. They were signs of success, gone on to careers in sandbox architecture, building block engineering, dolly rearing and scooter racing. There were chestnut twins and baby blues, onesie-clad musicians and peek-a-boo yoga instructors, apples and oranges of their proud parents' eyes, heroes of epic narratives, motivational pre-speakers each and every one of them. Drawing closer, I noticed the messages accompanying the triumphant moments, museum wall text for an exhibition in self-realization and actualization and affirmation. Life already imitating art.

"Maria (1.8kg) y Marta (1.6kg), nacieron 28 semanas, en sus tercero cumpleanos. ¡Gracias a los medicos de Swiss Medical!"

"Enrique, nacio 26 semanas, desde su primer dia del jardin. ¡Felicidades y muchisimas gracias a todos los medicos!!"

"Jorge y Eugenia, nacieron con 1.250 gramos y 1.1 gramos respectativamente, disfrutando tiempo del baño con sus papi."

I examined the father's eyes; elated beyond drained; contented beyond surfeit; ecstatic beyond fatigue. Here was a man who could take anything, could tolerate any tantrum, who would look to the heavens in gracious appreciation every time it was his turn to change a diaper. He had been to the gates and seen the void, and returned with his child safe in his arms. But what had he been through? What desperate pacts had he made? For how long had he dragged his frayed nerves through this "quarantine environment?" How many times had he soaped his own trembling forearms, cried into the sink, shrouded his bawling, tear-sodden face behind that choking mask? And where was his wife, absent from the photo? Was she behind the lens, or waiting in nothingness, beyond the void?

There were more snippets, too, merry vignettes from the other side. Life born at twenty-seven, twenty-six, even twenty-three weeks (twins, Elijah and Elisa). I examined the specimens, struggling against my own will to discern any evidence of their ordeal, any deformity, any dullness of expression or vagueness in their tiny apprehension. They had emerged, passed the bar, but were they unscathed? Did they carry any scars from their mortal battle? Any problems with their eyes or lungs? Blindness? Asthma? Worse? How was their coordination, their mental capacity, their emotional development? I suddenly became over-invested in the wellbeing of a whole cohort of life students I had never met, and likely never would meet. They were my child. Their parents were me. Our plight shared.

Wondering again if I had properly scrubbed my world-filthy arms, I heard my name and saw a doctor approaching with outstretched, lab coat limb.

"Congratulations," he offered in English, to my unending relief. "My name is Doctor Vee Maro. I'm your daughter's neonatologist. I understand your wife is also in intensive, up on four. This must be quite an ordeal for you. Well... we can go and see your little girl now."

I made to move, but my legs were frozen with panic. And shame. What if she was not perfect, as I had so confidently assured Evie? What if she was suffering? What if she was destined to suffer her whole life? The very thought stuck itself like a dart in my neck, filling my blood with cold, paralyzing poison.

"Hey, hey. It's still early," said the man with his hand on my shoulder, "but all indications are good. We've lowered her oxygen dosage and she appears to be coping well enough on her own. She's small, but she's strong."

My soul plummeted through every crack and caveat – "still..." "but..." "enough..." "appears..." – but though "coping" was not exactly "thriving," there was at least encouragement in the doctor's firm hold. He seemed to be saying, as he shook me gently, "It's *you* who needs to be strong for *her* now."

I scanned the corkboard again, the graduating classes of years gone by, toddling testaments to will and spirit. With a blind inhale, and a pulse-racing sense of *déjà vu*, I went to meet my daughter.

* * *

The room was warm and dark; womblike, I imagined. Except for the ubiquitous beeping machines and a few faint cries, the unit felt very much asleep. As my senses began to adjust, the space came to life one plastic, primordial pod at a time. It was like looking at a camouflaged ecosystem under a microscope and, after initially dismissing it as devoid of activity, you begin to notice one... then two... then a dozen and more distinct creatures, energy emanating, their movements forming a gentle chorus, then finally a grand symphony of life. I followed Dr. Maro, my guide, through the ancient darkness.

We passed by rows and columns of dimly lit incubators, mimicking the delicate balance of uterine conditions for their precious little passengers. I tried not to leer over the contents, the squirming bodies in saggy skin sacks, their delicate expressions painted on squash ball-sized heads, a mess of tubes and cables connecting them to monitors and drip feeds outside, in the real world. I could not help but look. They were so very unreal, a legion of fetal soldiers just pushing their way through, insisting on life. Occasionally, we passed a family member slouched by their own pre-infant's isolette, exhausted, staring at their sleeping little human, willing its wee lungs to keep breathing, its heart to keep beating on, to just keep *being*.

I fixed my gaze on Dr. Maro's white coat as it sailed past the rows of doll-like bodies, a live toy store of miniature vessels and pores and jellybean organs, pumping and squinting and gasping. From somewhere down one of the rows, I heard an adult-sized voice softly whimpering. I dared not look. Other muffled sounds punctuated the atmosphere. I trained my vision, blurred and moist, on the doctor's white sail ahead. My mind escaped to a late summer's afternoon, Evie and I on a friend's sailboat, out on the Chesapeake. We had cold Yuenglings in hand and the air was sticky with the drifting aroma from the Domino Sugar factory. The sunlight glistened on the water. Evie let her fingers trail along its surface, catching the energy in her hand.

"So when are you two going to tie the knot?" someone had asked.

"When we get back to Argentina, most likely. More than anything, I think Evie just wants an excuse to invite everyone down and show off the city, to have a grand, multi-national party with friends and family from all over the world."

"It's not just that," she had coyly protested. "I want to wear an elegant dress and dance the tango, too!"

"Don't laugh. We've been taking lessons. It's much harder than it looks. Well, for me, anyway. Evie seems to be getting along quite well."

"I've got a good lead is all."

"Ah, you two will do great," someone, again. "Just be sure to give us plenty of heads-up. We'd love to join you."

"And you know what comes after that?" another voice teased.

"Jeez, let 'em get married first. The kids'll come in due course. They always do."

In due course, of course. All in due course.

I stared up at the mainsail, billowing in the sunshine. The staysail (or was it the jib?) blew into view too. Nothing but blue skies. Blue skies and smooth sailing. Then the wind suddenly died and the doctor and nurse turned to address me in relay. When had she arrived?

"Podrias sentarse aca, señor." she beckoned. *"Espérame un momento, por favor. Espérame…"*

I sat down and watched as she reached her hands through two holes on the side panel of an empty incubator to fiddle with some tubes and cables. She must be readying the little bed, I thought to myself.

While the nurse prepped the various instruments, Dr. Maro gave me the vitals. "She was born at 31.1 weeks, 1,382 grams and healthy. Her APGAR was good and she's doing well. Marta, the neonatal nurse here," he nodded to his staysail, "fed her an hour ago."

"Yes, yes," I thought, "but where is she? Where is my baby?"

Marta felt around in the empty incubator, messing with the chords and tubes.

"We'll continue to monitor her," the doctor went on, "but so far, so good. Here, it's your turn to hold her."

From the corner of my eye, I saw Marta's arms extended. In hardly more than two hands she held a crumple of blankets, from which protruded a leg the size of my thumb. Instinctively, I held out my hands and received into them my swaddled daughter. Marta adjusted the tissue-square blanket and I saw her, her tiny face looking up at me like a ray of light glistening on the water. I thought of Evie's fingers, trailing gently through the wake.

"And here she is, daddy's little girl. She's been waiting to meet you. Now, if you open your shirt, Marta here will help her onto your chest."

"Ah, cangurito," soothed Marta as she adjusted the oxygen tube and other leads and lines. *"Cangurito con papa. Eso… eso… Muy importante."*

"We call it Kangaroo-ing," the doctor explained. "Like a pouch."

I undid my top two buttons and, with Marta's guiding arms, lowered my little joey onto my naked chest.

"The incubators help maintain a stable environment and allow us to monitor her vitals – heart rate, breathing, blood pressure and so forth.

Even so, there is nothing quite like the touch of a parent's skin. Here, now she's listening to your heartbeat."

My clock was just about ticking through my chest. "Can I... can I touch her face?"

"Of course you can. She's your baby."

I traced my giant fingertip along her forehead. Her little body wriggled into position, settling onto daddy's chest. I looked into her half-closed eyes and whispered the opening three words of that very first letter: We. Love. You. The vibrations of my voice emanated from my chest and through her tiny frame. I stroked her hair, fine like dandelion pappus, and fell into this soft chant.

We love you... We love you... We love you...

*   *   *

Evie was sitting up under her clean white sheets when I burst in with news from the second floor. Her eyes widened when she saw me, widened in a big moon face. She looked swollen, my Evie, lethargic.

"What did she feel like?" she breathed the words out.

"Oh Evie, she's sublime," I gushed. "I had her on my chest. Right here, against my skin."

"*Cangurito*..."

"Right, exactly. She listened to my heart and..."

"...and you told her..."

"And I told her we love her, Evie. Of course I did. Just as we planned. I told her many, many times. It was the first thing I said, in fact. And the last. I... I..." I had to catch a breath. Those damned stairs! "She's tiny, Evie. Tiny, but strong. Doctor Maro, he's the neonatologist, he said she's doing really well, that they might even be able to take her off oxygen soon. They've got her on this tube and, well... The nurse, Marta, she's right by her side. She's kind and warm and... She's lovely, loving."

"Off oxygen..."

"Yes, they're lowering her dosage now. The lungs are one of the last things to form, apparently, so premature babies sometimes need support.

They have this little blue facemask thing that feeds directly into their nose. But doctor Maro reckons…"

"Premature babies…"

"Right, there's a whole corkboard full of them, Evie. Their pictures. Like little survivors. All these preemies that grew up and went on to lead perfectly normal lives. Some of them were unbelievably tiny. Like less-than-a-kilogram tiny. Most of the really small ones were twins. The boys seemed to be smaller, I noticed. Not sure why. Anyway, anyway, our little girl is almost fourteen hundred grams, so… Oh Evie, she's so pretty. Her little eyes, these shiny little things, like light playing on water. I don't know whose features she has, but they're absolutely perfect…"

"…and you told her…"

"Evie, I told her. I… Evie? Evie? *EVIE!!!*"

* * *

Chapter VIII

A PATH TO FOLLOW

Dearest Little Love,

Well, you're only as big as a raspberry (at least, that's what the books say), but already you're filling our lives with immense love and joy. And sleepiness! We've been indulging in some long naps together, you and I. Naps before dinner... naps on trains... naps on planes. Your poor daddy must feel as though his wife has fallen into a coma! Who knew growing a little human would be so exhausting? Mercifully, we seem to have skipped the dreaded "morning sickness" stage. There were a few moments there, early on, when I thought I'd have to make a beeline for the rest room (once during the second act of Prokofiev's *Romeo and Juliet*, which would have been less than romantic), but thankfully the feelings passed. Otherwise, we're doing rather well, physically speaking. I even caught myself in the reflection of a tram window the other day and fancied my shape a little curvier. Hmm... overall not so bad, is it?

Plus, we get to dream together, you and I. That's one of my favorite parts about this journey so far: visiting you when we sleep. You come to me almost every night now. I don't see your face, exactly, but I feel you in our story, traveling right alongside me. You're like a light source, just out of the frame, but always comforting me and warming me (and occasionally reminding me just how influential hormones can be on the body!)

Sometimes I see you when we're awake, too. (Though this may well be a side effect of the fatigue!) Like just last week. We were in Stavanger, where mommy was born and where she spent time as a young girl, visiting family, and I thought I caught a glimpse of you in a crowd of teenagers. They were playing in the square right in front of the big church, where I used to sing and dance with my own friends. They were running back and forth and giggling, as children do. You were a splash of blonde hair, somewhere in the center of the group. The others were frolicking and jumping about and I swore I sensed you racing between their gangly teenage forms, a ray of light in an impressionist painting, something by Thaulow, perhaps. I imagined you laughing with them, your adolescent heart aflutter with excitement, rollicking in the eternal twilight. You'll love Norway. It's in your blood, you see. You come from a long line of adventurers. But that's another story, for another day. One could write a book, one really could...

You have so many experiences to look forward to, my Little Love, so many places to see and know. Already daddy and I are planning out a Grand Tour for you, a journey that will inspire and amaze. We'll go from Norway to New Zealand, Cambodia to Colombia and beyond. But for now, we're here in rainy London again, back where we began this correspondence. It's astonishing to think that it was only a couple of months ago when I told your Daddy that you would be joining us, along for the ride. I remember distinctly, standing in the bathroom after having just taken the test, looking at myself in the mirror. I could almost feel, in that very moment, someone else looking back at me. Was it you?

Already the seasons have changed. The leaves have fallen to the ground and the bare trees reach to the sky in tortured, Scheilesque beauty. The whole world has turned under our feet. I've been thinking a lot about life and death lately, with you, my own little energy source, emanating from within. Though it feels like you've been with me forever, I recognize we're now entering a new phase in this journey, in our own little life cycle. So I'm embracing each new day with an open mind. *Paso a paso* (step by step), as they say down on the Pampas.

On that note... we have a visit with the doctor here later this week (just a routine checkup, no need to worry your sweet raspberry head), then we'll head back to the U.S. to stay with mommy's family for a while. After that, it's back down to Buenos Aires, Argentina, to the end of the world, to look for a new family home. We'll find something cozy with plenty of light...and be sure to fill it with lots of love. Until then I'll be dreaming of you at night (and during our spontaneous naps) and looking forward to seeing you every day.

All my love,

Mommy

London, England
November, 2014

*   *   *

Good morning June,

Hooray, hooray! June 23rd is the day! It seems like an eternity from now, I know, but that's when we're finally going to get to meet you. The date is fixed in my brain and already I feel my whole self oriented toward its arrival. (As you can see, I've assigned you a new temporary birth-month name...subject to change, of course.)

Mommy and I took you to the doctor here in London this morning. It's freezing, by the way, but she is being very good and wearing nice warm clothes to keep you all toasty inside her belly. Anyway, the doctor examined you both using something called an *ultrasound*. Basically, she squirted a cool gel over mommy's tummy and, through the wonders of sonographic technology, we were able to get a glimpse of your little self! It was amazing, I have to say, even though daddy hates being in clinics and hospitals (all those beeping machines are enough to drive anyone mad!)

The doctor couldn't tell us if you're going to be a little boy or girl yet (though Nana and I have our suspicions...), but she did let us hear your heartbeat. So strong! To think that your organs are already forming, that your brain is beginning to take shape, miniature lightning bolts flashing around the hemispheres, your little self coming into being one neural connection at a time. Next will come your eyes (green like daddy's, or blue-gray like mommy's?) and facial features, then nascent thoughts and dreams all of your own. Well, you've got another six months for all that, of course, no need to rush there. Still, it's fascinating to think that you're already assembling, that you're a *you*, recipient of these meandering letters, with an *in utero* address all of your own.

Speaking of addresses, we've been on the move plenty this past month, our compact family caravan traipsing all over Europe. You've probably been to more countries in your mommy's tummy than most people get to in their whole lifetime. Next we're going to the U.S. to spend some time with mommy's family. But before that we have a few more days here in London, just the three of us. I can't believe it's already been two months since we learned that you were on your way. It seems like yesterday! Since then we've traveled by plane, train and automobile across France, Germany, Poland, Hungary, Norway… thousands of years of war and peace, all flashing by in a millisecond. We took you to plenty of monuments and museums, parks and plazas, churches and synagogues, grand archives of mankind's archetypes, his checkerboard past cataloged in living ruins. Your mommy is a devoted history buff. You'll love going to old ruins with her. She's a walking encyclopedia she is, full of names and dates and colorful imagination. Remind me to tell you about Tunisia one day, and the worst hotel room ever. And Cyprus. And Greece and Sicily and Morocco. Well, so many places, really. It's a funny old world, this one, balancing between countless contradictions and opposing forces, at once comedic and tragic, "Dionysian and Apollonian," as mommy would say, simultaneously rising you up and wrenching you asunder. It's a ride, if nothing else, and one I absolutely cannot wait to share with you.

In the meantime, you and mommy are resting peacefully, so I'm going to go order us some dinner. I wonder if you'd prefer her favorite Indian dish, *malai kofta*, or if a takeout *yasai yaki soba* from Wagamamas is more your speed. (Hamachi sashimi is out until June 24. Sorry mommy!) Either way, I'm sure you'll let her know.

With lots of love,

Daddy

London, England
November, 2014

* * *

Chapter IX

ON EAGLE'S WINGS

For ten days and ten nights the *Fushima Maru* was at port, Japan's imperial waters lapping gracefully at her mighty hull. Besides a few curious creatures, her passengers mostly remained on board, where repairs were made during the day and the band played on against the sounds of the cheery, post-war revelry in the brasserie of an evening. Bleary but relieved to be off the high seas, they read in their quarters or played gin rummy in the common areas or simply milled about, chatting idly on the twisted decks and casting apprehensive looks toward the strange harbor, off in the middle distance. Outside, the November air was cold and still and the moon glistened on the Yokohama waters. Behind them the vast Pacific settled, its typhoons and tsunamis safely bottled for now. Ahead, the Far East loomed tall, a prospect shrouded in mystery and doubt and general suspicion.

Miss Hilda Nilsen counted herself among that curious minority, who daily disembarked the great ship to conduct investigative probes into the new and strange land, but while the others went about in small groups and pairs, wide-eyed whites with confused expressions and scuttled senses, the young missionary mostly wandered the streets alone. She watched as the others recoiled at the foreign smells and pointed to the painted glyphs, splashed red on the weatherboard outside shops and huts and teahouses (they could barely tell which was which.) She eyed them as they narrowed to single file, squeezed through laneways thronged with bicycles and overrun with chickens and dogs, as they fanned lace-gloved hands under their noses, hiked their pretty dress skirts over puddles and stood upright and rigid when locals passed them by. She felt embarrassed of them, but equally self-conscious of her own conspicuous apprehensions. She was aware, too, of the squinting eyes trained on her own form, blonde and western-dressed and awkwardly tall. Asian expressions examined her from behind counters and under window sills, out of darkened corners and in broad daylight.

All the while, her father's words echoed in Hilda's ear: "Whenever we go out to meet the world, the world also comes out to meet us." They were intrigued too, these peculiar people, just as she was of them; like strangers in the looking glass.

What a curious world this was, full of community narratives and personal pains, localized episodes of mankind's eternal meditations. She imagined all there must be to apprehend in this life, all the unopened doors and unturned stones and unasked questions. As she ambled, she breathed in the smells of fish and eggs and burned tea, boiling away on open flames set out in front of the little huts. She met the darting eyes, but found she could not hold their gaze, that they averted, as if she had caught them doing something wrong, somehow foiled their furtive voyeurism.

For ten days she walked the dusty streets, the atmosphere filtering into her lungs and settling in a thin film on her skin. At first it was sour and pungent, full of overripe ingredients and raw meats and salty brines, but it soon grew milder, even oddly pleasant. Block by clutter, she began to map the streets and alleys and to recognize a few of the stall operators, one or two of whom she exchanged polite nods with and who bowed when she passed their modest enterprises. Occasionally she would stop by one of the many temples, to examine their little icons, curios of strange superstition, arrowheads of a lifetime spent abiding by their own creation stories and morality tales. She felt a soft pity toward the pathetic little figurines. The inwardness of it all seemed to her somehow sad, that pleasure and comfort should be derived from handmade objects, that worship should be turned toward an inner peace or (she had heard the word somewhere before, though she did not quite grasp the concept) *Zen*. Still, the devotees were polite to the point of being deferential and their courtesies very much impressed the young visitor. She was careful not to betray any sign of sympathy that might be interpreted as condescension, though she felt a certain tightening in her throat nonetheless.

She saw the Old Man only twice during those days at port. Once when they exchanged a few passing pleasantries in the brasserie, before the crowd shuffled them along on their separate ways, and another time toward the end of the stay, when he joined her on the quarterdeck for their customary twilight exchange. He had under his arm a folded newspaper and he approached with an unconcealed smile upon his face.

"You need not be relieved, Miss Nilsen," began the Old Man in his familiar, avuncular tone, "to discover that you are provided with onward travel." He turned the crumpled yellow pages to a schedule of some kind, written in a scribble of foreign characters. He had circled the relevant column. "Here, there's a river boat leaving the very afternoon we dock in Shanghai. You won't need to spend even one minute in that vile hotel. The *coolies* will help you with your luggage, so you needn't worry yourself about that, either. And we'll arrange for a message to be sent onward from port, to your mission in Hankow, informing them of your arrival time. You'll be on your way before the sun reaches the horizon."

Hilda was indeed glad of the news, but a certain melancholy sat heavy on her chest. Their journey together was coming to an end. Though she had only spoken to him briefly while in Yokohama, it was a comfort to know the Old Man was there just the same, in the same boat, as it were. Once in Shanghai, they would be separated, left to follow their own individual callings. And she would be alone again.

"Thank you kindly for the news," she started, "but I find that I *am* relieved to hear it, after all. Is there some reason I should not be?"

"Ah, because you never brooked any doubt, young lady. Not really."

They watched in comfortable silence as the sun set over the storied Pacific. The very next day, the *Fushima Maru* put out for Shanghai.

*   *   *

Hilda Nilsen arrived in China with both eyes open. What she saw there, in the heaving metropolises and amaranthine hillsides, in the cheeky grins of the school children and the milky eyes of the dying, took her years to fully comprehend. Yet, for all that, what she first noticed was not for her eyes at all, but for her nose. If the smells in Japan had arrested and enticed, they were nothing compared to the exotic mix China laid before her. Floral and acidic, heartwarming and gut-churning, scents she had never before imagined, much less imbibed, rushed at once to her senses. They were a teaser, a *taster*, she would later reflect, of a land swimming in contradictions. So she went, eyes open and lungs full, into the Middle Kingdom.

Wading into the human rush of the Shanghai port that first afternoon, Hilda found the mass of people occupied enough with their own business that they paid her scarce attention. Thus left alone, she tended to her various logistical concerns. Her American dollars she had changed with the ship's purser, who kindly pointed out the riverboat, its twin funnels silhouetted against the graying sky, which was to take her to Hankow and beyond. The "coolies," as the Old Man had called them, saw to her luggage and even transported her by rickshaw to the foot of the smaller ship's gangplank. The ride upriver was pleasant enough and went by largely without incident, save for some expected confusion with the new coinage and a few awkward moments with a talkative shipmate, who, Hilda suspected, had become a little jolly on some strong drink he smuggled onboard while in port. Steaming further inland, she watched as the city's drab buildings and factories yielded to grassy riverbanks and marshlands, punctuated occasionally by shantytowns and little fishing villages. Eventually, the scenery passed under her heavy eyelids as if on repeat. Sleep came at last.

When the riverboat reached Hankow, Hilda stood back to let the other passengers disembark first. From the deck she spotted, among a sea of Chinese faces, a conspicuously foreign expression, roughly the size of a nickel in the crowd. When she descended the gangplank, the man came over to introduce himself. Hilda had never before seen Erik Sovik in person, but she fancied she recognized his face from the church papers. Years later, she would confess to his wife that Mr. Sovik was nearer to being "hugged to distraction" by a complete stranger on that day than ever in his life, so glad was she to meet a missionary from her own church.

That first night she passed at the Sovik home in Shekow, just outside Hankow, with Erik and his wife. The rooms were modestly appointed in just the way she expected a mission house to be and the warm familiarity gave her some comfort after the terrific journey. Besides the Soviks themselves, there were other guests in the house, each coming and going throughout the afternoon. During dinner, Hilda encountered another man and wife who had been serving somewhere deep in China's interior; Chengdu, she thought they said. They were setting out for a long furlough to their native Norway after ten consecutive years on mission. Hilda could hardly believe their health and vitality; they were robust, red-cheeked and optimistic. Somehow she had expected, after such a long time working "in the field," they would be ground down, visibly fatigued. She could not suppress the urge to ask what, beyond complete surrender to the will of God, of course, had sustained them during their work.

"A good sense of humor," the man responded without hesitation. "It has helped us out in many a tight pinch!"

"Ah, and don't forget a strong stomach!" his wife chimed. The pair laughed as only couples that spend a long time together on the road, eating strange things, laugh about such matters.

The following morning, with a lovingly prepared lunch and some hard won intelligence from the field, the Soviks set Hilda off by train to Sinyang, where she was to spend her first ever Christmas abroad, before heading off to Peking to attend language classes shortly thereafter. Erik's brother, Edward, and a woman by the name of Marie Anderson, who had founded the local school there, would meet her at the station. Though she traveled by train a lot in those early months, the young missionary never quite grew accustomed to the way the locals moved around from city to city, their personal goods piled high in wicker clothes baskets; wash basins and teapots, live chickens and dirty linens and kitchen utensils, all out in the open, for the whole world to see. There was something both liberating and shameless in their manner, something she could not imagine witnessing in personal, conservative, Midwestern America. Everywhere she looked, Hilda saw people laden down with enormous loads.

The first important station north of Hankow, Sinyang was like dozens of neighboring cities in the region in that it was largely concealed behind great brick walls. It was unique, however, in that it straddled the border between what was then considered by many as North and South China. The railroad, which ran through the city on the way to Peking, was supposed to be an express but, like many such things in China at the time, it sometimes was, and sometimes was not. In any case, it was the westernmost railroad until one got to European Turkestan and, as such, commanded tremendous traffic. (Additional transport of goods – textiles, food and, when it was available, medicine – flowed up and down a nearby tributary to the Yangtze River.) A tunnel just to the south of the city, which connected the two regions, was a point of constant and bloody contention between warring political factions, each vying for control over the strategic passageway. Sinyang itself, a city of perhaps 60,000 mostly poor souls, was accessible by four main gates (North, South, East and West). These were drawn shut everyday at sundown, for safety reasons. Beside each of these ponderous gates were smaller doors, which could be opened quickly in case of extreme emergency; fire, say, or to let in refugees fleeing from nearby cities, which also came under frequent siege. The soldiers that patrolled the perimeter in their drab gray uniforms were, like soldiers in menial positions at all times and in all places around the world, bored to the point of general mischief and even open hostility. Rarely did a woman – much less a *foreign* woman – pass under their gaze without hearing some cheap joke or outright insult cast in her direction. It was not unusual for the soldiers to defect, sometimes *en masse*, to join the roaming bandits. Poor, even unpaid, wages and dangerous working conditions were the most common reasons cited for defection, although each man undoubtedly had his own story to tell.

Looking upon the imposing fortifications from her rickshaw, Hilda was glad to be in the company of her escorts. Edward, bespectacled beneath a thinning brown tuft, was keen and thoughtful, much like his brother. Miss Anderson, though quietly spoken and generally unassuming, was perceptive without appearing to be so, quick to understand a situation and just as swift to navigate her way through it. Though she was a good deal shorter (and rather plumper) than Hilda, the younger missionary felt herself looking up to her. She wore plain clothes and maintained her short, reddish hair in tight curls. Together, the threesome traveled around the city to the South Gate, where the school was located.

"We remain inside during the evenings," explained Miss Anderson. "Night time belongs to the bandits, I'm sorry to say. For the most part, they leave us foreigners alone, but we don't wish to test them just the same. They are a cruel gang indeed."

"We had hoped they might settle down a bit after the last rounds of looting and violence," added Edward Sovik. His voice was firm and Hilda got the impression he had confronted these bandits before. "Alas, the severity and frequency of their attacks seems only to have worsened. I'm afraid we must accept that there is evil here on God's green earth, Miss Nilsen, though we do our best to lead those who have strayed back to His graces."

Hilda watched the thick smoke plumes from the roadside fires, where people were burning their trash. In noxious clouds they rose up against the fading sunlight. "May the wicked forsake their ways," was all she could think to reply.

"And the unrighteous their thoughts," chorused her hosts, "Let them turn to the Lord, and he will have mercy on them, and to our God, for he will freely pardon."

They drove on in silence, the sun low in the heavens. A strange energy was building outside the city walls. Hilda Nilsen wondered just what she had gotten herself into.

*   *   *

When they arrived at the school, Marie Anderson took Hilda aside and explained that her students wished to sing her a welcome song, which they had been practicing in anticipation of their new teacher's arrival. Entering the school's internal courtyard, Hilda saw a hundred or more Chinese girls dressed in identical navy blue uniforms. They were lined up in perfect, military-style formation, arms by their sides. As discreetly as she could, Hilda whispered to Miss Anderson, "How does one say 'thank you' in Chinese?" The word sounded like the word for 'spoon' in

Norwegian, repeated twice, as a question. When the girls had finished their fine rendition, Hilda clenched her left fist, covered it with her right hand and bowed deeply.

"*Hsieh, hsieh*," she intoned with a volume she hoped would disguise her lack of confidence. The language skills Hilda would acquire later, in Peking, but for now, she must make do with these little impromptu lessons. To her own surprise, the girls seemed pleased with her effort, as did Miss Anderson. Thus she felt she got off to a passable start in what was otherwise a rather daunting situation.

After her hostess made some introductory remarks to the students, which she did in both Chinese and English for the benefit of all present, the girls were invited to form a line and meet their new instructor one at a time. One hundred (and more!) new faces, all trained on hers. "How am I ever to learn all these names, recognize all these individuals?" wondered Hilda as the girls filed past, bowing their heads and offering their heavily accented salutations as they went. Examining their fresh teenage expressions, under neat black hair tied back in blue and white ribbons, the newcomer realized that she, too, must look rather exotic to them. "Ah, but they only have to remember one face while *I*... why... how many girls *are* there?" She prayed that God might help her identify them.

Later, when the girls had retired to their dorms and the moon had taken its watchful place among the stars, the adults found their way to and from the dinning room for some informal pleasantries. The boarding school, which the women sometimes called "*Det Lille Hotellet*" or "The Little Hotel" in Norwegian, was forever hosting guests of all sorts, so that it was difficult to know exactly who was coming and who was going at any one time. Mostly they were fellow missionaries from the China Inland Mission and smaller, neighboring houses that, for one reason or another, could not support their own billet load. "We shall have to request one of the new '*revolving doors*' from the appropriations board," was one of Miss Anderson's frequent quips. The night Hilda Nilsen came to stay was no different, with a modest parade of women rushing in and out of the pantry or the laundry with baskets of white sheets or sacks of rice in their arms.

There was Sister Christine, a clumsy older woman who, despite having been with the mission *"since before your time,"* seemed always to be rushing to retrieve some forgotten item. "Never enough hands…" Hilda heard her say more than once that first night, as she dashed about hither and thither. Another middle-aged woman, Miss Hillary, appeared as slow-witted as she was cheerful. Judging by the path of her movements, her main role in the house seemed to be to misplace or forget things that the older Sister Christine could then complain about. Then there was a doctor and his wife (The Helstads? Or the Hellmans?) whom Hilda was introduced to briefly but who were, in any case, packed up and gone early the next morning, only to be replaced with some other pair. Besides these foreigners there were the Chinese cooks and cleaners, to whom Hilda, lacking anything of the language beyond her single, repeated word of gratitude, could do little more than politely nod and bow. All in all, it was a great confusion of characters and conversation.

Once the general commotion in the dining room settled and Miss Anderson had seen Edward Sovik off to his own residence, Hilda offered her apologies and made to retire for the evening. In the dimly lit hallway she saw one of the Chinese helpers approaching. She was younger than Hilda and wearing a sullen face. Feeling the Spirit upon her, Hilda motioned silently to the young woman, offering her a look of smiling encouragement. "What exaggerated calamity could this young lady have endured," Hilda thought to herself, "that I might not be of some ready assistance." She made to bow, but the woman brushed past her.

"I am no fool," she declared solemnly, in plain English. "It is you who still has a lot to learn about our land, our people." She then muttered something in Chinese and marched off down the hall. Hilda was taken aback by the woman's abruptness but, having had such an otherwise pleasant day, she determined to retire without paying it any mind.

The following afternoon, when they were alone, Hilda asked Miss Anderson about the young lady from the hallway. She had no intention of making a disturbance of her own, so she broached the subject gently.

"Ah, so you have met Ling," Miss Anderson smiled in response. "Now there is a complicated soul. Her parents were killed in the Boxer Rebellion when she was still a baby in arms. She was lucky to escape with her own life. By His good grace, her grandmother brought her here after the rebellion was eventually put down. She has been with us ever since, but still she has a complicated relationship with foreigners. She is a devoted woman, Ling, and an honest worker. You will come to like her, I suspect."

But Miss Nilsen hardly had time to think about Ling. In the days and weeks that followed, the young missionary committed herself to her work and prayers and, when she found a moment, to learning what she could about Chinese culture. In addition to her lessons, where she would take the girls through basic religious instruction and some rudimentary calisthenics, she had a Christmas show to organize for the mission and no shortage of duties to perform around the house. "Never enough hands" she even heard herself say once. From the time she rose in the morning, no later than 5:00am, until she fell onto her pillow, exhausted, of an evening, she found that she had not a moment too many. After supper she rarely lingered, as she was keen to return to her room and record the events of the day in her diary, including whatever new words she had learned. The few times she encountered Ling, she was grateful that nothing more than silence passed between them. "I have enough on my plate without her *complications,*" Hilda thought to herself. Besides, she was to leave for Peking shortly after the (western) New Year, where she would spend the summer before returning to Sinyang in the fall. "Maybe the Ling girl will be gone by the time I get back," she imagined one night, though she dared not waste the good Lord's time with such a petty prayer. He would know what to do, after all.

"Do not be wise in your own eyes," she reminded herself of Proverbs, "but instead fear the Lord and shun evil."

*   *   *

On the morning Hilda set out for Peking, Miss Anderson had the ladies of the house form a line on the front porch to wish her a safe journey. There was Sister Christine and Miss Hillary, standing as always in an awkward pair, plus Edward Sovik, who had made his way across town that very day to accompany her to the station. In addition, two young women from Ohio, who had come to stay in Hilda's vacant room while they waited for accommodation at the nearby Methodist house, stood in the sunshine and shook her hand warmly. (Always a great confusion, this revolving roster of guests.) At the end of the line, even after the cooks and general staff, stood Ling, her countenance as gloomy and petulant as ever. Hilda, for her part, was determined to begin her travels in a positive attitude, so when she came to the grim-faced woman, she simply smiled and bowed her head. Ling made no movement, either to show affection or disdain, and so Hilda thought nothing more of it. She waved again to Miss Anderson and the other woman and climbed on the rickshaw with Mr. Sovik. Secretly, she was glad to be heading to Peking, where she hoped a basic grasp of the language would help her better serve His purpose in this strange land.

The train ride from Sinyang to Peking was a long one, filled with the usual clamor of wicker baskets and household paraphernalia and squawking animals. Hilda rode in silence, listening to her fellow passengers as they hustled on and off at the various stops, dragging their worldly possessions around the vast country on their backs. What a culture this was, she ruminated. In the daily routine and discipline of the mission boarding house, she had almost forgotten what the rest of the society was like outside those walls; the chaos; the sheer scale of humanity existing here, belonging both to the present and the past. This was a history that stretched back thousands of years, long before God gave His only begotten Son to the world. What plan had He for these people, these "virtuous pagans," as Dante described those whose only sin was that they were simply not exposed to Christ's teachings? She tried to comprehend them. Generation after generation pressing on in darkness, never feeling the warmth of His Light, yearning and struggling and perishing without ever hearing His Word upon their poor, heathen ears. She shuddered at the thought and, looking around the dirty train cabin, felt a renewed sense of catechetical duty, a desire to spread the Good News as far and wide as she possibly could. To rescue those condemned to that limbo of the soul, where their own ignorance denied them passage to the eternal glory of heaven. But it was no use doing it with eyes wide shut. First, she must learn the words and the ways of her new country. And, of course, she must hold true to the path He had set for her.

The week before she left, Miss Anderson told Hilda that there had been some bungling with her accommodations. Apparently the dormitory room that was assigned for her was let out to another missionary who had just arrived from America and had nowhere else to stay. Hilda expressed no concern and, recalling the Old Man's words from the *Fushima Maru*, took it as an opportunity to prove her faith. A few days later, news came that alternative arrangements had been made for her and that, "as fortune would have it," her new room was in one of the finest houses in all of Peking, that of Dr. James H. Ingram and his family. Hilda welcomed the word, but felt no relief, for she had brooked no doubt. "The Lord never closes a door in the face of one of His children," she bowed her head to Miss Anderson, "but that He opens another one farther on."

Upon arrival, Hilda discovered that the Ingram household not only lived up to its reputation, but quite exceeded it. The doctor himself, an esteemed Pennsylvania-Dutch physician, had been in China some thirty years. On top of his considerable medical work, he was also an authority on the Chinese language and had even written a textbook, which was used in the missionary language schools. Dr. Ingram's wife, whom he met while serving in the field, had then been a nurse. They had six children together, who rotated through the house on their way to answer His callings over this ocean or that horizon. A most worldly brood they were! Mrs. Ingram herself, meanwhile, applied her considerable talents as a gracious homemaker. People from different legations across Peking would consult her on all manner of practical concerns, from where to find the best supplies to how to secure a capable Chinese for this or that position. Dinner was served at Mrs. Ingram's table at 7:00 pm sharp every evening (except for Sundays, when she followed a full roast lunch with a light supper at 6:00 pm). More often than not, there were guests of some distinction in attendance. So the young Hilda Nilsen met people of importance she never would have encountered had she stayed in the language school dormitory. The Lord had his ways, she thought.

Oftentimes, when Mrs. Ingram went to the markets to buy food or clothing or artworks, she would invite Hilda along. Whether it was to impart some lesson or simply for the company, Hilda was never quite sure, but she was grateful for the experience just the same. She watched with keen interest as her host bargained with the shop vendors ("one must bargain for *everything* here," she would say, "it's almost considered an offense not to.") She observed, too, how the doctor's wife treated the locals with a kind of firmness they seemed very much to respect, and how she often made use of certain "non-textbook" language to further endear herself to them.

One unseasonably fresh afternoon, while the two women were walking back from the central flower markets, Mrs. Ingram turned to Hilda. "Now, I know you said that when you left America that the hardest thing to leave behind – besides your family, of course – was your mother's piano. Well, later this week we are to receive into our own house a very fine instrument from one of the other missions. My own children have no use for it, as, for all their myriad talents, an inclination to musicality is not to be found among them. It is Dr. Ingram's and my wish, therefore, that you take to it as if it were your own."

Hilda was without words, but Mrs. Ingram was not done with the surprise yet.

"As for lessons," she continued, "for you must never remain idle in any of your God-given pursuits, we have arranged for a Russian gentleman to instruct you. Dmitri Pavlovitch, a professor at the Petrograd Conservatory of Music, was obliged to leave his homeland on account of the Bolshevik disturbances there…"

At this the younger woman could not help but break in. "I… Why Mrs. Ingram, I…" Hilda found herself on the verge of dissolving to tears when her kindly benefactor took her by the shoulders.

"It is not for us to question the turbulent world in which we live," she assured, "only to make the most of the opportunities the good Lord sets before us."

Hilda found the grand instrument, and the tutelage of Professor Pavlovitch, a welcomed respite from her intensive Chinese language studies. She was even grateful when, to her already heaped agenda, she added frequent invitations to perform short, post dinner recitals for the Ingram's many and distinguished guests. Indeed, it seemed to the young missionary that the Lord had opened a whole world of opportunity for her. She only wondered how best to take advantage of His Grace, so that she might serve His Will the better.

*   *   *

Among the many outings to which Mrs. Ingram invited Hilda were the weekly excursions to a pensioner's villa that she, with the help of some interested Chinese locals, had established a few years back.

"The Chinese people are an intensely family oriented people," she explained to Hilda during their first visit to the home. "But that has its drawbacks, too. Elderly people without family are often left outside society, with no one to care for them or see to their health and dignity, much less prepare them spiritually for what awaits us all."

Hilda called to mind the forgotten figures she passed by daily on the street, elderly men and women covered in newspapers, sleeping rough under the dripping eaves. She wondered what had become of their families, their brothers and daughters, sisters and sons. Where had these people gone? She thought of her own family, how they so often fed and boarded people they had never met, and welcomed them in from the cold.

Though ostensibly preferable to the dirty, crowded doorsteps outside, the villa itself could hardly be termed luxurious. There was a dank smell about the place and the old, broken roof tiles let in the skies when they rained. Still, it was relatively clean and provided basic shelter from the worst of the weather, which turned deathly cold during the winter months. In the front section of the building were a simple kitchen, a pantry and a communal dining hall with a long wooden table at its center. In the back, behind a small concrete courtyard, were two open rooms with rows of cots pushed against the walls, on which slept thirty or forty trembling souls at any one time. Out back there was a water closet with a washbasin, which the men and women shared. As for the residents themselves, although their board was free (subsidized by the mission), they were expected to contribute to the daily running of the place, each according to their own condition. For those able to do so, there was always a floor to sweep, dishes to be washed or vegetables to peel. Mrs. Ingram was adamant that such work helped maintain a sense of community and build a moral purpose. In addition to such quotidian duties, residents were also encouraged to participate in regular religious instruction, although attendance was not mandatory and many remained skeptical until the end. Being as it was the only such facility in Peking at the time, there were always fewer beds than bodies in need of them.

On one visit, Hilda noticed a new resident, an elderly woman whom she had occasionally seen begging in the *hu-tong* laneways around the flower market. She was in a particularly poor way, her bare feet gnarled and swollen, the splintered yellow toenails months or even years from proper care. Her clothes were filthy and tattered at the knees, the calloused skin on which she had spent so many years in desperate prostration. Hilda felt a deep urge to ask the woman her name, to somehow reach out to her, but she fought a strange revulsion for the pitiable creature. She looked like a caged animal, with furtive glances and skittish movements, as if she had been raised at the end of a stick. When the residents were called to the dining room for lunch, Hilda noticed the woman remained curled on her cot, her naked feet bent under her ragged body.

When they came to visit the following week, the woman appeared even worse for wear. A vile stench emanated from her cot, an effluvium so putrid that the other residents had dragged their own cots away from her in disgust and lined them against the opposite wall. From there they sneered and made uncouth gestures toward her, to which she responded with an occasional hiss or snarl of her own. Again when mealtime was called, the woman remained huddled in her filthy rags.

Ashamed of her own cowardice in having not approached the woman the previous week, the young missionary ventured out onto the street, where she bought a large Chinese doughnut from one of the vendors there. She brought it to the poor wretch and knelt down beside her, ready to administer some soothing words of redemption. The stench was suffocating and it was no small miracle that Hilda was able to stand it at all. She dared not inhale as she gently held out the offering. All of a sudden, the woman's scabbed arm darted out and snatched the coal-burned food from her grasp, squirreling it away under her mud-caked rags. Hilda later recalled how the whites of the old woman's eyes had come alive in that moment as though, far from accepting friendly alms, she was fending off some vicious predator. The younger woman recoiled in fear, then fled the room out into the summer heat, a feeling of shame and disgust gnawing at her own stomach. The bile rose in her throat and she repressed the urge to be sick in the gutter. The old woman's smell, like burning flesh, clung to her sweat-damped clothes. She returned home with it cloaked around her still, hot and heavy in the breathless humidity.

The following week, Hilda was obliged to join the language school in practice for an upcoming musical event at which she was to accompany the chorus with a piano recital. Though she knew she must return to the villa, she was grateful for the break and the distraction. When she finally visited again a fortnight later, she found herself mildly relieved to discover the old woman absent from her cot; a bedraggled man with droopy eyes and a long white chin beard had taken her place. She must have moved on, Hilda thought, or perhaps the other residents had finally turned her out.

After supper that evening, Hilda asked Mrs. Ingram about her.

"We cannot help those who are not ready to help themselves, my dear." The hostess turned her straight face toward the sink and continued. "The others did their best, but the devil had taken that woman's soul long before the gangrene took her by the flesh."

Before climbing into the precious comfort of her bed that night, Hilda fell to her knees and prayed for her own family, that they may be delivered into His waiting arms with dignity and grace. It was many years before she could forget the smell.

*   *   *

Oftentimes during her stay, the Ingrams would invite Hilda to escape the city with them for a daytrip or even a weekend. They would fill their picnic baskets with fresh peaches and breads and cured meats, and head off into the cooler, surrounding hills. Sometimes they would visit the grounds of the Empress' Summer Palace, where they would lay their blankets out and give thanks under the glorious shade of the ancient armand pines. Other times they sought out spots by the Great Wall, or near one of the many pagodas or jade fountains. The countryside was so utterly majestic, so completely removed from the filth and squalor of city life, that Hilda often forgot she was even in the same country.

Late one summer afternoon, after the long, dog days had fallen behind them, Dr. Ingram informed Hilda that the family would shortly be departing for their annual journey to Inner Mongolia. The doctor had lent his medical advice to a member of royalty in the region some time ago and, after passing many a subsequent night up in the hills over the ensuing years, had grown very fond of the place indeed.

"You must feel free to stay on here at the house," he went on, to the young woman's ill-concealed disappointment, "...or you may join our little caravan for the experience, if it suits your studies."

Hilda could barely contain herself. She spent the following week happily buried under double duties in order to free up her schedule and, but for a dentist appointment that she could not move for the morning of departure, was all but ready to head out.

"We'll go on ahead and line everything up," Mrs. Ingram called from her husband's side, waving a gloved hand off the back of the rickshaw, "Just remember, take the four o'clock to Kalgan, the city with the twin gates. We'll meet you there."

When the young Miss Nilsen arrived at the Peking station later that afternoon, her luggage in tow, she was as ready as she had ever been to get out of the muggy, clotted metropolis.

"One for Kalgan," she said to the man behind the ticket counter in Chinese, proud of the progress she had made in her language classes.

"Changchakow!" the man barked, without looking up.

Hilda repeated, firmer this time, "Kalgan. One for *Kalgan*."

"Changchakow! *Changchakow!*" came the equally louder, repeated response.

Hilda mustered her words as best she could. She explained that *Kalgan*, to where her 4 o'clock train was due to depart, was a city with two gates; one opening into Inner Mongolia, the other into China.

"Changchakow," the man nodded without expression as he handed her a ticket.

The Lord sure has a lot more faith in me than I sometimes do in myself, Hilda thought as she made her way to the platform.

Ignoring the secret relief she felt when the train did, in fact, arrive at the appointed destination, she was nevertheless glad to see the smiling Ingram faces there to meet her. They had set up camp in the nearby hillside, a short ride from the station. For perhaps the first time during her stay in China, Hilda was beginning to feel as though she were a part of something, like she belonged to this little family in some way, united in their common cause.

One day while camping in the hills, a few members of the group decided to hike up one of the lower mountains that bordered China to the south. So they set off with water canteens in their packs and chocolate bars in their pockets "in case of emergency," as Mrs. Ingram had explained when handing them out. Weary but exhilarated, they reached a suitable viewing platform just before noon. The doctor pointed out six provinces rolling out before them in China proper. It was truly an incredible sight to behold.

Scanning the vista, Hilda espied a black spec circling above them, high up in the nameless sky. "Look, it's like a period," she explained to the others in her English teacher manner. It continued circling, then became a dash with several periods around it. "A semi-colon, no... wait! A... now what would you call that?" The formation grew larger as it fell until, of a sudden, it was close enough for Hilda to make out an adult eagle with a clutch of five or six little eaglets on its back. They appeared homely enough with their long, scrawny necks, barely able to hold up their oversized beaks and hairless heads.

As Hilda was taking their measure, the adult eagle swooped out from under them again, leaving her little fledglings to wobble and sputter in mid air, their wings grasping at the empty space, slipping a dozen or so feet at a time. The chirping eaglets continued their fall until they dashed right past the platform of astounded onlookers. Hilda covered her eyes as the birds struggled to arrest their fall. Unable to resist, she peered over the edge, only to see the helpless things plunging toward the earth, hundreds of feet below. Then, one by one, they began to find the wind in their winglets, to fly. Only one continued to plummet. Hilda's nerves screamed inside her as she looked on. Just when it seemed too late, the great eagle swooped down under the fledgling, catching it on her back. Hilda's heart was in her mouth. She felt as if her own stomach had gone off the edge.

Next, without warning, as if a zipper had been pulled across the sky, a torrent of rain poured down from above. Hilda hadn't even noticed the clouds gathering, and here they were emptying themselves on her head. The convoy raced down the mountainside toward camp, the chocolate bars liquifying in their saturated pockets. Hilda kicked off her shoes at the entrance, discarded her outer clothes and leapt into her hammock. She found her Bible and turned at once to the concordance. There it was, in Exodus 19:4, the Lord reminding the Israelites, "Remember when I bore you on eagle's wings." How many times, already on this journey, had she felt as though she were standing on the edge of an abyss, plummeting into the unknown, only to be spirited to safety in God's cradling hands? She bowed her head in prayer.

Not long after the journey to the Mongolian hills, it came time for Hilda to return to Sinyang. She was eager to see Miss Anderson and Edward Sovik and the others again. Perhaps she could even afford a little patience for the Ling woman, too, for the young Miss Nilsen by now felt herself a little older and, God willing, a little wiser.

*　*　*

Chapter X

CLEAN WHITE SHEETS

T he Father of Medicine, Hippocrates, first described the symptoms of eclampsia in the 5th Century BC. He observed the rapid onset of bolt-like maternal convulsions and, indeed, the term itself, *éklamps(is)*, derives from the Greek word for lightning, or "sudden flash of light." Zeus only knows what frightful conditions his patient found herself in at that time, what filth and ignorance and terror filled the atmosphere as the horrified onlookers stood helplessly by their loved one's side. Hippocrates attributed the condition to a disturbance in the "four humors" but, despite considerable advancements in medicine over the ensuing two and a half millennia, the pathophysiological causes remain largely a mystery.

All this I read about later, as I tried to piece together what had happened to my dear, my lovely, my precious Evie. In the moment, however, when the lightning first struck, there was no time for research or logic or teary retrospectives. There was panicking to be done.

* * *

It is a strange phenomenon indeed that, when your entire world is summoned into question, when your oh-so-sure footing slips from beneath you and you turn to see the loosened rocks disappearing into the fathomless cavern below, your mind does not necessarily go to the places you might expect. There comes a time for deep philosophizing, of course, for profound meditation and Kubler-Ross' well-known stages of grief. But in the shock of the moment, all that goes to the wind. When confronted with an unthinkable future, it makes a certain amount of sense that the mind would seek to blanket itself in the familiar, oft-remembered past. What else could it do, when the senses are sending it messages it cannot, *will not* compute?

And so, as I watched the life drain out of my dear Evie, her eyes rolling back in her soft moon face as a pool of blood formed in the cotton valley between her legs, my mind focused itself not on the immediate, unthinkable danger, but on that which was palpable, graspable, simple:

Clean. White. Sheets.

My Evie was happy to economize on many things – to take a metro instead of a taxi, for instance, or to settle on *Prosecco* or even *Cava*, simulacrums of the costlier French original – but when it came to accommodations while on the road, a woman had a right to draw the line somewhere. And so Evie drew it there, right under <u>clean white sheets</u>.

One impromptu summer sojourn, a surprise to celebrate Evie's twenty-somethingth birthday, I even went so far as to learn the phrase in French. A few expat friends had relayed uninspiring stories regarding Tunisia's budget accommodations, so I wanted to make sure I had at least the basics covered. Return flights from Dubai (where we were then residing) would be straightforward enough, but who knew what the Carthaginian hoteliers had in store for unsuspecting tourists of limited linguistic alacrity? (Arabic and the local Tunisian dialect having proven out-of-the-question-difficult.) And so, along with "*une chambre avec douche*" and "*quelque chose avec une vue*" I committed "*draps blancs propres,*" to memory, neatly filed under "hotel vocabulary."

"Oui, oui," the réceptionniste d'hôtel assured us on arrival to his (*ahem…*) establishment. He employed one sun-leathered hand to swat away any remaining doubts while, into the other, he received my credit card. "Draps *très* blancs, *très* propres."

At a snap of the man's fingers, a hotel flunkey appeared and promptly relieved us of our luggage. Our room, with the promised view and aforementioned linens, would be ready later that afternoon.

"Enough time to visit the baths?" Evie enthused.

"I suspected you might say that. Yes, of course, Dear."

So we spent the golden afternoon wandering the ancient Roman thermae, the cool Mediterranean breeze washing over our perspiring brows. Evie was in her element. Happily I followed as she held forth on Antoninus Pius and the "five good emperors," reimagining scenes under the imperial colonnades.

"Of course, the Jews tended to contrast 'bad Hadrian' with 'good Antonius,'" she sallied forth, "but just to walk in their footprints is thrilling enough for me. Why, Marcus Aurelius himself might have sat right *there* [pointing eagerly], under that very archway, making mental notes for his *Meditations*."

There was nothing quite so rewarding as taking Evie to an ancient ruin, whether for her birthday or some other anniversary or, better still, for no occasion whatsoever, other than the ongoing celebration of life itself. She became a monument to behold in and of herself, my historical adventurer, agog among her new old surroundings, overcome with playful eagerness, backstroking in the timeless past.

"Think how the citizens must have finally felt at rest, decades of peace settling into their souls, after so many years of war and rage had emptied their blood into the seas."

I followed Evie's gaze out over the wine-dark waters. My own soul I felt at ageless peace besides hers. After the waning daylight forced our little expedition into retreat, we wiled away an hour or two at a *café du tabac* nearby the hotel. The summer heat dissolved into a few sweet rosés, and the conversation turned toward our own "imperial successors."

I began the negotiations at six. Evie, I knew, wanted one or two, but she seemed in the mood for some impish teasing nonetheless.

"Oh, I don't know, Love. Didn't you hear my little Nerva–Antonine oration this afternoon? History argues pretty well for adoption, don't you think? Recall that Marcus' son, Commodus, was the beginning of the end for the Roman Empire. What does that say for biological progeny?"

"Yes, yes. You are too clever, my Dear," I raised an empty glass and bowed my head in mock defeat. "But perhaps Machiavelli overlooked something in his hypothesis. You said that the predecessors to the 'five adoptive emperors' actually had no biological sons of their own and, as such, were *forced* to adopt. It was not by heavenly design, in other words, but out of human necessity that the one succeeded the other in the way they did."

"So, you're saying if we *have* a choice…"

"And we do, don't we?"

"And what of the Commodus Factor?"

"He was a megalomaniac. Maybe his daddy didn't love him enough. I don't know. Anyway, that won't be a problem in our house, I promise you."

"So, forget Commodus?"

"Forget Commodus."

Evie smiled her honey-sweet smile. "Well, you sure know how to talk to a woman."

Shortly thereafter, our heads swimming in uncut wine and ideas of succession, we were back at the *petit hôtel*, ringing the bell for *le réceptionniste*. As he was apparently nowhere to be found, it was the flunkey who saw us to our room, where he had earlier deposited our cases. The little man flicked on the lights and, before they had time to illuminate the space, scampered off into the darkness of the hallway behind us.

Evie's sigh was audible. Not only was the room *sans vue*, a fact she might have overlooked for a night, but the *draps blancs propres* were nowhere to be seen. In their place, a filthy cot was covered in stained yellow sheets, acned with cigarette burns.

So my dear, patient Evie passed her very first night in Carthage, winning hands of *bezique* against her slightly embarrassed partner as he swatted horseflies and stomped on the not-occasional roach.

Clean white sheets was the very least she deserved, I recall thinking to myself at the time. And now they were sullied…

When I came to, standing in my own shoes by Evie's hospital bedside, I found myself waving frantically at the rushing nurses.

"Draps blancs propres! Draps blancs propers!"

By then Evie had lost consciousness altogether, but still the blood kept seeping into the clean white sheets.

* * *

Evie's room was suddenly awash in clean white lab coats. A semicircular shield of them stood guard at the foot of her bed, their arms reaching in to remove bedding and apply bandages and swabs, to attach crimson transfusion bags to intravenous lines, to handle machines and flashing instruments, and to bundle a hyperventilating husband from the room.

"What's going on in there?" I demanded, "what's... *que esta pasando*... what's... Evie!"

A pair of nurses held me by both arms and talked to me at once. I caught verbs, but could not grab the conjugations, heard nouns but did not grasp the tense.

"What do you mean Evie 'was' stabilizing?" my mind and body struggled against the desperate confusion, the confused desperation. "The bleeding 'has stopped' or it 'will stop?' Well is it 'pre-eclampsia' or 'eclampsia?' And what does that even mean? Where is the doctor? Where is he *now... ahora?*"

Behind the nurses I caught flashes of the patient's form through the window... her matted hair... her bloodied abdomen... her bloated legs, limp and flopped down on the red-brown sheets. The doctors swarmed around her, attaching tubes and handling her heavy, swollen limbs, her convulsing white torso. Then the blinds closed and the terror of not knowing, of not seeing, began to set in. My own pulse, overflowing with cold, urgent blood, started to thump incessantly. Presently, a doctor appeared, as if summoned by the very sound of it.

"Señor, please. Please calm yourself. I am doctor Laso. My team and I are working with your wife now." It sounded like a collaboration. "It is normal to experience some additional bleeding after an induced cesarean, though postpartum seizures are not so common. Tell me, does your wife suffer from diabetes? Any kind of nephropathy? Kidney disease?

No? Renal disease? No? Well, Doctor Kostas is on his way now. In the meantime, I ask you to please wait outside. I will keep you informed. Please, your wife is in good care."

I collapsed into a plastic chair immediately outside the room. My legs were stiff, my mouth and eyes wide open. And dry. The nurses were saying something to me, but I couldn't hear their words. A siren of clean white noise filled my ears. My skin crawled under a film of cold sweat and the thrill of nausea passed through me over and again. Somewhere in the distance I heard Dr. Kostas' voice. Vaguely I recognized his shape coming down the hall. He looked at me through unseeing eyes and, mouthing something I could not process, passed directly into Evie's room. The door closed once more. For an anguished eternity, I sat there, staring at the unmoving blinds, the unturning doorknob.

It occurred to me that Evie never really took to Dr. Kostas, never really liked him. His ways were too casual, too familiar for her strong, independent sensibilities. In short, Evie did not appreciate being spoken down to.

"He talks to me as though *I* were an infant," she complained after one routine visit. The sun was high in the sky and we were walking back to our apartment through Plaza Vincente Lopez. Off in the distance, children were playing on the slides and seesaws. The air was full of musky scent. Underfoot, the path was carpeted with fallen jacaranda flowers. Iconic Buenos Aires.

"And what's with all the baby talk?" she went on. "The 'here's a piece of cake' and 'here is too much *churro*' and 'here's a *choricito*' nonsense while he's poking away at my stomach. It's embarrassing enough as it is, to lay down like that with my enormous belly exposed and vulnerable. Why can't he just talk like an adult, a professional?"

"He's just trying to reassure you, Evie, to help you relax."

"Well, he sounds like an idiot."

I could not argue with that. It was annoying even to me, and I was not the one being pressed and prodded and examined. Still, he came highly recommended and he worked with the very best hospital in the city. Besides, Evie had not exactly had the easiest pregnancy to date, what with the weight and the blood pressure issues and the Aspirin and so forth.

"Maybe it's a language thing," I offered. "Maybe it's… Evie, I don't know…"

"Well he should be speaking Spanish, not gibberish. Besides, he's Greek-Argentine anyway! He probably read the Hippocratic Oath in the original. He's, he's… *uhh…*" A wince caught her mid-stride. She raised a hand to her stomach.

"Now look, Evie. *Evie!* You can't stress yourself like this. It's not healthy. Not for either of you." Easy enough for me to say, I was not the one whose body was in secret revolt. *My* cells were fine. *My* platelets were not mounting an internal mutiny. *My* body was not digging trenches, about to go all napalm and scorched earth and A-Bomb, to wage bloody, merciless war upon itself.

"I know, I know," she breathed. "You're right." And I know Evie wanted to believe I was, that everything would be all right, even though her body was screaming at her, urging her to bolt in the opposite direction, to reverse course, to beware the imminent danger. "I just want this to be over. I want it to be June already, to be nursing our little girl in our new place, beginning our life together as a family. All this waiting and worrying, it's not for me." She took my hand in hers. "It's not for *us.*"

As I replayed Evie's words in my mind, I began to feel an ire rising in my gut, a ripening indignation aimed at something, *someone.* Just then, the emergency room door opened and in walked Dr. Kostas. He was drying his hands with a clean white towel. I saw the sweat on his temples before I heard him say, in those placating, saccharine tones, "Evie is going to be just fine, but her blood pressure needs to come down. And you need to relax. Doctor Laso and his team will be caring for her from now on, but I will be on call around the clock in case she needs anything. But don't you worry. She's in good hands now."

What did that mean, in good hands *now?* And why did *I* need to relax? A squall of interrogation began to form in my head, but before it could gather strength, a nurse took me by the arm and diverted my attention toward Evie's room. The door was open. As I entered, I could hear the Greek's retreating footsteps fading down the hall.

* * *

If Evie was awake, it was only barely. Her eyelids were beyond pale, her lips almost translucent. Fresh linens had been placed on top of her shivering body. They still smelled of hospital bleach. Or the room did. I watched for a second from the threshold, the hallway light casting my own shadow across her bed. Evie's chest rose and fell, shallow seismic activity beneath the cotton tundra. Behind her semi-inclined mattress, a wall of knobs and monitors, switches and panels, buttons and flashing lights. Leaning over her on either side, like grieving relatives tossing handfuls of dirt into an open grave, stood twin metal stands bent at the hip. They had transfusion bags for heads, their spindly, claret-filled arms reached down to clasp at her withered veins. Evie's forearms, whiter than white sheets, were swollen with edema, puffed up and stretched like sausage balloons at a child's birthday party. She looked as though she had been dragged ashore, found facedown. My poor, darling Evie. I almost wept when she stirred.

"What are you doing in the doorway," she asked, turning her pinhole eyes toward me. Her face, too, was bulgy. The edema. "Have you been to see her yet?"

"I.., I…"

"What did she feel like? I dreamed you two were together, that she was resting peacefully on your naked chest. *Cangurito*-style."

The words dropped from her colorless mouth like anvils onto my sternum. Involuntarily, I exhaled. What did she remember, my Evie? Had she felt the convulsions, the lightning bolts seizing her vital organs? Did she recall the blood at all, gushing like water from a punctured kiddie pool? Had she seen my face, petrified with terror? Witnessed my own frantic, panicked episode? I drew a long, slow breath. I had to keep it together, to shield her from the horror, the razor-edge of reality, to keep her as still and present as possible. I tried not to look at the tubes, emptying vital juice into her veins, tried not to imagine the needles tearing at her clammy dermis, tried not to notice the monitors, advertising her waning signals to anyone who cared to notice them. I moved closer. I touched her hand. I smiled.

"I told her mommy loves her, Evie. That we both do." My eyeballs stung from the salt, but I dared not blink free a tear. "And I told her mommy was just having a little rest, that she's doing well."

This seemed to land softly. Evie closed her eyes again. I was about to whisper something else when I felt a hand on my own shoulder. It was Dr. Laso. (All these physicians, and for one little family!) He motioned for me to step outside. Gently, I let Evie's sleeping fingers slip from my own, onto the sheets, and followed him into the hallway.

Under the fluorescent light, I registered Dr. Laso's appearance for the first time. He was a tall, thin man with gray hair to match his goatee beard. Unlike pudgy Kostas, he carried himself with a dignified, educated bearing. He wasted no time on small talk. In fact, I strongly suspected he had never used the diminutive 'choricito' in his life, not even with his own children.

"Your wife has a hypertensive disorder known as pre-eclampsia. The convulsions you witnessed before were a symptom of that condition. There are others, but I hope to avoid them. Right now, pathology is running a series of tests so we can do a platelet count and monitor her erythrocytes, her red blood cells, to see if there is any rupturing. Any lysing. If there is cytoplasm in the surrounding fluid, we will have to render a new diagnosis." He paused, not so much to take a breath as to be sure I was absorbing what he said. "The situation is dynamic. You should be aware that this is a very serious condition, but also that she is in excellent hands. My team is the very best in the country. Right now, she needs to rest. My staff will keep a close eye on her. Meanwhile, I suggest you go and see your daughter. I understand she is also in intensive, down on two. Well, we'll be here, whatever you need."

And with that Dr. Laso shook my hand and marched determinedly off into another room. I peered through the opened blinds, my Evie drifting soundly between the land of the waking and the dead. What could I do to help her now? What could I do to make her stay? I felt no tiredness, no exhaustion. I could and would do whatever was necessary, even if that meant nothing for now. And so I blew my *stilleven* wife a kiss, and went to see her baby daughter.

* * *

I descended the stairwell, dark, deep and foggy in my head. The elevators must have been out of order, for the shrinking spiral was thronged with other travelers, bound to similar paths. I imagined Dante's limbo; "Crowds, multitudinous and vast / Of babies and of women and of men." An in-between world, lingering on the verge of death and the everlasting. Virgil and the virtuous pagans. What had these poor children done, to suffer so, to be detained in this bleak landscape? Some for eternity…

Nurse Laura (as her name tag reminded me) went over the hygiene procedure again and admitted me promptly into the womb-like conditions where my little girl lay cradled. I scrubbed up and passed by the corkboard, eyeing those little graduates, on their way to becoming men and women of great worth. The room was dark and warm.

"*Buenas noches, señor,*" Marta greeted me with gentle, smiling eyes. Was it nighttime already? It was impossible to tell inside the hospital. It was like a casino, with no natural light or clocks, just beeping machines and tiny roulette wheels. Red or black. Life or death. Marta motioned to the incubator beside her and to the naked infant inside, bathed in blue light. I recognized the tiny form even with her baggy eye mask on, saw the spot on her forehead where I had first laid my lips, recalled her milky smell as if she were soft against my cheek. She lay on her stomach, face to the side, downy back to the lights. Her sheets were fluorescent under the indigo rays.

"*Luces bili, señor,*" Marta nodded. "*Luces bili. Por la ictericia. Bilirrubina, señor.*"

"Don't feel bad. These are not words one learns in your average 'Spanish for the street, not for the test' course." Doctor Maro, who presently joined our bilingual bedside confabulation, shed his own light on the situation.

"She's doing remarkably well, you see." He appeared genuinely impressed. "The bili lights here are routine really, nothing to concern yourself over. The phototherapy treats jaundice common to newborns, especially in premature cases. The blue light you can see breaks down the bilirubin in her blood, which is produced when her body builds new red blood cells to replace her old ones..."

I peered in through the plastic and tried to fathom what was going on. The cellular functions and wavelengths of light, the dynamic systems morphing and adapting to a new and changing environment, life forcing its way through the darkness and into the light. A whole universe at play in one infinitesimal organism. The stirring miracle was overwhelming.

"...and no more oxygen." Doctor Maro had been talking all the while. "She actually came right off. Remarkable." Again, the most important man in the room seemed sincere, earnest even. I could have cried from relief. "Well, Marta is here to monitor her temperature and other vitals. She's quite taken with your little girl. There are fighters in this world. Marta herself is one."

I glanced over at the nurse, her baby-smoothed hands, her skin creased with age and practice, with instinctual care. She was turning my little girl in her gentle grasp, resting her on her back in her own private isolette. There was her little blue tummy with all its organs, the skin-shallow veins lost under the bili lights. She wriggled and jerked her pasta limbs, the minute tendons and ligaments engaged in the great, cooperative effort of life. And not a cry, not a wince from her glorious face, nestled under the giant, parachute eye mask. Thank you, Marta. My heart swelled. *Thank you.*

Doctor Maro laid his hand on my forearm. "We're still in the early stages, young man, but the signs are good. Very good indeed."

The elevators must have been functioning again when I ascended through that limbo membrane, for the staircase was empty. Spiraling up from the depths, I felt cleansed and optimistic, baptized in the waters of hope. I drew the abundant oxygen into my own lungs in fat, chunky gulps, feasting on life with every step forward. The energy spread through my body, carried through my vascular system, reaching out through my climbing limbs.

I arrived at Evie's doorstep in a state of near euphoria, just in time to register the vacant panic etched on her face as she slipped, once again, into unconsciousness. The blood red sheets formed the last image I saw before I was once again ushered out of the room.

* * *

She was right there, my Evie, on the other side of the door. And yet, she was a thousand miles away from me. I could almost hear her labored breathing, feel her salty tears falling on the green bathroom tiles. I pressed my hand against the wood, imagining (willing) that she might be doing the same. Forming a bridge over the vast expanse of our fundamental misunderstanding. Again I begged her to come out, to just talk things through, but she had locked the door. She could be stubborn when she wanted to be. So, we sat, she on her side of the threshold and I on mine, for what seemed like days.

I ran over the argument again in my head. "The Big Euro-Discord" we would later call it. Basically, Evie wanted to keep moving, on from Budapest and on from London and on from Stavanger and on from *wherever*. The peripatetic life, lived out to its ultimate conclusion.

"What's in a place anyway, huh? What's so special about a dot on a map? It's just where we happen to be in any given moment. It's not *us*. It's a coordinate. A position. Life is movement, or at least it should be."

"I get all that, Evie, at least in the abstract. And to a certain extent, I agree. But that's not what I'm saying."

"You're saying we need to find 'a place.' But why do we need to stay somewhere, *anywhere*, if we don't want to?"

"That's not what I mean either, Evie." We had been over this, I thought. "Look, we're people, Evie, people with friends and families who love us and want to see us, to grow with us. And to see our own family grow with them. That's all. It's," I struggled to find the right word, then fell on exactly the wrong one, "it's *community*."

"*Community*? Since when were you all about community? Ok, well my community is scattered all across the planet! Wherever we 'end up,' as you keep suggesting with such suicidal finality, we're going to make *someone* unhappy. Disappoint some members of this '*community*.' We can't please everyone. So why not live life on our own terms?"

"Again, I'm not saying we can't travel, Evie, only let us put down some roots somewhere. Find a home base. Something familiar. We can't keep doing this, just up-and-leaving whenever the wind changes direction. Even the weather has patterns!"

She was quiet a long time after that, evidently processing something I had not yet considered but that was about to land on my neck like a millstone.

"Well I'm sorry," her voice had changed, stepped backward, away, "but I'm not that person. I can't just 'put down roots' or 'settle' or whatever you just called it. I don't want to follow some prescribed pattern, another 'general circulation.' I want to paint my own way. I thought you did too?"

Gravity doubled in an instant as the realization of what she was saying weighed on me. Was this an… (I could barely admit the word to myself) an… *ultimatum*?

"I wanted to paint it together, Evie. You and me."

Silence. Excruciating, unending, soundproof silence.

Another door opened and I saw Dr. Laso standing before me. I wiped my face, ready to meet the news head on. What, Dr. Laso? Tell me *what*!

"I'm afraid your wife's condition has worsened. Considerably worsened."

Wait, *wait!* No, no. Not that. Don't tell me *that!* But he did…

"She has developed what we call HELLP syndrome."

"Help?"

"H.E.L.L.P. Essentially, her red blood cells are rupturing, which is releasing cytoplasm into the surrounding fluid. Additionally, her liver enzymes are at highly elevated levels, which may indicate damage to the organ, preventing it from functioning as normal. Finally, her blood platelet count is low. Very low. Platelets help the blood coagulate, which prevents hemorrhaging…"

This last part I understood. "So, apart from everything else, you're basically saying she can't stop bleeding?"

"We're monitoring her condition and considering some options. Corticosteroids have been shown in some cases to help increase platelet count, but we have to be very careful with her hypertension."

I stared at this man, his big educated brain throbbing away in its protective case, the thousands of hours of seminars and training, cramming for tests, stuffing that incredible mind with dynamic scenarios and multivariate analyses, the millions of medical words filed away in his encyclopedic memory, the lab work, the operating rooms, the decades of experience, practicing for this very moment.

"So… what's next? What do you need to do?" The imperative. The unanswerable imperative. What do you *need* to do?

"Well, her blood pressure needs to come down. She's at 220 over 130. We need to get that down to a manageable level."

"Okay," I reasoned. "I can understand that. So what's the treatment? What's the *cure*?"

"Unfortunately, the most commonly recommended course of action has already passed."

"Which is?"

"Your daughter."

[My blank look]

"That is, delivery of the baby. And the placenta."

"But she's already…"

"Do you have anyone here with you? Where is her family?"

"Her family? They're in the United States. They're all the way…"

"You need to call them. They may wish to get on a plane and fly down."

"What? Now?"

"Your wife's situation is critical. We need to reduce her blood pressure or we risk multi-organ failure. You should call her family."

"I understand…" But I did not. Not really. Not in any meaningful sense of the term. The words I could comprehend, yes. But the significance was decidedly, stubbornly *in*compressible. Words, like abstractions, are easy. I could think of a million, just to describe my own position. Ineffectual. Unable. Inept. Impotent. Helpless. Impuissant. It was the real world application of the doctor's sentences that I could not process. And I tried. Multi: many, plural, more than one. Organ: Heart, lungs, kidneys, liver, etc. Things required for life. Failure: …

And there I stopped. Dead.

"You should call her family. And spend some time with your daughter. She needs you, too."

Need. There was that imperative again. I nodded, struck dumb. My mind began to close down. Became small. Focused. One. Thing. At. A. Time.

And so... Into the stairs. Instructions from [name tag says] Laura. Wash hands. Corkboard. Smiling faces. Darkness. Beeping machines. Plastic pods. Bili lights. Nurse Marta.

But now, what was she doing, this Marta, this saintly courier? Delivering a swaddled life force into my hands...my arms...my sobbing embrace. I looked into my daughter's face and experienced pure and perfect love, an atomic burst of tenderness and affection. To my overwhelmed self she appeared as an angel, an oracle of some universal truth or wisdom, a messenger from the pre-life, the un-life, come to bestow an answer to my deepest question. And so, not twenty-four hours into her earthly existence, two months before she was even due to *be*, I found myself on bended knee, in the strange and humbling position of asking my baby daughter for the strength and guidance I had for so long assumed would flow in the opposite direction.

* * *

Chapter XI

YOU'RE A GIRL

Dear (*drumroll please...*) Daughter,

That's right! You are going to be a little girl! Daddy's dearest daughter! Can you believe it? I'm going to confess a little something to you here, just between you and me: I think I secretly hoped you might be a girl all along. Not that I wouldn't have loved a bouncing baby boy around the house, too. It's just that you have such a strong, independent mother, you see, so fiercely intelligent and unique. If ever there were a role model for a little girl, your mother is that person. Of course, this may mean losing the occasional vote when it comes to democratic decisions around the dinner table, but I'm happy to surrender to the will of the in-family female majority, if that's what it comes to. (And who knows? Maybe you'll have a little brother in a year or two, a wee man to help rebalance the electorate.)

Jesting aside, the main thing of course (*of course!!!*), is that you and mommy are happy and healthy. The doctor here in Houston says you are progressing well and that mommy is doing a great job taking care of you in her belly. We'll check in again when we get down to Buenos Aires after Christmas.

On that note, there really is no place better to pass the holiday season than right here, in the United States. It seems like a magical time and place to be a kid. Everywhere I look I see smiling faces and decorations and fathers carrying their little girls high up on their shoulders. Now, I don't wish to rush you when I say, I can't wait to hoist you up on mine, to show you the world that awaits! The seasons, the festivals, the many celebrations. It's truly a wonderful time to be alive. For mommy, the scene here is pretty familiar. She spent a good deal of her childhood in the U.S., so everything from the Macy's Day Parade to the giant ball drop on New Year's Eve, with Hanukkah candles and Christmas lights and everything else in between (including the madness of holiday sales!), is part and parcel of the season for her. To me, it's still like a scene from the movies.

You see, when daddy was a little boy, growing up in Australia, we had Christmas on the beach in the middle of summer. In place of a sleigh pulled by reindeers, Santa Clause rode in on an inflatable red rescue boat and handed out candy canes to us kiddies as we jumped up and down on the white-hot sand. Not exactly snow-covered rooftops and roasting marshmallows by the fireplace, but it was an experience of a kind. Like your mother, you'll grow up with all kinds of stories and traditions, from Australia to America, and Argentina, too. A "third culture kid," is the term mommy often uses. "Cosmopolitan," I say. You'll be a real woman of the world, and we'll do everything we can to help you along your way. To wit, a few basic promises…

1. I will always value you as an individual and listen to your concerns and opinions;
2. I will never rush to judgment;
3. I will do my best to offer you guidance when and where I can;
4. I will never, ever, take you for granted.

Now, as much as I look forward to the opportunity to fulfill these promises, and more to come, you've got more growing to do, and your mother and I have plenty to take care of before your big arrival. So, you just sleep tight in there and enjoy your mother's nurturing care.

All my love and thoughts,

Daddy

December 2014,
Houston, USA

My Dear Girl,

Well, that was a whirlwind! A few weeks home with the family and
I'm more exhausted than when we began this journey! I do love visiting
the U.S., but it can be overwhelming at times, especially during the "silly
season." Every meal is a grand occasion, a cause for celebration, with more
food than one can possibly consume. Luckily, I was "eating for two,"
but even so... Then there's the Christmas sales and the constant media
barrage, encouraging everyone to "consume, consume, consume!" More
house! More car! More *stuff!* It's a lot to take in. I still find it a culture
shock going back, even now, and I spent half a childhood there! Still, it
was lovely to see everyone and to share with them the most important
news: You. They were all thrilled, of course, glad to see their own little girl
is finally "adulting." Hmm...

I don't know so much about that, but I do know it feels good to
be back in the "Paris of the South," where the pace here is slow and the
weather is fine, if a tad warm, given my (our) current state. And what,
exactly, is/are our current state/s? Let's see... I'd say, Determined (state
of mind), content (state of heart), robust (state of nails), shiny (state of
hair), bumpy (state of belly)... Ah, but you knew all this already, didn't
you? I wonder if you feel these developments in me, just as I feel them
in you? That would be an interesting thing to study, wouldn't it, the
way we communicate with one and other, in utero? I read the other day
that nursing infants actually send chemical signals through their saliva
back to their mother, informing them what antibodies they need and
even changing the contents of the milk their mothers produce. Like
customizing an order at Mom's Milk Bar. Isn't that amazing? Anyway...

I'm just happy we're here. And I'm especially happy to see your
father back in his element, in Buenos Aires. He finds it very appealing,
the way of life down here, writing in the cafés during the day and strolling
the wide, leafy boulevards of an afternoon, hands behind his back. He
could have been born in 19th century Vienna, your dad. Or Prague. A
romantic, wandering from coffeehouse to coffeehouse, talking to any old

soul about the state of the world. He's interested in people, you know, especially the little one I'm carrying around. So, settling down here suits him just fine. As for me, I'm coming around to the idea, if only because I don't have the energy required to lead the wandering lifestyle at the moment! (I barely have the energy to get to lunch without taking a quick power nap!) Moreover, Buenos Aires is as good a place as any to spend a couple of years as a young family. They're perfectly Latin regarding the whole approach to child rearing. Why, just the other night we were leaving a restaurant, it must have been past 11 o'clock, when a woman walked in pushing a stroller with her husband and two boys under 5 in tow. Nobody so much as blinked an eye. Dining so late would be grounds for child abuse in some "first world" countries, but not here. The waiter just smiled and, when the mother began nursing her youngest, right there at the table, he promptly brought her a glass of water. That's what I call *civilized*.

So yes, a year or two here will do us just fine. We'll find a place to live while your daddy finishes his book, something cozy and "us." Then we'll see what's next. I can easily imagine moving to Mexico City or Medellin or Mumbai in a couple of years. Or taking you on a grand tour, stimulating your burgeoning senses with the smells and sights and sounds from around the world. There's a lot to see out there, my little one, lots to experience and explore. But for now, I'll let you (and me) get some sleep. We're going to meet our new doctor here tomorrow, a Doctor Kostas. I'm looking forward to hearing all about your progress, now that we're almost halfway!

All my love for now,

Mommy

January, 2015
Buenos Aires

*   *   *

Chapter XII

LIGHTS OUT

M iss Hilda Nilsen watched the country pass by her window, first in drab city grays and browns then, gradually at first, in splashes of field green and sunflower yellow and sky blue. The train was heading south, back to Sinyang. As the vista expanded to include the mountains off in the distance, Hilda caught her own reflection in the window. She thought she saw in her face a new maturity, a certain seriousness to her expression. She tried to imagine the young woman who had traveled north along those tracks to Peking, six months earlier, with scarcely a native word on her tongue. She had seen a lot since then, the young missionary, had learned something of the ways of the land and its people. Enough to recognize how wide-eyed and ignorant she must have seemed back when she landed in this strange place. Enough, at least, to know she had a lot more to understand still. As she contemplated all that had come to pass between then and now, in her own short life and in the life of the country itself, she gave thanks for the many opportunities the good Lord had afforded her, to grow and to better serve Him.

There had been Dr. Ingram and his dear wife, of course, along with their troop of children, forever marching off to heed this or that calling, hearts full of faith and conviction. To Hilda, they were truly an inspiration; a shining example of what one small family unit could do to affect the whole, a tiny pebble cast into the world, sending great ripples out across a glass-like pond. There were the daily trips with Mrs. Ingram, to the flower markets and the food stalls and the little clothing stores, where she observed the ways of the people, in their businesses and on the street. The haggling. The bargaining. The jostling. The begging. The swarming, sweating pandemonium of that oversized village. She began to understand, too, beneath the pointing and shouting, the unseen thread stitching it all together. There were little rituals, Hilda had noticed, that seemed to accompany every aspect of Chinese life, from selling a fish to painting a door to burning a stack of joss paper at the foot of a sacred icon. There was an attention to detail, an order of action, that the young foreigner had not noticed before, when she first arrived in Sinyang. Everything had a place. A purpose. Was considered part of a grander plan, however chaotic and confusing that unspoken framework might at first appear. She watched closely the way Mrs. Ingram navigated this invisible web, how she handled her own affairs, the way she spoke to the help, the guards, the vendors in the square, the old men and women sleeping rough on the concrete stoops, how she treated them with equal parts respect and firmness, and how they, too, responded in kind. Every day brought new experiences and challenges to her mind and heart, just as it brought new tastes and smells and images to her senses.

So, too, she listened of an evening, when meals were served in the Ingram's well-appointed dining hall. There she heard dignitaries hold forth on matters of political importance, became attuned to the wide-ranging concerns of visiting leaders from neighboring missions, to the news they brought and the insights they shared. It was a period of unusual tension in the ancient kingdom. The country was undergoing a grand metamorphosis, at once cultural, societal, political, philosophical, in which every aspect of Chinese daily life was called into question. With the Wuchang Uprising in 1911, two thousand years of dynastic era had come to an end, and yet nobody quite knew what was to replace it. In the gaping power vacuum, elderly Confucian scholars argued with young army officers over the proper role of government in civil versus military matters. There were spirited disputes on street corners and in the teahouses, in prominent homes as well as prison cells. Older Chinese men debated the importance of the Xinhai Revolution or the Boxer Rebellion, military flashpoints that had exposed an essential weakness in the country's centralized powerbase. A few even remembered the Taiping Rebellion, or recalled what their fathers told them about it. Younger men, eager to establish their own mark on history, exchanged romantic tales of cult figures like Yuan Shikai and Dr. Sun Yat-sen, demi-gods who had led great armies in revolt against the long-cast shadow of the past. The transformation colored everything. In the countryside and on city streets, warring factions vied for regional power with former military cliques of the imperial Beiyang Army, a holdover from the fallen Qing Dynasty. It was a time of warlords and strongmen, exiles and revolutionaries, of loyalties pledged and promises betrayed. Alliances were formed and abandoned, seemingly at whim, and often with grave consequences. The transition of power was erratic, unpredictable and almost always soaked in blood. Hilda listened to the doctor's learned guests with equal parts fear and fascination. In public as in private life, the Lord had lighted her way and she was grateful for these lessons, especially during such a tumultuous time in history, when men had so strayed from His path. Nightly she prayed for wisdom and courage, both for herself and for those around her.

Along with the human (*all too human!*) elements of life, there were also moments of arresting natural beauty, sublime intervals when the sun shone through the clouds, however briefly, onto God's green earth. Amidst scenes of heartbreaking violence and despair, there were the peaceful afternoons spent picnicking in the shade of the Great Wall, visiting the jade pagodas and strolling the many ancient sites. There were the long weekends camping along the northern borders, far beyond the city walls, the endless starry nights suffused with the sweet smell of honeysuckle and flowering jasmine. There were hillsides blanketed in peonies and the taste of buttery yak milk and the enduring warmth of the locals, who opened their hearts to the wandering visitors. There were hymns sung and prayers offered, too, and baptismal waters to wash anew all the Lord's children. They rushed by her now, these scattered scenes, as the colors raced by her window on the long train ride back to Sinyang.

Edward Sovik was there to meet the young traveler at the station platform, as he had done on her very first visit. He was pleased to see her and said as much, though he was otherwise mostly quiet on the ride down. He appeared tired, she thought, his brown tuft now salted with gray. As they approached the city's Southern Gate, late in the afternoon,

Hilda noticed graffiti painted in bold red characters, high up on the wall for all to see:

He who shall not3 work, neither shall he eat.

The soldiers, smoking and laughing at their posts, seemed to be at no effort to remove the message. Suddenly chilled, Hilda wondered what manner of strife had passed through these gates since she was last within them. Crossing the threshold, she felt the guards' eyes fall heavily on her movements. They seemed emboldened, these leering men, their old, garrison-styled ribaldry imbued with a new and cocky lawlessness. She turned her own gaze away, toward the setting sun, but it had already fallen below the high brick walls.

*   *   *

When she arrived at last to the school, Hilda was glad to see Miss Anderson come to meet her, along with the other women of the house. Her host too had aged, she noticed, the months having settled themselves around her eyes and on her softly rounding shoulders.

"The Ingrams send along their prayers and very best wishes," Hilda remarked after their embrace, remembering her gracious hosts in Peking as they had waved goodbye to her from their porch.

"I was happy to receive word from them while you were away," replied Miss Anderson, warmly. Hilda saw again her bright red curls, remembering how they bounced when she talked. And yet, there was something missing from the glint of her eye. "They were most glad to have your presence in the house. The Ingram children are forever traveling hither and thither. I think Mrs. Ingram, in particular, was fond of your company. Especially your help at the pension. The doctor, too, spoke highly of your talent at the piano. Under a Professor Pavlovitch, I gather. Most impressive. We must showcase your refined skills here for our own girls."

Hilda blushed. "You're very kind, Miss Anderson. Though I'm afraid I benefited from the good professor's unlucky exile, which may soon be over, God willing."

"Yes, I heard he planned to return to Petrograd before the year's end. One hopes the situation in Russia improves, though one has one's doubts. Still, we make do, don't we Dear, with what we are given." An earnestness persisted in the woman's voice, laid there by years of habit. "Now come along. There's work to be done, and your hands are most welcomed in sharing it."

Though the old school was more or less as Hilda remembered it, the place seemed far more crowded than before, almost as if the space itself were smaller. Sister Christine was there, fussing about between the kitchen and pantry, forever exasperated that her own workload should be multiplied by Hillary's absentmindedness. There were the cooks and cleaners and the women who tended to the gardens. Ling was there, too, though she kept strange hours and Hilda rarely encountered her presence, either in the hallways or at meal times. In addition to the regular staff, the guest list seemed to have swelled considerably too. ("Must put in for that 'revolving door,' muttered Miss Anderson.) Moreover, it was not always clear to where these visitors were headed next, or when, so that the dining room and sleeping quarters became quite crowded indeed.

"I don't know how she manages," Hilda overheard Hillary saying to Sister Christine one morning, while they were folding bed sheets in the laundry room. "Why, she's got more than double the guest roster as last year, and still more are due every day. It's like she's running a hotel!"

"Like *we're* running a hotel more like it," retorted the Sister. "Look who's doing all the foldin' and the sweepin', eh? You and me, that's who!"

"We all put in, we do."

The truth was, everyone was working longer hours than before, picking up slack where they could, helping to hold the place together. Only Sister Christine ever complained, but even her heart was not really in it. She could see the strain on Miss Anderson's back and would sooner die than shirk her own duty in any way. Besides, if ever there was a time to dedicate oneself to the Lord's work, this was it, when the country seemed to be breaking apart around them. The political situation lingered on the edge of every conversation, colored the background of every plan, fought its way into the tension of every moment.

"They're closing the Chengdu mission," Edward Sovik announced over dinner one night, "and half a dozen more in the interior. At least temporarily. It's just not safe anymore. I'm afraid the situation is getting desperate."

"The situation," as everyone well knew, meant banditry. Looting. Violence. Chaos. In recent months there had been a wave of desertions from the imperial forces, soldiers who had abandoned their posts *en masse* and crossed over to join the roaming gangs. Some, who felt they had been lied to or cheated out of their wages, were bitter toward the old guard. Others welcomed any excuse to flout the army's strict rules; young men who were all-too happy to be swept away in the romantic notions that have accompanied all such revolutions throughout history. Many, many more were simply desperate; tired, starving and at the end of their rope. Their choice was made for them.

As the great empire rotted from the head, the limbs flailed and the body convulsed. Civil services, such as they were, had long been on the verge of failure, a point they now seemed to be crossing. Food shortages were becoming more and more frequent, as were the attendant medical emergencies. The rivers were choked with filth and the streets bled acrid smoke and pollution. The very earth seemed sick, as if in revolt against the sins of the men who dared walk upon it. As the weeks grew into months, the swelling crisis became all-consuming, the inevitable destination of virtually every passing thought. Over the high city walls the swirling winds brought the smell of death and decay. Not knowing what was to come, Hilda prayed for peace and guidance. Both would prove hopelessly elusive in the darkened days ahead.

*   *   *

It was around this time that Hilda became acquainted with a certain Mr. Chu. Nobody was quite sure how old Mr. Chu was, or when he first came to follow in the Lord's path, but it was generally accepted that he was among the first Chinese Christians in the province. He was known and acknowledged both on the streets of Sinyang, where the shopkeepers and stall owners stopped him on the corners and asked him for a word, and within the inner walls of the mission school, which he visited regularly. With a long white beard and kindly, aging eyes, he was a favorite among the schoolgirls, who would gather about him in semicircular groups to heed his wizened advice and to hear stories of the "olden times." In his coat pocket, tucked in a worn old matchbox, Mr. Chu carried with him a cricket, which he used to entertain the girls, who giggled along at his ventriloquist antics. Hilda liked to watch his shows, in which he would spin parables into conversations with his cricket, bringing the Word to life for the clapping children. She thought of him as a kind of patron saint, or maybe even a Santa Claus-like figure.

Eventually the day came, sometime late in the fall, when, like all God's creatures, Mr. Chu began to feel the weight of his age bearing down upon his shoulders. Content with the universe and his place within it, he requested that his family and friends construct for him a simple thatched hut, high in the hills beyond the city walls, beyond the rice paddies, where he might pass his final days, close to the earth and the sky and the water that the Lord made for all his earth-bound travelers. In this peaceful setting, he informed the women of the mission, he would prepare himself for delivery into his creators' waiting arms. The modest dwelling was completed in no time and, within a few weeks, Mr. Chu was waving goodbye to the city he knew so well. The townspeople bid him heartfelt farewell and the mission girls, who sang for him a chorus of heavy-hearted hymns, cried as they watched his stooped frame pass beyond the schoolyard for the last time, his cricket tucked away safely inside his pocket.

It was a short time later when Miss Anderson approached Hilda in the kitchen. The younger woman was washing up some dishes after supper.

"I'd like to make a trip to see our dear Mr. Chu," the older woman began, somewhat wistfully, peering vaguely off into the distance. Miss Anderson, too, had grown older with the passage of the seasons. "Word is he is in his final days. We should be there to offer him any comforts he might need. He has proved himself a great pillar of strength for the community. Now it is our turn to cradle him."

Hilda could see the dying man's face now, patterned with time. She imagined herself washing his feet and dabbing his brow. "It would be an honor to tend to our friend in his hour of need," she replied.

"Excellent," Miss Anderson went on. "We'll set out tomorrow in the morning, then, just the three of us."

Hilda had the sudden realization that they were not alone. She turned, not without a small fright, to see the Ling girl standing in the doorway behind her.

"Yes ma'am," replied Ling who, until that very moment, had not so much as uttered a sound.

"Besides," continued Miss Anderson, "it will be good for you two to spend some time together. We live in trying times, girls. If we are to make it through them and carry on the Lord's good work, we must learn to gather our allies close." And with that, she left the young women to themselves. Embarrassed, Hilda muttered a hurried excuse and made her way directly to bed.

The following morning, with the dimmed sun still low and heavy in the sky, the unlikely threesome set out on foot for Mr. Chu's hillside retreat. Miss Anderson walked in front; the two women followed close by her footsteps, their eyes downcast to avoid the soldiers' lingering gaze, their lips sealed to idle conversation. It was the first time Hilda had ventured outside the city walls since returning from Peking, and she was nervous at the prospect of what she might discover beyond their limits. Passing beneath the Western Gate for the first time, she subdued a chill as it corkscrewed up and down her spine. She was determined not to let the Ling girl sense her anxiety. Any pretense to indifference was soon surrendered, however, as the true extent of the surrounding squalor met the three women head on.

At first it appeared as though some slow-moving natural disaster had roared through the countryside; the rumbling destruction of an earthquake, perhaps, or a tsunami that had somehow made its way far inland, the waters of which had receded to lay bare the rot and decay of a society smashed to smithereens in its turbulent rage. On closer inspection, however, it became apparent that the carnage was not the result of some sudden, unexpected event sent from the heavens, but of the slow, torturous grind of neglect and apathy, a society degenerating at the fringes before finally collapsing in the middle. The winding dirt road, which led up into the hills, was pockmarked by a pathetic display of debris; old furniture, broken kitchen utensils, soiled rags and torn clothes. Dogs, mangy and skittish, prowled the scene in rabid packs, sniffing at the scattered piles of rubbish and scratching through the rubble. Little fires smoldered up and down the pathway, their noxious fumes, dampened by the previous night's rain, hung low in the pungent yellow air. The smell, at once organic and toxic, was thick and inescapable, and it seemed to seep in through one's clothing and into the skin. Above the impenetrable, amber-green haze, the late morning sun cast its light almost entirely in vain.

The journey itself was long and silent. In Miss Anderson's wake, the two young women soon fell into a dreary step, the unspoken words between them somehow understood. For months they had heard of the misery and deterioration beyond the city's protective walls, of the relentless havoc wrought by the bandits. They had heard the screams and howls too, sounding off into the echoless night. But this was the first time either had encountered the brutal reality on the ground. Hope, it seemed, was all but left to the hounds. The few remaining peasants shuffled along the streets aimlessly, as if wandering through a waking nightmare. Their doors had been kicked in, their possessions looted, their larders raided and their livestock slaughtered or burned alive. Resistance, it was well known, was invariably met with the very harshest of penalties. Public displays of rape and torture were not uncommon. What remained was the very absence of civilization, the faithless path to barbarism and brute animalism. Nature; tooth and claw.

Through the post-apocalyptic scene the women trudged, their noble mission a collective beacon propelling their one foot mechanically in front of the other. It was not until they neared the foothills, an hour or so march out of town, that the human carnage began to thin and, eventually, gave way to the cold indifference of the shifting dirt and sand. Slowly, the road began to incline as it wended into the fainting mountains. Hilda allowed her mind to drift out over the preceding miles, assuming an aerial view of the scorched terrain. What hath man wrought for himself here, she wondered, in this strange and forsaken land? To what fate had he condemned his wretched soul? Lifting her eyes for a moment, she noticed something ahead in the distance, off to the side of the road. It appeared as an abandoned bundle, or laundry bag, hidden in with the bushes. Miss Anderson and Ling had apparently seen the same thing, for the three slowed to a collective crawl as they approached the shapeless form. In the blistering noon twilight, it was near impossible to make anything out for sure, but Hilda fancied she discerned some clothing; a shawl perhaps, or a torn duvet. Then the reality dawned. Passing by, they saw protruding from the pile a human leg, stiffened with rigor, in torn military fatigue. The naked foot was gnarled, the sole badly bruised and beaten raw. The shinbone was broken just below the knee, so that the limb angled off like a swastika. The blankets flapped silently, uselessly in the breeze. Dumbstruck, the women stood in the middle of the deserted road, gaping at the severed appendage, until a passing eddy delivered the shock of rancid flesh to their noses. Hilda felt as though she might be sick. A cold sweat passed over her brow, then she noticed in her hand Ling's trembling grasp and heard her soft whimpers smothered in the dust. Without knowing who had reached out to whom, the two women squeezed tightly and held their breath for what seemed like an eternity. At last Miss Anderson mumbled a quiet prayer for victim and perpetrators both and, after bowing their heads for a solemn moment, the ladies shuffled off along their path. In the distance, they could hear the dogs howling into the sour noon haze.

* * *

Having traversed the hillsides and the plains, the three traveling women came at last upon the elderly man, asleep in a manger. His cot, made from the wood of a converted feedlot, was pressed into the far corner of the single room. Next to his bed was a cushioned stool and low-set table, on which were scattered a few meager belongings, a shaving blade, a candlestick, a world-weary bible. And an empty matchbox.

Through the window above his bed poured an apologetic afternoon light. Aside from some splintered cracks in the thatched roofing, it was one of only two light sources in the room; the other being the doorway, the threshold of which the three women presently crossed.

Mr. Chu did not wake with a startle, but rather stirred gently, a slow smile forming on his crusted old lips before he knew even to whom this reflexively sanguine expression would be directed. It took his cloudy eyes some moments to make the figures out against the soft light, his mind still longer to recognize them absent their usual context. When he finally did apprehend their mission, Hilda thought she sensed in his countenance a subtle disappointment, as though he had long been expecting a trinity of angles, come to deliver him at last into his maker's waiting hands. Denied this fate yet another day, he wasted no time placing himself in his guests' debt.

"You do me the greatest of pleasures, dear ladies," he spoke to them in clear and practiced English. "Just when a man feels he has enjoyed all that the good Lord might bestow upon him, he is gifted the delight of youthful company. Bless you." The mottled sunshine fell on the earthen floor, barely sufficient to illuminate the rest of the space, as the women stood aside from the entrance. Hilda registered a washbasin off in the opposite corner, above which hung a framed triptych of watercolor butterflies, gifts from the mission schoolgirls. Nearer her there was a little kitchen table and a lopsided cutting bench, too.

"My little pets," remarked Mr. Chu, nodding in Hilda's direction as she eyed the dancing butterflies. "Never a day passes they don't still bring me joy."

Hilda remembered the schoolyard faces, the girls and Mr. Chu's, then noticed again the empty matchbox. "Gone to tell his stories elsewhere," said the old man's wiley expression.

Onto the table the women emptied their rucksack, which contained some bread and vegetables, plus some sweets the girls had baked for their favorite ventriloquist and a special greetings card, on which was drawn a tall thin man with a long white beard holding in his hand a cricket the size of his head. The speech bubble read, "And for today's lesson, girls…"

Hilda recalled the children's mirth when they had entrusted it to her. She handed it to Mr. Chu, who let out a wholesome laugh of his own, as if he had been in on the joke all the while.

Across the room, Ling quickly got to peeling the potatoes and chopping the napa cabbage, while Miss Anderson went to fetch some water from the well around the back of the premises. Hilda, meanwhile, acceded to Mr. Chu's invitation and sat next to his mattress on the little cushioned stool. Seldom did he forgo an opportunity to practice his English.

"You are a long way from home, my dear girl," he observed without condescension. "Tell me, why do you travel so far, to be with us in this remote part of the world? Is there nobody in your own country in need of ministering?"

Hilda, conscious of Ling's ears, waited for the other women to resume chopping before offering her response. "So far as I know the world, Mr. Chu, and that indeed is very little, I find people all over wanting for the Lord's guidance."

"I see, I see," the old man muttered. "And tell me, when did you, yourself, first hear of His Word?"

Again Hilda timed her reply for maximum privacy. "My father is a man of God, Mr. Chu. I grew up in the church, since I was a little girl. I guess I have always felt His word, even before I knew what it meant."

Mr. Chu nodded. "A church man, huh? How very interesting. And tell me, child, what have you come to know of our ways, here in this land? I hope we Chinese have brought something to teach our visiting guest."

Again, there was not the slightest trace of patronization in Mr. Chu's voice, but the question nevertheless put Hilda on guard. She thought a long while as Ling's chopping sounded in her ears.

"I have learned that the bird does not sing because it has an answer," she said at last, "but because it has a song."

The old man crossed his fingers on his frail chest, their little spider veins intertwining at the knuckles. The wry smile did not depart from his lips for a second. He seemed satisfied, even impressed.

"I see you have studied the proverbs." He spoke in slow, deliberate sentences. "I am glad they speak to you. Tell me, dear child, what worries you? Do not be shy, for we all have concerns. What is it that occupies your young mind of a night, before you lay your head to rest? God willing, I may offer you some more proverbs, that they may assist you on your journey."

Again Hilda contemplated Mr. Chu's question, watching the slow rise and fall of his ancient hands upon his threadbare shirt. Many times she had seen him entertain the young schoolgirls in the yard. Many times, too, had she seen him on the street corners, engaged with elders in deep discussion. It was a gift, she recognized, to be able to transcend age and conversation with such felicity of wit and charm, to speak to the young and old with an open heart. "That the good lord might know such company yet," she heard herself thinking, happily.

"I am not nearly so knowledgeable to entertain such grave concerns as you, Mr. Chu," she bowed her head in sincere reverence then, after looking toward Ling, added quietly, "but I do hope to know some courage in this life, if only to better serve His will."

Mr. Chu turned his milky eyes to his young interlocutor, crouched uncomfortably beside him. "My dear child, nothing is quite so bold as timidity when it is tested. And these are nothing, if not testing times, yes?"

At this they smiled together.

"There is much to learn, and to prove," Hilda agreed.

"And you will do both, in good time," Mr. Chu reached his bony hand out, until Hilda held it in hers. "Remember," he took her eyes in his, "be not afraid of growing slowly; be afraid only of standing still."

At that moment, Miss Anderson returned with the water. She surveyed the room with some satisfaction and, catching the end of the bedside conversation, joined in herself.

"Reciting proverbs, are we? I've got just the one: Talk does not cook rice."

With that, the four of them broke into a familiar laughter. It was the first time Hilda could remember ever seeing Ling smile. She was not nearly so stern as she remembered her; in fact, she recognized a certain reserve in her new friend, as if a common shyness had been all that stood between them until now. They exchanged a contented glance and set about preparing the food for Mr. Chu, who sat quietly on his makeshift bed, watching the day's fading light through his open window.

Later that evening, after Mr. Chu had bade them farewell and agreed to receive them again soon, when tummies were full and spirits high, the visitors set off down the hillside for the long trek home. The moon was full and plump in the sky, its reflected light cast across the ground like a great silver lake. The women walked in single file, along the ribbon-thin paths that crisscrossed the terraced rice fields. Miss Anderson set out in front, Hilda next, and finally Ling behind. The stars shone across the pools of water, undisturbed in the still night air, so that heaven itself appeared to catch their every step.

Hilda was contemplating the celestial beauty gathered around her when, of a sudden, she heard Ling's gentle voice sound off behind her.

"Night drew her sable cloak, and pinned it with a star."

The girl then began to hum a gentle tune, the honeyed melodies of which Hilda had never before heard. Whose words were those, she wondered, that they might reach across the universe and touch a forsaken orphan, lost in a forgotten kingdom, on this still and starry night? In silent meditation they walked on, trailing soft notes through the peaceful fields, unified in adventure, courage brimming in their breast, toward the mighty chaos that lay below.

* * *

As the countryside collapsed beyond the city walls, the friendship between Ling and Hilda grew ever stronger each passing month within them. Though harried by the unrelenting demands of the household, they made sure to see one and other as time permitted and, when that was impossible, used such moments to motivate themselves through the din and dirge of the endless days. Sometimes, if half an hour opened itself up in the afternoon, they would walk the gardens together, exchanging childhood tales amidst the scent of hanging geraniums, sweet osmanthus and planted apricot trees. Sparingly at first, then with growing confidence, Ling revealed to her American friend tales from her time growing up in the mission as a distant, introverted schoolgirl. Though she seldom spoke of herself directly, she recalled in remarkable detail how Miss Anderson and the others had changed with the passage of years. Their lines, postures, general habits. It was in this way Hilda learned, as she had secretly suspected, that Miss Hillary was once considered quite the fair maiden, when she arrived at the mission almost a decade earlier. Of course, that was before she fell under Sister Christine's regimental orders and, subsequently, awoke one day to discover herself wholly devoted to the Lord's service, as if by sheer force of habit. The two of them giggled at the thought of ditzy Hillary as a desirable, coquettish young woman, and still more at Sister Christine's unspoken jealousy when the young suitors would pay their hopeful visits.

"The good Lord helps any man intent on leading astray one of Sister C's flock," Ling would laugh. "She's not one to be on uneven terms with, that woman!"

"Not unless one wishes to meet their maker in a hurry!" agreed Hilda, with a demonstrative shake of her fist.

So the pair laughed through the sweet, shortening afternoons. Often, too, they would linger beyond supper, volunteering to relieve one or another of the cleaners from their duties in order that they may pass a few moments scrubbing floors and dishes together, sparing each other the tedium of unaccompanied labor. Observing their growing closeness with some affection of her own, Miss Anderson scheduled the two young women for simultaneous duties whenever she could, usually once or twice a week.

Hilda found herself delighted to discover in Ling a very eager listener, and so seized on the opportunity to transport the two of them back over the Pacific, to the prairielands of her distant adolescence. She recalled Sundays in the little red church on the hill, its white steeple reaching up into the moody spring skies. She introduced Ling to the wide open spaces of her youth, invited her to swim with her brothers and sisters in the cool fresh waters of the nearby lake and to lay down in the long grass, where they would fill empty hours making storyboards out of the drifting clouds, marveling at their casual, backlit metamorphoses. Ling would listen intently and ask questions about Hilda's family. Her mother, in particular, was a subject of endless fascination.

"What was it like, having her in your life every day?"

"I guess I didn't think about it much at the time," Hilda confessed, her heart suddenly weighed down by the invisible absence. "She was kind to us children, though, and a dutiful wife, I think. She had a musical heart, too, and would often play to us after supper."

"And did she teach you? The language of music?"

"And the piano, yes." Hilda allowed herself to become lost in reverie. "We were all musical in that way. Our mother's children. We could each of us hold a tune, but I was the only one she instructed on the piano."

"I guess she saw something there…"

"Maybe. Well, I'd like to think so. You know, I sometimes feel her by my side, reading to me, even still. She wore her hair in long braids in those days. Sometimes they would fall loose and hang down by her shoulders while she turned the pages for me. She washed her hair with flaxseed oil. Whenever I smell it, I close my eyes and I think of her."

"It must have been wonderful, to know your mother like that. Almost like knowing your future self, in a way…"

Though she was the last to indulge in self-pity of any kind, Hilda sensed in Ling a profound longing for a life that could never be, a permanent melancholy that would accompany her all her days. Still, she answered Ling's questions about her own parents and, in some way, hoped that the recalled stories might paint for her friend some version of that unlived experience. At least, she prayed as much.

It was on one such evening, the day's chores nearing completion and the schoolgirls safely asleep in their dorms, when the two young women found themselves folding bed sheets together on the mission veranda, overlooking the inner courtyard. The moon was still in its first quarter and its dimmed silvery tones fell softly on the gardens below. The leaves on the apricot trees appeared as though made of cement, while the pond reflected the wisps of smoke as they sailed across the apathetic night sky above. Beyond the city walls, the regular cries and howls were beginning their frightening chorus. The bandits would soon be on the prowl, their bloodlust growing ever more daring under the fading lunar lamp. The mission had lately taken to hanging a Red Cross flag over the entrance gates as a way to deter would-be invaders. Besides the regular, enrolled students, the school now housed a growing population of teenage girls from around the city; daughters of wealthy parents who wished to place their heiresses out of harm's way.

"Tell me again about when the Persians came to stay with your family," Ling prompted, her eyes automatically scanning the school walls. "Did they really stay for the whole summer?"

Hilda had told the story a dozen times or more, always with new anecdotes or recollections. She searched her memory for a fresh angle, the taste of a new and foreign spice, perhaps, or some curious cultural contrast over which they might discover a laugh to pass away the time. As she searched her past, she suddenly saw the color drain from Ling's face and her eyes widen in the darkness. Their conversation immediately froze, the unspoken words falling like knives, cutting the breathless air between them. With her body otherwise perfectly still, Ling mouthed the word already on Hilda's lips: "BAN-DITS!"

In the glass reflection of the double French doors behind Ling's head, Hilda saw what her friend espied over her own shoulder; above the school walls, a quiver of razor bayonets glinted in the soft light. Boots could be heard shuffling clumsily in the dirt beneath them. Then, in icy silence, a pair of ladders were gently leaned against the bricks. Like a deadly serpent, a writhing muscle of blackened scales poured over the walls and into the schoolyard below. The weapons of terror sliced through the still air as the bandits scampered for cover under the verandas and behind the bushes. A white fear gripped at Hilda's throat as she watched the breach in helpless silence. It was like a virus infiltrating a cell, filling it with poison. She felt nauseated, as though the bandits were already crawling over her skin, under her clothes.

With a slow motion of her head, Ling bade her friend creep back inside through the door, ajar behind her. Hilda prayed the old hinges would not creak as they moved stealthily through the dark.

Once inside, Ling whispered clearly, "Go to your room and fetch what you need, but keep only small change in your outer pockets. Meet me in the girls' upper dormitory, along the left wing, when you are done. The others will cover the main hall downstairs."

Willing her granite legs to motion, Hilda did as she was told while Ling crept silently in the opposite direction, to her own quarters. Within a blurred minute, they were kneeling together outside the girls' room upstairs. It had only recently been converted from storage space, so as to house the overflow from the worried townspeople. Hilda was on the verge of saying something, daring her words to break the stillness, when they heard a cracking shot fired from below. The deafening sound whipped around the halls and up the staircases, shattering the silence throughout the house. From the other side of the door they heard the girls cry out in panicked terror. Ling and Hilda lunged into the room, closing the doors behind them and urging the girls to remain quiet and calm. Together they ushered the clutch of petrified teenagers, matchstick legs trembling under their nightclothes, into a walk-in linen closet in the rear corner of the room.

Wild shrieks could be heard beneath the floorboards as the bandits raided the other rooms. Another shot pierced the night, this one fired from somewhere outside in the courtyard. Then another. And another. The women and girls huddled together, ducking their heads below the imagined trajectory of stray bullets. A confusion of men's voices could be heard, shouting over one another. Next came the machine-like stomping of military boots along the halls. Within a few minutes, they were advancing up the stairs. They heard the French doors smashed open, the glass panels shattered in the process. The girls huddled still closer, quivering and whimpering in each other's arms. Silence blanketed them for a second, as they drew their collective breath. Then... SMASH! A flash of light burst through the closet door as it flung wide open. Long dark shadows began grabbing indiscriminately, wrenching the frightened girls from one and another's desperate grasp, flinging their gangly bodies in a squealing heap in the middle of the room, where they once again clustered together, making tiny balls of their prepubescent bodies. They were like hunted prey, herded together before the kill. Somewhere in the confusion, Ling and Hilda were tossed in among the bewildered girls. Instinctively, they pressed themselves to the front of the heap, placing their own bodies between the jabbing bayonets and the cowering mass of childish limbs and tears.

There was a rush of commotion and shouting as the men all seemed to be yelling at once, thrusting their knife-mounted guns at the women and children. Rising to her knees in center-front, Hilda felt the barrels of several guns raised to her forehead, like so many spears around a cannibal's fiery cauldron. Was this it, she thought? Before her mind's eye, Hilda Nilsen saw the long grass of the prairies and the little red church up on the hill. The shouting mouths fell mute and she heard, instead, her mother's delicate, alabaster hands dancing along the piano keys. Over her brow and down her neck, the cool, fresh water from the lake washed away her fear. "If this is to be the end, I pray the Lord to receive my soul," she poured all her courage, all her pumping lifeblood into her invocation. "If it is not, then consecrate my mind, Dear Lord, steel my resolve that I might give unto you my faith everlasting."

Hilda felt a moment of stillness pass over her body before she was suddenly knocked aside. It took her a second to realize it was Ling who had shoved her and, having scrambled to her feet and thrown up her own hands, stood shouting at the encircling predators in rapid-fire Chinese, "We have no money! We are a simple church mission! We have no money! Leave us now!"

For a moment, the men trained their gun barrels on Ling. They seemed to grow silent as they let this hysterical woman flail about and scream in their faces.

"Leave us now!" she pinned her puny shoulders back then, realizing the men were paying her no attention, she spat at their feet. Silence followed until, mouth by fouled mouth, the men started to laugh. They roared in violent peels, shrieking louder and louder, cackling into the night. Ling's wiry frame shivered with fear, but still she held her ground. Hilda thought she could bear no more. She made to stand again herself when, abruptly and without warning, one of the men stepped forward behind a gnarled face and straggly whiskers and, swirling his long rifle in his hand like a baton, jabbed the butt of the gun smack into Ling's open cheekbone, dropping her stunned body instantly to the floorboards with a single, vicious blow. As the aggressing man stooped over Ling's unconscious slump, one of the school girls, a chubby little student named Ma, hurled her velvet change purse at the man's head. Missing him altogether, the sack tore open against a hanging lantern, scattering the cash coins across the floorboards. Instantly, the men dropped to their knees and began scraping up the little holed disks, like boys falling on scrambled marbles in a playground. As they crawled and clawed at the rolling metal, a series of gunshots suddenly rang out across the courtyard. The glass from the double-paned French doors shattered under the shower of bullets and the men, already on their hands and knees, beat a hasty retreat from the room on all fours. Lying on her back, heart pounding in her chest and Ling's unconscious body next to her, Hilda watched as the bullets ricocheted off the ceiling plaster above, shards of glass raining down from the dusty clouds. Suddenly, she felt a sharp pain in her right temple, then darkness and silence engulfed everything.

*   *   *

Chapter XIII

INTO THE ABYSS

S ome in the West say there is a process by which all things, at all times, are becoming their opposites. Writing two and a half millennia ago, Heraclitus employed the term *enantiodromia*, from the Greek (Romanized) *enantios* – opposite; and, *dromos* – running course. "Cold things warm," he observed, "warm things cool. Wet things dry and parched things become sodden." So too does day turn to night, just as darkness comes to light. And life, precious, vibrant life, in all its pain and love and glory, succumbs eventually to the nothingness of death. One is not necessarily apart *from* the other, rather a part *of* the whole. Harmony is to be found in "reflexive tension," explained the clever old Ephesian, "like the bow and the lyre." His was a philosophy dependent on the constancy of change, like the river into which the same man cannot step twice, both because the river has changed and so too the man.

Evie, of course, had her own take on the theory.

"There must be moments of transition," she intoned, "when things overlap. Like gray areas, when something is both itself and its opposite."

The afternoon sun was setting across the Danube, beyond Buda, casting its long summer light over the Fisherman's Bastion (Halászbástya). Evie sat solemnly amid the iron shoes of the Cipők a Duna-parton memorial, a monument dedicated to the thousands of human beings who were lined up along the riverbanks during WWII, and coldly transported from the land of the living to the realm of the dead. She let her bare feet hang above the brown, lapping waters and continued her solemn contemplation.

"Pregnancy, for example, seems to me one of those stages, where the mother is both supporting life and tempting death at the same time. I mean, you don't have to go back far before you start encountering some pretty horrific maternal mortality statistics. But even more than that, all living things are in the process of dying, decaying, atrophying. It's part of the natural course, one side of the grand cosmic equilibrium. We are not... then, for a brief time, we are... then we are not again. Forever. It's something we talk about all the time, you and I. It's neither good nor bad. It's just... what it is."

I listened as I wandered between the empty, *emptied*, footwear. One hundred and twenty shoes lined up in uneven steps, hastily discarded by trembling limbs, all facing the same inevitable direction, ready to step into the same and ever-changing river. I tried to imagine the street sweeper, donning his work boots for the last time as he was marched, carbon steel barrel pressed between his shoulder blades, from his gloomy room in the nearby ghetto. I thought of the hopeful woman squeezing her toes into fashionable sling backs, purchased after months of thrift and discipline. Did she have in mind an interview? A dance? A first date? How could she have known she would one day step out of them and into a watery grave? Then a tiny pair of Mary Janes, size two or three, set a child's arm-length from her mommy's hollow flats. I imagined the little hands clasped so tightly, shivering in the cold, watching the light disappear behind the western bank. Life, then...not.

The palette overhead was changing from warm to cool. I turned at a pair of vacant kitten heels and made my way back towards Evie, who sat staring off into the distance.

"The mother is like a conduit, her body breaking apart as she feeds and fuels the next generation, transferring her vitality from her ancestral past, down through her present, and off into the future. Woman and child are not separate entities at this point, but parts of a whole. Not opposites, as in mirror images; more like opposing points on the same circumference."

Evie buckled her own shoes and took my outstretched hand. The moon was in its place now, gathering far off stars under the diffused light. Later, at dinner, the subject came up again.

"You know," I ventured, the afternoon's iron laces still knotted around my mind, "he also wrote that 'war was the father of all, king of all.'"

"Who? Heraclitus?"

"The very same."

"Context?"

"Unsure. He supposed that war, 'rendered some gods, others men,' that 'he makes some slaves, others free.'"

Evie rested her chin in the palm of her hand. Over her shoulder, the bells of Saint Stephen's Basilica rang out under a lamenting slate sky. She waited until they finished before arresting her gaze from the heavens. "You know, I watched you by the river today, walking between those unfilled shoes. It's so sad, what they did to all those poor people. War is a scourge, no doubt. I go down to that spot every time I'm here, to watch the waters pass under the bridges. To declaim against the seemingly *un*changing nature of man, now and then, old and new."

Her expression flooded with a profound longing, a desire to reach beyond her grasp.

"As for Heraclitus," she went on, "I don't know what he meant by that. Perhaps he was talking of an inner struggle, an internal conflict of some kind, like the way a person wrestles with his own mind. Some, if they are fortunate, find freedom therein; others madness…"

"Maybe, maybe." I thought of those pitiful size twos, petrified in their penultimate step. My head rang, the timeless bells reverberating within. "Or maybe he was merely observing that war is part of the repeating cycle, a grim inevitability to which we are all condemned."

Evie held my stare, as if balancing a thought on the tip of her consciousness. On the verge of articulation, toes dangling over the edge, she demurred. In place of words, she brought my fingers to her lips and held them there in her warm, vital breath.

A week later, she was ready to leave the city. It was around this time I suggested we might think about "settling down," finding "a place" where we could rest and raise a family of our own. Shortly afterward, we were battling our way through the trenches of the "Big Euro-Discord."

She on her side of the door, cross-legged on green tiles; me on mine, marching back and forth on polished parquetry.

To this day I'm not sure what scared Evie most; the idea of perpetual transition, the "gray area," or the thought that things might go on the same as they always had; the certainty of death inevitable; or the possibility that she might never really live.

Either way, something had to change.

*   *   *

I awoke to a dull ache in my side. (For how long had I been asleep in this chair, blanketed by the sound of Evie's beeping machines, the wooden arm carving a space for itself between my lower ribs?) Shifting carefully my position, I peered up over the edge of Evie's bedside railing, not quite knowing what I might find. I held my breath until I determined that she was not holding hers. I watched the gentle undulation of those clean white sheets, the rise giving way to the fall, the fall in turn filling with the rise. Slow and cyclical. Cyclical and slow. I exhaled.

Then I remembered the critical fraction. What was it? Twenty-two over thirteen? Two-twenty over one-thirty? Oh, the pressure!

"Her blood pressure needs to come down," Dr. Laso's words printed themselves from my memory, like a computer spitting out data to be analyzed later by unsmiling men in over-starched lab coats. "Risk… multi-organ… where is her family?"

Wait! Evie's family! Had I called? I could not recall. I could not recall. Instead, I trained my mind on the numbers-at-heart, refocused on the printout. What had Doctor Laso said? Two-twenty over one-thirty. Systolic over diastolic. Pressure exerted when blood is ejected versus pressure exerted between heartbeats. I could not bring myself to think about that downtime. The bleak eternity between pulsations. That gray area. That dreaded transition phase. I rubbed unconsciousness from my own eyes. Before me flashed a graphic from ninth-grade phys-ed. class, fuzzy on the overhead projector screen. The plastic sheets were transposed like a jigsaw puzzle; venae cavae, superior over inferior; atria, right and left, upper over lower; valves, mitral and aortic; veins in, arteries out.

And lo! The central engine of the great human machine, pumping life through the system, carrying oxygenated blood to far off limbs, animating existence itself. Truly, a sight to behold!

Ruminating on the anatomy of a heart, I drew myself to Evie's side. She appeared pale. Her lips drained. Her waning face, gibbous in the soft hallway light. Her angelic form cloaked under the crisp cotton pall, floating somewhere between worlds. Gently, I pressed my fingertips to her wrist, feeling the radial stream of her aspirin-thinned blood flowing under my nervous touch. Oh my poor, helpless Evie! Where have you gone? Still she lay, unmoving, unflinching, unusually unanswering. A thick, coagulated silence filled the room. And all the while, beneath my fingertips, pulse…pulse…pulse…

"…for this is my blood of the new and everlasting covenant," the priest declared in his country Irish brogue, "which is poured out for many for the forgiveness of sins."

I felt Evie's hand in mine, supple and alive, and I knew from her clasp all that she did not then have to say. Never a friend's wedding did she miss and this, for one of her dearest friends, would be no exception. Outside the little church, a gentle breeze blew through the heather and over the verdant hills. Beyond the meadows, in neighboring county Cork, a young mother on her way to town sensed that the weather might be turning.

"May you feel no rain," continued the priest, safely perched in his sanctuary, "for each of you will be a shelter to the other. May God be with you and bless you, may you live to see your children's children. May the wind be always at your back, may the warm rays of sun fall upon your home…"

After the service, back at the nearby reception hall, the water of life really began to flow. At one point, between "Mo ghrá Thú, a Thiarna" and some incomprehensible, tear-filled speeches, Evie and I stepped out together, into the emerald night. I gave her a look that said, simply, "So?"

"Well, there's a lot of imagery in there, that's for sure."

"I warned you."

"And everyone seemed to know their lines."

"Lamb of God, you take away the sins of the world, have mercy on us. Lamb of..."

"Yes, yes. Well, I thought it was rather moving, just the same."

"You didn't have to sit through twelve years of daily masses as a child," I laughed in reply. "But yes, it was a heartfelt ceremony. Of course, that says nothing about the truth claims undergirding Catholicism itself..."

"I'm not sure that's for me to say. In any case, it's true that a great many people believe it to be true. That, to me anyway, is far more interesting."

"Belief, for better or for worse."

Evie smiled, the way she smiled when conversation slipped beneath surface level, into waters she found deeper, more rewarding. "You know, some people think it's mythology that we have to thank for our survival, that, without our ancestors' ability to spin yarns, tell tall tales, create collective narratives, our own particular branch of the human experiment, that is to say, sapiens, would have long been left bare..."

I smiled back at her, the smile I always wore when I found Evie in her element. She read my expression, correctly, as "Go on..."

"The theory, which might be a kind of myth in and of itself, goes that, sapien overcame his otherwise stronger, more adapted homo competition – neanderthalensis, for example, or floresiensis, or erectus – because he was able to harness the power of his imagination. Through that fiction, he was able to build group cohesion on a scale not before seen. That meant organizing and collectivizing modes of peace, and of war."

"Not all myths are created equal," I wondered, aloud.

"Anyway, it's just something I was reading the other day..."

Of course it was, Evie. Of course it was.

Overhead, meanwhile, irascible Zeus had apparently grown peevish. The young mother from Cork had been right; the weather had indeed turned, much for the worse. Sheltering under the reception hall eave, my thoughts returned to the afternoon service, where the priest was still holding forth...

"By the power of this sacrifice, O Lord, accompany with your loving favor what in your providence you have instituted, so as to make of one heart in love those you have already joined in this holy union, and replenished with the one Bread and the one Chalice. Through Christ our Lord."

Chorus: Amen.

Evie's delicate hand in mine, I closed my eyes and leaned once more on the old Roman church pew, smooth and time-worn against my ribs, and let my mind drift off, over and beyond the meadows, into the gathering squall.

* * *

There are no clocks in eternity, no sundials to mark the time beyond Dante's darkened wood. Still I descended, in my own hypnagogic limbo, toward that fated oblivion. There I found myself on the brink of an abyss, a melancholy valley leading down from the tear-drenched earth on which I stood. From that darkened lowland rose unending wailings and a mist such that, though I gazed into its depths, I could not make out top from bottom, side from side along the winding path.

From beside me rang her familiar voice, its timbre deathly pale. "Let us descend into the blind world now. I shall go first and you will follow me."

My own reply, in unseen space, "But how shall I go on if you are frightened, you who have always helped dispel my doubts?"

Said she unto me: "The anguish of the people whose place is here below, has touched my soul with the compassion you mistake for fear. Let us go on, the way that waits is long."

So she set out on our path, circling that first ring of the abyss. Here the deafening sighs filled our ears and caused the timeless air to tremble. From the multitudes, crowds of women and infants too, arose such quivering lamentations as to wrench the heart asunder. Theirs was a sorrow without torment, a yearning without hope.

"Do you not ask who are these spirits whom you see before you? I'd have you know, before you go ahead, they did not sin; and yet, though they have merits, that was not enough, because they lacked baptism, the portal of faith elsewhere embraced. And if they lived before Christianity, their worship was not deemed as fitting unto God.

"For these defects, and for no other evil, they now are lost and punished with just this: to have no hope and yet to suffer eternal longing."

A harrowing sorrow seized my being on hearing her words, for we had known and studied together great minds, since seen suspended in that torturous limbo.

"Tell me, Dearest, did any ever go – by his own merit or others' – from this place toward blessedness?"

She who understood the meaning between my words replied: "It is told by one who came before me here that, when he was himself new-entered, he beheld a Great Lord enter here; the crown he wore, a sign of victory.

"He carried off the shade of the first father, of his son Abel, and the shade of Noah, of Moses, the obedient legislator, of father Abraham, David the King of Israel, his father, and his sons, and Rachel, she for whom he worked so long, and many others – and He made them blessed; and I should have you know that, before them, there were no human souls that had been saved."

Onward we continued, these words passing between us as we pressed on into the wood, thronged by many spirits. Our path came by the room where I had slept, the chair now vacant, the clean white sheets empty. There I beheld a mighty fire, beating back a hemisphere of shadows. Though it burned at a distance, I could still make out, in that clearing of light, the faces of nobler persons.

Said I: "O you who honor art and science both, who are these souls whose dignity has kept their way of being, separate from the rest?"

And she to me: "The honor of their name and deeds, which echoes in the realm of the living, wins for them heavenly grace, and holds them in its timeless embrace."

Then another voice, unknown to me: "Pay honor to the estimable poetess; her shadow, which had left us, now returns."

When the strange voice subsided, I saw approaching a group of six, two in front, flanked by four. In aspect, they were neither sad nor joyous, but contemplative just the same.

"Look well on the pair who hold the sword in hand," she said to me, "for they move before the others as lords. Those shades are of Homer and of Sappho, the consummate poets; the others are Horace, satirist; next Ovid; then Lucan and, the last among them, Virgil.

Exalted so in such high company, we moved together toward the light, where we came upon a splendorous castle, encircled by a tranquil stream and seven towering walls. With these sages I passed through the seven portals into a flowering meadow of green. Those personages gathered there carried in their grave and solemn features a great authority. Moving toward the lustrous path, I beheld all those assembled, there on the enameled green. Those great-hearted souls were shown to me, so that I yearn again to dream of such a place.

Flanked by Hector and cunning Aeneas stood Penelope, bright faced and fair. Among them too was falcon-eyed Caesar, standing ready in his armor, and too many more to name. Raising my eyes a little higher, I espied the man who claimed nothing he didn't know, seated in the philosophic family. To his right side stood Plato, to his left the Father of Logic, Aristotle. Behind them Democritus, who put the world to chance, and Lucretius, who would set it back to order. Then Epictetus, Zeno and Seneca did follow. Next Thales, Pythagoras and Anaxagoras. Then Hippocrates, he of medicine, and Euclid the geometer, alongside Hypatia, mother of mathematics. And watching over them all, that clever old Ephesian, Heraclitus.

Many more did gather, in that vast and timeless assembly, too many, in fact, to recount here. For though my eternal quest impelled me on, the heavy sleep upon my head was of a sudden smashed by an enormous thunderclap, so that I awakened with a force, transported through the unconscious portal, to my dying guide's whitened side.

* * *

The storm itself began before the first raindrop touched the ground. Long before the convection cycle swarmed to life; before the electro-conductive plasma formed into those massive cumulonimbus cells, reaching up into the stratosphere; prior even to the sun's ancient energy radiating off the earth, there was a time when, deep in the galaxy's molten core, the cosmic matter was settled.

"Anions and cations," declared Evie, somewhat proudly. She was leaning against the railing of our little *terrazita*, here in Buenos Aires, surveying the brewing tempest as it gathered energy on the eastern horizon. I can still see her in profile, hair blown back in the outflow, standing on the edge of the building, as if pitching into the future from the hull of a mighty vessel, pressing forward into the coming weather. Between us and the far off clouds lay the *Cementario de la Recoleta*, its five thousand or so vaults an upper-crust cross section of the nation's history; presidents and intrepid explorers; writers and celebrities; doctors and generals; knaves, crooks and heroes, interred in elaborate marble mausoleums, Deco and Nouveau, Baroque and Neo-Gothic, spires reaching toward the heavens. Beyond them, villa miseria (#31), a slum of some forty thousand souls, living, or barely *existing*, hand-to-mouth. Then came the waters of the grand Rio de la Plata, widest river in the world and theater of many naval battles, the silver vein along which so much of the continent's resource wealth once sailed.

Raising a sundowner to my lips, I cast my windswept captain a quizzical glance. "Anions and…?"

"Cations," she cheerily replied, enraptured by the climatic, climactic event unfolding before her. "Negatively and positively charged ions, respectively. To think that there are opposing forces battling for control over the weather right there, in those billowing columns, and that the result should be a late afternoon's lightning show for us, front row on our little terrace…" Evie left her voice on the wind and came to sit beside me, on our flimsy plastic deckchairs (newly purchased for this very occasion).

Sighing, she took my hand in hers. "This was the right decision. To come here, I mean. Buenos Aires. I do feel at home here, in a way."

Beyond the river, a sheet of lightning illuminated the sky. The thunder would soon come rumbling in. I could feel the energy in the air, the charge. "I'm so glad you're happy, Evie. Wherever we are together, that's our place, our home."

"Be it Buenos Aires or Paris," she raised her own glass, "Budapest or… wait, what do they call the 'Paris of the West' again?"

"Uh, Detroit?"

"No, not of the *Mid*west. Although that could be fun, too…"

I mustered my very best Bogart: "We'll always have…Detroit?"

"Ok, so that doesn't have quite the same ring to it. In any case…"

Just then the heavy green skies lighted and the slow-falling dominos began to disturb the atmosphere. Gusts of wind whipped down the concrete canyon beneath us, along Avenida Las Heras and up toward the parks.

"Ooh! Here we go!" Evie leaned forward in her chair, like a child at a fireworks display, yearning to get closer to the action. "I just read something about this on the plane. You know, these types of clouds only last a short time. Maybe half an hour or so. There's just too much energy built up to sustain…" a bolt of lightning forked across the sky, searching, searching. "Wooow!" Evie cried, her face positively glowing with excitement. "So, right now there's a massive static charge between the clouds and the earth. If we could only slow the whole thing down, we'd be able to see the process in action. It's amazing. And it all starts with a tiny spark inside the cell, a flicker of life, a molecular phenomenon in the eye of a towering storm. Then a stream of electrons shoots out of the base, looking to discharge its energy. Like a reconnaissance mission. Oh! [pointing] There's another! That stream only travels about thirty or forty meters then, stopping for a few billionths – *billionths!* – of a second, it splits in two. The strongest vein continues on its journey towards ground, while the other dissipates in mid-air. The path less traveled. This is just the initial bolt, mind, something called the *stepped leader*…"

I drank in Evie's enthusiasm like a parched desert catching the first drops of the season. Such complete surrender to the majesty of life! Such inspiring awe! Such wonder and vitality, flowing through my dear Evie's circuitry! I thought of her heart, racing away with the story.

"The leader, it has this incredible build-up of energy, but it needs a signal, a route to follow. So, what happens? The leader attracts an opposite stream of *positively* charged ions! Isn't that amazing? These streamers flare up from the earth, existing for just a tiny fraction of a second. They can be anywhere from an inch in length to hundreds of feet. When leader and streamer meet, they create a path, a *connection*, along which the lightning literally bolts from the heavens and grounds itself in the earth. There are even ways to predict the pathway, something to do with 'flux lines,' I think. But anyway, isn't that just incredible? All these variables, these opposing forces, coming together to give life to lightning? And all ignited with a single spark…"

The rain was teeming down across the river now, the skies a pyrotechnical display offered up by the Gods. I took Evie's hand in mine as we looked out together, over the silver river, into the terror and the beauty.

* * *

Seven blocks and seven years away, lightning struck again. Evie was awake, but not conscious; or conscious, though not awake. More likely, she was somewhere between the two, suspended in limbo, wading through her own vast, darkened abyss. I could no longer tell, lost, as I was, amid the storm clouds of white-hot fear and torrential desperation. I gripped her hand and felt her waxen body convulse, the light flashing through her frame, seizing her organs and electrifying her flesh. I saw her focus retreating behind her eyes, heard from her bloodless lips a kind of low, pained groan, as though it were summoned from some other realm. Face drenched in the pouring rain, I tried to bring her back, urged her to remain there with me.

"Stay with me, Evie. I'm here with you. Please, Evie! Stay…"

The doors crashed open and the fluorescent tubes overhead burst to flickering life. Light flashing. Flashing light. A storm of medics converged on the scene once more, swirling around my brave Evie, reluctant conductor at its center, pitiful streamer, waving in great bolts from the heavens above. Still I held her hand, refusing to let go.

"Come on, Evie! Stay with us now! Please, Evie..."

Of a sudden, the energy drained from the heavens and the skies turned black.

* * *

There were many such storms that night. I remained by Evie's side for them all, feeling her slip away from me, her life force extinguishing, one dissipated cell at a time.

"The lysing is getting worse," Doctor Laso explained. I no longer saw his face; only heard his words as they fell dead in front of me. "Her blood cells are rupturing, but the immediate concern is disseminated intravascular coagulation. There remains considerable risk to both her liver and kidneys. The situation is dynamic, of course, but if either of these organs fail, we will have to consider the likely and imminent onset of multi-organ failure..."

* * *

It was sometime early in the morning, when the heavens parted and the pelting rains and thunderbolts abated for a few, miraculous moments, that Dr. Laso advised me to visit the second floor.

"There's nothing you can do right now," he said in direct, medical-speak monotone. My vision was so bleary I could barely make him out in the shadows. I felt for Evie's hand. Two nurses were changing the transfusion bags. Red for blood. Yellow for plasma. I had not even noticed them come in. On and on the machines beeped in the background.

"Look, I have some important tests to run," Laso continued, "so I'll be right here, in the room." Then, sensing my reluctance, "I'll page NICU myself, directly, if anything changes. Now go. Hold your daughter. Draw your strength. We're here."

Moments later, I held our squirming infant, and stared into the future. I searched her crystalline eyes, peered out beyond the storm and across the abyss, to the other side of Evie's life circle, where my little archangel lay cradled in her daddy's arms. Then I heard myself say something I will never forget for the rest of my life.

"I'm so sorry, little girl… it looks like this might just be you and me."

* * *

Chapter XIV

IN BETWEEN
HERE AND THERE

Good morning, little lady.

Daddy here, just checking in to say "G'day" and to remind you that you're loved to the moon and back. You're actually asleep right now…or at least, mommy is. I can see her, laying on the bed next to me, here in our little bedroom. She looks so peaceful. So restful. Sometimes, when she's sleeping, I put my ear up to her stomach to see if I can hear you. Occasionally, you'll give a little kick or an elbow. It's amazing, to feel your presence, your movements. To know that you're already growing so much. Your little organs and features coming into being. I can't imagine what it must be like for mommy!

Well, we've got some busy days ahead of us. Only four months (to the day) until your big arrival and we're still looking for a place all of our own. We're renting a little corner apartment here in Recoleta. It's on the sixth (top) floor of a beautiful old French-style building. It's small, but it has plenty of natural light. That's something we're looking for in the new place, mommy and I; lots of light. (Side note: I just found out the other day – from your mother, of course – that the expression here in Argentina for giving birth is "dar a luz" or, "to give light." Isn't that poetic? Gotta love the Latins for their passion!) So yes, lots of light. We also like high ceilings, crown moldings, wooden floors, that type of thing. And three bedrooms; one for mommy and daddy; one for you; and one to "grow in to." Of course, anywhere the three of us are together will be perfect (as mommy helpfully reminds me), but I really am trying to find something I know we'll all like. It'll be the place you grow up in, after all. At least for the first few years. Your mother is a tough one to pin down, you know. We haven't even settled here yet and already she's dreaming of the day we three can up and travel to some distant land. She's quite the explorer, she is, always wandering off in her mind to exotic places in search of adventure. Truth be told, it's one of the things I love most about her; that she's forever seeking new horizons. I remember seeing her passport for the first time, when she came to stay with me in New York City. It was overflowing with stamps and visas written in Cyrillic and Arabic and Korean and many languages besides. I thought of my own, comparatively blank document and, right then and there, determined to hitch my wagon to hers, to get out and see the world with my intrepid travel partner. It's been quite the journey, let me tell you. One you're about to join us for and that I cannot wait to share with you.

In other news, my book is coming along, page by page. I'm not working on it as much as I probably should be, given everything else that's going on, but I'm making steady progress. It's funny, you know, what we come to do in our lives. Some folks become doctors, others housemaids, still others horticulturalists or waiters or electricians. One person develops an affinity for words, another for sounds or visual arts or culinary tastes. It's a wonder to contemplate and observe, one's talents and proclivities evolving over the years. Why, just the other day I was thinking about what you might like to do in your life, what might inspire you and catch your attention. I guess we'll begin discovering that together soon enough. I can hardly wait.

Love always,

Dad

Buenos Aires
February, 2015

Dearest Daughter,

It's just on sunset here and I'm sitting in my pajamas, looking out over the city, enjoying a cup of chilled chamomile tea (which, as it happens, you seem to really enjoy, too). I love the way the sun takes so long to set here, far from the equator. There's something about the slowness of the transition, the elongated, liminal state, that gives pause for thought. I sometimes think about all the sunsets across all the skies around the world. All different perspectives of the same phenomenon, each experienced in a totally different way, but universally accepted as something worthy of our attention. Some sunsets are over in a moment, like those in the Arabian desert. In other places, like Norway, whole months pass by when the sun never really sets at all, merely dips into the horizon, creating a Lynchian kind of twilight across the sky. I wonder how these varied, astronomical aspects affect people in different places? Could Impressionism, for example, have taken off in Ecuador? Or did it simply not have the time of day? Did it need those long, crepuscular hours, light stretched thin across the heavens, inspiring all those great artists? Hmm…

One day we'll sit, you and I, in a little café in Florence or Paris or Sarajevo, and we'll discuss all the "hmm…" moments in life. You'll ask me a question and I'll say, "You know what? I don't know the answer to that. Let's think it through together." And you'll weigh in with your ideas and I'll contribute mine and we'll order another round of espresso or *café au laits* or *kafas* and we'll talk until sunset and beyond. (The colors are changing here now, from warm oranges and pinks to cooling blues and violets. The rooftops are changing color, too…or reflecting it differently than before. Another "hmm…" for later.)

Sometimes, when I'm alone (or rather, when *we're* alone), I like to imagine conversations we'll have together, one day in the future. Just *being* together, in one another's company, will be fantastic. Only last week I dreamt that we, you, me and daddy, were on a train together, somewhere in Europe. We were traveling through a lush valley, in Bavaria, perhaps, somewhere in Central Europe. Daddy was making notes on his writing pad, sketching out marginalia and underlining passages, as he does.

You, seven or eight years old, were coloring in one of your drawings. Pretending to look out the window, I was studying you in its reflection, watching your young hands glide across the pages, bringing them to life with your imagination, creating like no one was watching. Your hair fell across your face, so I couldn't quite make out your expression, but I felt your emotion through your action. You were calm, focused on bringing out the potential of that blank page, bringing it to life, as it were. I looked to see what you were drawing and saw, there on the page, a happy little family, sitting on a train, traveling through a forest. You, me and daddy. It was so very sweet; I could have cried from joy. The following morning, while in the shower, I recalled the dream and thought, "If that's how happy a dream of reality can make me, just imagine what it will be like when that dream turns into reality!" I thought about this for a long, long time and, when I finally got out of the shower, I was so faint I had to go lie down again. Daddy, sweety that he is, brought me a long glass of water and kissed me on the belly.

"Take care of our little lady in there," he said to me. I told him not to worry his handsome face. We three are going to be just fine.

All my love and dreams,

Mommy

Buenos Aires

February, 2015

P.S. We've been to see Dr. Kostas. Not my favorite man in the world, I must confess, but as long as the developments are positive, so shall I be. Kisses!! ~ Mommy

* * *

Chapter XV
ONE AND ALL

H ilda woke to the blurry outline of a man leaning over her. She blinked, willing her eyes to focus on the strange yet familiar figure. Gradually, she made out his wiry frame, then the deep lines on his forehead and his long, wispy beard. It was Mr. Chu, the old Christian from up in the hills. She noticed that his cheek was deep purple and badly swollen. Still, he tended to his patient with one open eye, dabbing her forehead gently with a cold compress. The water felt cool and refreshing.

"Where are we?" Hilda thought. Her senses were slow to feed her information. Then she remembered the glinting bayonets, heard again the sound of shots fired and saw the cackling yellowed grins of the surrounding jackals. She felt her pulse begin to race and her muscles stiffen.

"The girls!" the scene rushed back to her in a sudden shock. *"What happened to the girls? And the bandits? Where were those vile and godless creatures?"* She made to speak, but a splitting pain shot like a lightning bolt from her temple through her nervous system. Then she felt the muscles in her neck fall loose in Mr. Chu's ancient, cradling arms.

"Shhh." The old man's soothing tone washed over her. She felt his fine white beard brush her cheek. It smelled vaguely of flaxseed oil.

Mother. Ah, mother.

"I'm here," came the voice. "I've got you, my child. Shhh."

She laid her head again in the outstretched arms, felt the time-worn skin against her own, and sighed a long, deep breath.

Shhh… I've got you, my child. You're here with me now…

"How long was I out?" the young woman asked when she came to again some while later.

"Long enough," replied the old man, a kind smile forging its way under his ripening bruise. "You're doing well."

"But the girls!" she gasped, working herself up again. "The girls… they're?"

"All safe. All safe." His voice was calm and tender and dusty with time. "All safe, praise the Lord."

Hilda let out another long sigh. Then she remembered the smell of plaster falling from the roof, feeling the rubble raining down on her until… Again the room began to spin. She made to move, but another pain, a dull ache in her side, prevented her. "What about the men? The bandits? Are they…?"

"Gone, for now," the old man calmed her. In his wrinkled hand he held the damp compress against her throbbing temple. "They're gone, for now. You're here with me, my child. You're here now."

Here, now… here with me… with me, my child…

She pictured the words in her mind, kneading them over like dough, feeling them mold to her hands, and then squeeze through her grasp. A soft light fell through the window and onto her face. She could see the tiny rainbow ribbons, refracting in the dust.

"What's happening?" she asked the old man, her head groggy with a confusion of thoughts and colors. "What's happening to us? To all of us? In this country… this world… in this life?"

Mr. Chu turned and wrung the compress into a little bowl on the bedside table. Hilda saw there the old man's meager belongings; his shaving blade, the burned-down candlestick, his weathered old bible. And atop the Good Book, the little matchbox.

"Oh that," the old man smiled. "You remember Mr. Cricket. He's even older than me, you know. Older than the universe itself, some say. Shall we ask him?"

He held the little box to his ear, sliding it open just enough to hear what the creature might say. "Hmm…" he nodded along. "Very interesting, indeed!"

Then, turning his wizened countenance to Hilda, he continued in warm, becalming tones: "There are some here in the East who believe in a process by which all things, at all times, are becoming, even *being*, their opposites. The *Yi Ching*, or *Classic Book of Changes,* was begun more than two and a half millennia ago. It is a Chinese text that gave rise to, among other philosophies, that of the ying-yang. This is the idea that, although forces may appear to be contrary, even oppositional, they are in fact interconnected, interdependent and complimentary when observed as part of a unifying nature. Masculine and feminine; active and passive; fire and water; even life and death. Within a thing itself, there exists both *yin* and *yang* components, as represented by the ancient symbol. Scholars have attempted to explain the apparent paradox of *duality within unity* by giving it names, "dualistic monism," for example, or "dialectical monism." But when you see the whole for what it is, realize that life and death are part of a unified phenomenon, just as summer and winter are components of a greater universal cycle, the paradox vanishes, like a ghost in a dream."

The old man took the compress again and gently dabbed Hilda's forehead. She felt the water was cool on her skin. "All is one," he repeated the mantra, "and one is all."

Mr. Chu spoke slowly, as if transmitting an eternal knowledge beyond even his own comprehension. Hilda saw in his expression a deep, eternal serenity, the creases around his mouth and eyes worn by time itself. As she drifted from consciousness once again, she thought to herself: Here is a man who has seen the face of God.

*　*　*

It was late the next morning when Hilda finally woke. She found herself in one of the dorm room cots, on the ground floor of the mission. The doors were opened to the interior garden and a soft breeze played in the drawn white curtains. She could hear someone breathing on the next cot, behind her. Turning over gingerly, Hilda saw that it was Ling, asleep under the sheets. Her cheek was badly bruised and a gauze bandage was wrapped around her head, covering one of her eyes. The dried brown blood on it gave Hilda a mild shock. For a few quiet moments she monitored the slow rise and fall of her friend's breathing and collected her thoughts. Her own head pounded, as if she had been the one bludgeoned with the butt of the rifle. She closed her eyes and concentrated on the cool breeze. After a few minutes, she heard footsteps coming down the hallway. Miss Anderson entered.

"Ah, you're awake," she said in a low, soothing tone. "We were wondering when you two might rejoin us."

Ling, too, had woken, her one eye peering pitifully out from beneath the spattered bandages. It appeared red and sore, Hilda noticed, as though she had been crying in her sleep.

"Here," said Miss Anderson as she rested a tray of tea and cakes on the little bedside table, which was otherwise empty, between them. "The girls made you these. They want to see you both well again as soon as possible. They're very proud of your bravery, you know. Very proud, indeed. We all are."

The matron of the house stood there a while, looking over the two young women as a mother might tend to her sick children. She appeared overworked and decidedly worse for wear, but her expression was one of pleasure and satisfaction. She seemed to want to say something, but stopped herself. Inside Hilda's own head a great many questions circled, but she could scarcely apprehend a single one before they blew away again in the late morning breeze.

"Well, I'll let you two rest," said Miss Anderson. Hilda thought she saw her bow ever so slightly before she left the room.

When the doors closed, she turned to Ling. "Your eye…"

"Will be okay," nodded Ling.

Hilda looked upon her battle-wounded friend. The two of them there, in the student's cots, on the bed sheets they had so often washed and folded together; it all seemed suddenly absurd. They let out a strained laugh, which brought pain to both heads.

"Thank you," they managed to say at last, more or less in unison.

For three whole days Hilda and Ling convalesced together in the dormitories. Most of the students had gone home to stay with their parents while the school was brought back to order. Between overseeing some minor repairs (to broken windows, door jambs, the upstairs ceiling) Miss Anderson called on her patients herself, both in the morning and the afternoon. For their parts, Hillary and Sister Christina brought them meals in bed and tended their various bumps and bruises. The young women had never seen "Sister C" so attentive. On the third day, the little fat girl, Ma, was permitted entry for a few minutes on behalf of the other students, who were ever so eager to learn how their courageous heroines were recuperating.

"Oh, but it was you who saved us all!" cried Hilda, when Ma presented she and Ling with a crumpled stack of Get Well Soon cards. "You and your purse of cash coins, to say nothing of your bravery and quick thinking!"

The girl blushed, her eyelids fluttering like butterfly wings over moistened pupils.

"And don't you worry," added Ling, "we'll get every last one of those coins back for you, Miss Hilda and I will. Don't you worry a thing."

Ma bowed deeply, the tears now running fast down her chubby red cheeks. "No price, Miss Ling. No price, Miss Hilda." And she bowed. "No price too much for you."

That night, after the last of their visitors had departed, Hilda turned to Ling and, with a heavy chest, asked the question she had been asking herself these past few days, but which she could not clearly answer: "Were you... afraid?"

There followed a long silence. "I was," Ling replied at last, "but not the other night." Another moment passed. Outside, the day sounds quieted and the evening sounds began. Dogs. Men. Animals. Ling collected her thoughts, like a child organizing a jigsaw puzzle. Her pretty face, shadowed and bruised, was hardened by concentration. It seemed to Hilda as though she were arranging the pieces for the very first time.

"When I was a young girl, I was frightened all the time.... especially during the night... When I learned that my parents had been taken away... that the bad men had come to steal them... when I was old enough to know what that meant... that someone had kidnapped them... probably tortured them... and killed them... but had left me...

I was scared that... that..." she paused, unable to quite find the right piece.

"You were scared they might come back *for you*?"

"No, no. Not that..." Ling took a deep breath and answered, "I was scared that they *wouldn't* come back... that they would leave me here, *alone*... I was scared that my parents had been taken away and sent to heaven... and that..." her voice began to tremble "... that if the bad men didn't come back in the night... that I might never see them again."

Hilda listened, unable to breathe, unwilling to disturb her dear friend's searching confessions.

Ling continued. "For many years I prayed that the bad men would come again... that they would take me away and kill me, too... so that I would one day see my mother and father again... that I could leave this life and finally be dead... dead with my family... I lived in hope that we would be reunited... until..." Hilda watched Ling's eye glistening in the pale moonlight. Softly, in a child's voice, she began to whimper.

"It's ok," whispered Hilda, vaguely recalling Mr. Chu's words. "I'm here. I've got you."

"Until I realized that... if the bad men *did* come back... if they *did* kill me... it would only mean my prayers *had* been answered... and that... because I had *wished* for death, *selfishly*... because I had *desired* death... and my sinful wish had come *true*... that I would not be permitted into Heaven after all... and that after... that after suffering all through this life, I... I would be condemned to suffering in the next, too... "

Both women were crying now, the shock of the attack and the gravity of Ling's confession filling them with such emotion. They wept for a long time, wept as two people who realize at last that they are not alone on this earth, that they have one and other. Comforted in this thought, the sobbing gradually subsided.

"But the other night," Hilda managed at last, when they had calmed down some. "You said you weren't scared? Why?"

Ling looked at her friend, the tears welling up again. "Because... when I saw you standing there, in front of us..." her voice trembled under her quavering smile, "... so brave and... so strong... I knew that here on earth, I had you… and that you… that you and the girls were surely worth saving… if only I could."

A gentle rain fell outside in the courtyard, washing away the sounds of the night in its mist. The moon's silver light filtered through the curtains.

*   *   *

Life at the mission went on. Outside the gates, too, times were hard. Month passed into month and the country fell deeper into despair. Wherever people gathered, they talked of the growing violence in and around their cities and villages, wrenching their once peaceful communities asunder. The fragile system of "alignment politics," which had, until recently, ensured that no one warring faction could gain control of the vast land, was now breaking wide apart. As the balance of powers tilted in favor of one warlord or another, subordinates often betrayed their commanders with bribes known as "silver bullets." The resulting era of treachery and paranoia meant that even suspected double-dealing was punished in the most severe manner. In hushed and suspicious tones, forever wary of listening ears, men exchanged stories of these vicious warlords and the roaming gangs of rebel bandits, while the women told of the unbelievable horrors visited upon so many innocents, men, women and children too, who were caught in the middle of the epic struggle for power. There were public executions, after which bodies were left for days as a reminder of who was in charge. There were brutal beatings and torture and rape, and even instances where, after the killings were done, there was nothing of the bodies to leave, except for the dogs. The tales were gruesome and appalling, but humanly irresistible, so they passed from village to village, city to city, until the entire Middle Kingdom lived beneath a pall of fear and subjugation. At first this new reality seemed incredible, unbelievable. Then, as one season followed another, as sin begat sin, as one ghastly crime succeeded the last, the people grew accustomed to the atmosphere of death, such that many could not remember a time when violence was not a part of their everyday life. Just as the political situation worsened on the ground, so too the heavens above seemed to conspire against the people with a series of floods in the south and the west and droughts to the north and the east. There was famine, pestilence and plague, such as would test the faith of Job. Everything was extreme in those darkened days, when even the weather could not be trusted, when gods and men became monsters both.

During the spring of Hilda's third or fourth year in Sinyang, the skies unleashed floods of such unrelenting ferocity and duration that even the elders, notoriously stoic when facing the inevitable vicissitudes of life, beseeched the heavens for mercy. The torrents began in the far northeast, along the Mongolian border, and swept over vast plains and valleys, soaking the earth to its very roots, drowning anyone and anything in its path and driving wave upon wave of hapless peasants from their homes and farms. Those that could, traveled by rail, on the great "fire-eating dragon," as they called the train. But transport was slow going and intermittent, as warlords had commandeered the railways so as to move troops and supplies between their own strategic strongholds. Roughly half of the traffic running from Peking to Wuhan was used for arms and for armies, forcing great droves to travel on foot, their meager possessions tied to their bent and breaking backs. They followed, this woeful multitude, along the iron tracks, camping beside them at night and when their legs would no longer carry them. Many perished on the journey, their families forced to abandon the deceased to shallow graves before pressing on themselves. Those that did arrive, that managed to survive by some grace or miracle, carried with them filth and disease and the unforgettable, inescapable stench of death, so that the human flood, too, became an unrelenting force in and of itself.

Early one afternoon, when Hilda and Ling were returning from town, they saw a young boy, of perhaps five- or six-years of age, loitering nervously in front of the mission. His little chest was bare, his face smeared with dirt and his clothes little more than rags, tied at his ankles and waist. When they approached, he puffed out his chest and chin, as if to demonstrate his fearlessness. As the two women drew closer, they noticed a skittish movement behind the small boy.

"Look, a sister," gasped Ling.

Perhaps half the boy's age, though much less than half his paltry weight, she too was shabbily dressed and filthy. Her eyes were sunken in boney cheeks. Her hair was matted to her head and caked in grime. "*The poor thing*," thought Hilda. She held out her hand, but the little creature cowered behind her brother's spindly legs, like a beaten dog. "*What must this tiny person have seen already, in her short and miserable life?*"

The young boy stepped aside and took the little girl by the arm, thrusting her toward the two women. He said something in a dialect Hilda could not understand. The little girl bowed her head. Then he nudged her little body, frail and weak, forward again. At first Hilda could not understand what was happening. She turned to Ling, whose face was contorted with anguish.

"He is trying to…" she struggled to find the words. "Hilda, this boy is trying to sell his sister. He says his family needs money. They are starving."

Hilda looked at the children before her. God's children. She tried to understand the kind of world that would abandon children to such a wretched state, but she could not. There was no understanding. For these poor people, there was nothing. Ling took Hilda by the arm and they passed into the mission.

"We cannot be in the business of buying children," Miss Anderson explained to them, not without a deep sorrow of her own. "Here," she held out a paper lunch bag, the ones provided daily to the schoolgirls. "Give them this to share, but don't let any other beggars see. Our resources are already stretched and we have many to care for here. Take them around the side, by the garden, and hand it to them there. But tell them there is no more."

The young women did as they were instructed. Hilda was at first surprised to notice the anger on the little boy's face. He seemed both annoyed and disappointed, in a childish way. Then she realized: food meant no money, that these women would not be buying his sister, and that this small offering was all they would get today. With tears in his eyes, the little boy took the bag and first helped himself to its contents of meat dumplings with rice and breadcake. He ate with his grubby hands, stuffing the rice into his mouth and chewing ravenously. Behind him, his sister waited in obedient silence, her scrawny shape bowed at the head. Hilda saw her vertebrae, poking at the skin on her neck. When the boy had finished, he turned to his sister and threw the bag at her feet. Then he barked something at her and walked off. Without looking up, the little girl fell to her knees and tore the bag open, grabbing at the crusts and picking out every last grain of rice. When she was done, she walked slowly off in the direction her brother had gone, head hung low. Ling took Hilda's hand and, together, they returned to their chores, their own hearts sad and heavy.

The following day, Hilda was coming back from town alone having just paid some bills and sent off some mail. Turning onto the mission street, she felt her stomach sink when she saw now a group of children standing at the gate. There were the two from yesterday, plus two more little boys and two new scrawny sisters, hanging about their ankles. The feeling of their eyes on Hilda as she passed through the gate was almost unbearable. Hilda knew the mission could not support the entire population of starving children. She understood that resources were slim and that everyone was already doing the very best they could with what little they had in hand. Yet, there seemed something unforgivable in turning one's back on such wretched, forsaken little creatures. Something unholy, even. That night she prayed. She prayed deeply, asking the Lord to send her something, anything that she might be able to share with the children, to relieve their suffering.

The next day, at around the same time in the afternoon, Hilda went to the front gate of the mission. When she saw that there were no children there, she wept. Until sunset she remained on watch, waiting for their tiny, pathetic forms to reappear, and when they did not come, she wept some more. At dusk, Ling found her friend by the gate and, again, brought her back inside, empty and disconsolate. Some days, it almost seemed to the young missionary that there was no redemption, no savior, no grace at all in this long-forgotten world.

*   *   *

So the seasons passed. Some brought with them tragedy and great sorrow, others small triumphs and moments of patient solemnity. Gradually, Hilda grew into her role in the mission. She helped Miss Anderson with the workload, which seemed only to grow with the years, and even assumed some of the administrative tasks, like balancing the accounts and drafting petitions for fund raising activities. During those rare moments she found her afternoon or evening free, Hilda would practice the piano or send letters home to her family, who seemed to her to live in a different world entirely.

The Sinyang mission remained open during the whole school year, except for the summer months, which Hilda passed with the Ingrams at their home in Peking. Although she looked forward to those trips with cheerful anticipation, when she would join the family on their excursions to the North Lake and the Western Hills, for picnics by the Jade Fountain or by some lost nook that Doctor Ingram knew along the Great Wall, Hilda always dreaded her time apart from Ling, who, because she was without family or home, stayed on at the mission year-round. Since the dreadful episode with the bandits, when the women had stood side by side in the face of death, the two had become inseparable, bonded by shared experience. They were grateful for each other's company and found in one another a loyal confidante with whom they could share their deepest confessions and doubts. Oftentimes they stayed awake after dark, either talking in sleepless circles of their grand hopes and fears, or simply discussing the activities of the day. Sometimes they ruminated on the future, too, imagining what it might hold in store for each of them.

"Someday I would like to see your country," Ling said to Hilda one night, after the others had turned in for the evening and the two friends lay awake in their dormitory cots. "You have seen so much of mine, I should like to know where you came from also, to see the places of your childhood stories, as you have told me them so many times."

Hilda remembered the lake and the little red church and saw her clear-eyed siblings. "We will go together," she promised, visualizing the scene as it played out on the ceiling, "and I will show you my own little corner of the world. My family will be happy to finally meet you, though from my letters they probably feel as though they already have."

They lay silently for a time, smiling in the dark at the imagined future before them.

"Will you go again to Mongolia with the Ingrams this year?" Ling asked after a while. The school holidays were drawing near and, with it, that bittersweet summer period they would spend apart.

"Yes, I think so," replied Hilda, silently wishing she could take her dear friend with her everywhere she went.

Ling hesitated, slightly embarrassed to ask, "You will write me though?"

"Of course," Hilda assured her. "And you too. I want to hear all about..."

"Hillary and Sister C's fascinating adventures?" joked Ling. "Why, I'll be sure to keep you up to date on *all* the missionary gossip."

The pair laughed, happy and content in the company of a true friend.

The following week, Hilda set out for Peking. She and Ling embraced by the mission gate, where they promised to meet again at summer's end.

"Keep well, sister," said Ling.

"And you, sister," returned Hilda.

They held each other once more and, through misty eyes, waved each other goodbye.

* * *

The Ingram family expedition was to be a special one that summer. Some years earlier, the good doctor had tended to a Mongolian prince who was said to be "sick unto death." There had been a good deal of apprehension on that first visit, as the Mongolian royal family put little faith in western medical practices but, being in a state of desperation and having heard miraculous tales of this "foreign specialist," they invested their hope in Doctor Ingram. When the young prince made a full and unexpected recovery in less than a month, they were overwhelmed with joy and, when it came time to part, implored the doctor and his family to come back and visit whenever they could. It had been some time since they last made the journey, owing to the various and unpredictable matters involved with the raising of six children but, with the older ones now off to college and working various mission posts, the Ingrams were ready to set off once again. And so, with tents, bedding and food enough for the journey, with a few close servants and their assorted equipment, and with Hilda as their family guest, the good doctor, his wife and two of the younger children set off from Peking. Their first stop was Kalgan, the border city of twin gates, which Hilda had had so much trouble with on her earlier trip. There they took three covered passenger wagons, along with a water wagon and a half dozen riding horses, and headed north into the vast plains. The caravan followed alongside a wire cable, which ran from Peking all the way to Urga, Mongolia's capital, and then on toward the Siberian border. For most of the journey, there were no roads, so the wagons stuck to the dried river beds when and where they could. Later, when the rains came and the rivers became swollen, they had to remove their footwear and wade across, leaving the horses to pull the supply-laden wagons through the mud and rushing water.

To Hilda, the journey was absolutely magical, both a welcomed break from the violence and heartbreak of Sinyang, and a timely reminder of His goodness and grace. She missed Ling terribly, of course, along with Miss Anderson and the others, but she was mindful not to dwell so much on her own personal longings that she might miss this wonderful opportunity which the Lord had so benignantly laid out before her. Instead, she tried to capture the precious moments in her memory, so that she could retell them in her letters and, when the summer ended, animate them in person, when she would once again see and embrace her dear sister and friends. In this way did she remain close to Ling, even as the distance between them was great.

Sometimes, the convoy would pitch the tents outside little villages of a few dozen Mongol yurts. The overnight rain would patter gently on the canvas overhead, filling it with great puddles that had to be poked with broom poles every so often, so they would not weigh down the roof and collapse the whole thing on their heads. Hilda would look at the yurts and think how appropriate they were for the weather and, by comparison, how odd and clumsy their own accommodations must appear to the locals. Then, in the morning, they would open the tent flap and see a whole sequence of curious eyes staring at them, little Mongolian children standing in the cold rain, shivering, who could not resist coming to see the strange foreigners that were crossing their lands. What a sight they must have been!

Other times they stayed in little inns or even homes, where they were welcomed as guests. Hilda noticed the pride with which their host families showed Doctor Ingram and his party off to their Mongol neighbors. It seemed to be a point of honor among them to be able to accommodate these wandering missionaries on their travels. They grew particularly excited when, on occasion, the good doctor told them they were on their way to see the prince and his family. A few even gave gifts or offerings to pass along, requesting that he bless their family. The homes were modest but comfortable, especially compared to the dampness of the tents. Some of the larger ones had long brick structures inside them, called *kangs*, that were several feet wide and with a flat top. Around the sides were a series of vents, in which the Mongols would light little fires to warm the inside, making a kind of altar that heated the whole room. During the day they would lay their wet clothes on top to dry and warm them. Then, at night, they would unfurl their bedding and sleep right there, the red clay bricks warming them from beneath. It was a real treat to be given a position on top of the *kangs*, one that Hilda enjoyed a couple of times at the doctor's kind insistence.

"It's an essential part of the Mongol experience," he would say. "Something for you to put in your letters."

During the long travel days, the caravan would stretch itself out over the rolling terrain, the horses and servants forming broken lines between the wagons as they wended along ravines and plodded up and down the hillsides. Sometimes Hilda would go riding with one of the Ingram children, threading a line between the wagons, from head to tail and then circling back again. Often, she would take shelter from the midday heat in the back of a wagon, reading a book or else composing letters for Ling and the rest, filling them with colorful descriptions of the local people and the vast, unending countryside surrounding her in all directions. Other times, usually in the cooler afternoons, the doctor or his wife would conduct little side expeditions, and an interested group would go foraging for wild mushrooms or ride off to inspect an ancient ruin. Once they came upon a site where one of Kublai Khan's palaces had stood.

As Doctor Ingram explained, "The fifth Khagan of the Mongol Empire, Kublai Khan was grandson to Genghis Khan and reigned in the 13th century. The Mogul Empire at the time stretched all the way from the Pacific Ocean to the Black Sea, from Siberia in the north right down to what we know today as Afghanistan. Kublai was the first non-Han emperor to conquer all of China…"

Hilda surveyed the boundless land in awe and wonder. What earthly power this man must have commanded, she thought. And yet, time and the elements had all but returned the once-formidable palace to the earth, so that now there was only a large, rounded hill, around which ran a crumbling stone fortification. There were a few remaining towers, here and there, which they poked around. At the windswept base of one such tower, Hilda spotted glistening in the light some imperial tiles in golden yellow and peacock blue, a few paltry remnants that the marauding bandits had somehow overlooked. She considered slipping one into her pocket as a souvenir, but it somehow seemed disrespectful to the order of things, so she left it where it was, there on the ancient stone, to turn to dust in its own good time.

*   *   *

At some point along the journey, the caravan came upon a Swedish Mission. Hilda had no idea how they found the place; it seemed to her as though they had been wandering aimlessly for days. She was even more surprised when, after the doctor and Mrs. Ingram exchanged familiar pleasantries with the woman who ran the place, a Miss Wuckland, the latter turned to Hilda and, apparently recognizing her as distinct from the party, announced that she had received correspondence under her name from Sinyang. Hilda was about to exclaim her astonishment when she remembered that the Ingrams had passed this way many times and, after all, she was the only Westerner who was not obviously part of the family. She accepted the letter with gratitude, amazed at the way word traveled in this modern age, even to the farthest reaches of the earth.

"There is no place to which the Good Word does not travel, Miss. Nilsen," replied Miss Wuckland. She was past middle-aged, but bore herself with excellent posture and poise. Hilda liked her instantly.

As the following day was a Sunday, the camp rested on the grounds of the mission, where they set up their tents near the sheepfold, over by a knoll just off the perimeter. As a rule, they never traveled on Sunday. Instead, Doctor Ingram would often lead them to a mission he knew beforehand, where they could join the local mass on the Lord's day. If they were too far afield, they would simply take a load off in the middle of the plains or by a stream, where they would break bread and give thanks together, right there under the open skies.

The letter, which Hilda read by candlelight in her hammock directly after supper, bore Miss Anderson's signature. She had written to wish the young missionary a "safe and educational passage" and to remind her that school was to begin on the usual date and that her presence was "eagerly anticipated." There was no mention of the goings on at the mission house, other than that there was, as usual, "much to do." Finally, she asked that Hilda pass along her "warmest regards for the Good Doctor and his wife, to whom we all owe a great deal."

Hilda folded the note and put it in her breast pocket. It felt strangely significant, though she could not have said why. That night she tossed and turned in a restless sleep, as the bleating of the nearby sheep kept fitful rest at bay.

The next morning, they walked the short distance to a little chapel overlooking the mission, where they took the holy sacraments with a gathering of Mongol and Chinese Christians. The hymns were sung in all three languages, simultaneously, and Hilda thought they sounded just fine, even if nobody present, save perhaps the doctor, could quite understand what everyone else was singing. After the service, Hilda asked him whether he thought she had time to visit the prince and make it back for the beginning of the school year. She suddenly felt a disquieting urgency to return to her post.

"We're in His hands, of course," the doctor assured her, "but there should be ample time for the remainder of the journey, provided the weather holds out."

Hilda was glad to set out before sunrise the following day. She even rode up front, in the lead wagon, so she could keep an eye on the weather ahead. By midmorning the skies were painted an uninterrupted blue. Before long, the young missionary was dozing with her head on a blanket, her Bible opened on her lap, its pages blowing gently in the breeze.

* * *

CRACK!

A piercing sound split the afternoon skies in two. Hilda roused from her slumber to find the gathering clouds hanging low and heavy over the caravan. The thick smell of burnt charcoal and sulfur wafted through the moist air and into her wagon, which had at some point come to a standstill. She heard the cock of a rifle pin and had just enough time to cover her ears before…

…*CRACK!*

…another shot echoed off into the distance.

Her hands still cupped over her ears, Hilda looked back toward the rest of the convoy and saw the doctor and one of the men kneeling behind a cluster of boulders, just off the track. Their rifles were pointed across a hollow, towards a shadow atop the adjacent gorge. Hilda squinted her eyes, struggling to make out the form.

CRACK!

Another round fired off, but still the figure remained, undeterred. Then a cloud cleared for a moment and Hilda saw the animal clearly; a lone gray wolf. The men fired a few more times, but the distance was too great. Eventually they packed it in and set off again.

For three humid, overcast days, the wolf trailed them. It appeared at dawn; a haunting apparition borne of the night. Through the morning hours it would pace along beside them, shadowing the winding caravan through valley and ravine and over the rolling planes. Sometimes, it would disappear for hours, even a whole afternoon. Then it would emerge atop a nearby ridge late in the day, cloaked in the shimmering dusk, or stalk out from behind a blue-gray rock face on the other side of a creek bed. When they thought they had a good shot, the men would halt the wagons and aim their rifles, but to no avail. The wolf would pose, its lean and wiry frame held unnervingly still, as if daring the men to take it out. Then, as their exasperation grew, it would vanish again, receding into the misty haze like a ghost. The weary travelers remained inside the wagons, as much to escape the heat as to avoid the haunting beast.

At dawn break of the fourth day, the creature was nowhere to be seen. The party searched the surrounding hillsides through trained binoculars. The men even rode the perimeter on horseback, to ensure they were in the clear. "All good," was the verdict.

"Probably returned to the bleating flock," thought Hilda as she resumed her letters.

After a sweltering morning spent tracing a deep riverbed, the heavens finally broke open, emptying a torrent onto the wilting, dawdling caravan. It rained, non-stop, all afternoon. Forced from the riverbed, on account of the rising waters, the caravan took the long way around the mountainside, trudging slowly higher against the falling skies. It was nigh on dusk when they finally reached the palace grounds. Only when they passed through the gates and rounded the long, paved drive which led up to the main building, did the rains eventually cease, as if in polite deference to the occasion.

The prince was there to greet them, accompanied by his younger sister, the princess, and a small entourage of loyal retainers, who held multi-tiered umbrellas, like little pagodas, over their masters' heads. They were turned out in the most fantastic dress, thought Hilda, admiring their intricate silver jewelry and finely embroidered costumes in crisp white and peacock blue. She was reminded of Kublai's lost palace, unoccupied now, long forgotten to the patient winds. The prince himself was a handsome man, with high cheekbones and equally square shoulders. He greeted each member of the visiting party, including the servants, with a gracious smile and dark, unwavering eyes. Hilda noticed that, when he came to the Ingram children, he even bowed his head slightly, a high and noble sign of respect for the future of a family to which he owed his very life. His sister, the princess, followed a pace behind. She, too, bore a refined and timeless air, with eyes set like gems in the family cheekbones and a wrap of raven hair adorned with exotic feathers atop her lofty head. A fan of silver necklaces she set off with a single brooch, which seemed to catch even the faintest light. When she came to Hilda, the princess allowed herself an approving smile, which put the young missionary immediately at ease.

Following the greetings, the Ingram party was left to shower and refresh themselves. The doctor and his wife would stay in the main building for the duration of their visit, while the children and servants were invited to enjoy the traditional yurt accommodations that were dotted amongst the grounds. That night there was a lavish dinner of lamb stew and fried dumplings and vegetable pastries. Hilda thought she had never eaten so well. The meal was followed by more celebrations and even a princely toast, in which the host welcomed the long-absent guests back to his lands. When the man himself raised a cup, even the children were allowed a ceremonial sip of the traditional *airag,* fermented mare's milk. Not wishing to offend, Hilda touched it to her lips and found, to her ebbing surprise, the bitter taste not altogether revolting. There was dancing to follow, and tea served with little cakes. Then came plates of cheese and meats, and more dancing, too. Watching quietly from the side, the young missionary was glad to observe the doctor and prince had fallen into cheerful conversation together. The journey, she thought, had been quite the success.

*　*　*

Later that night, Hilda saw the wolf again.

It was high noon, and the wagons would not budge. They were stuck in a riverbed, deep and narrow, the mud caked solid around the creaking wooden wheels. The horses brayed in the stifling heat, their coats beaded with sweat, but the red clay earth would not yield. The blue ridges rose high and sheer on either side, focusing the sun on their trapped caravan. Hilda sat alone in the front wagon, the reins in her blistered hands. She squinted into the burning haze, trying to figure a passage forward.

Then it appeared; regal, indifferent, unperturbed by the fact of their presence. In long, deliberate strides it marched across the dried gravel, directly in front of them. Lowering its powerful head, the wolf turned to face them, its golden eyes unblinking in the white-hot midday glare.

The horses reared up on their hind legs, yanking at their bridles and fighting against their load. But still the wagons would not move. The men emptied their rifles in a cloud of smoke and the piercing *CRACKS!* echoed up and down the canyon. Standing its ground, the wolf unsheathed its wild fangs and snarled. Overhead, a kettle of vultures began to circle, the writhing shadows painting a deathly ring around the wagons below.

Hilda watched the creature carefully. It did not advance, but rather appeared to be waiting for something, anticipating some movement of theirs. Of *hers*. She let the reins fall from her hands. The horses lowered their heads. Cautiously, sniffing the ground in front of it, the wolf paced toward them.

In its golden amber eyes, Hilda thought she sensed a deep sadness, an unmet longing of unfathomable profundity. Her own simple fear began to recede and, without knowing why, she climbed down from the wagon and began to walk towards the creature. The wolf moved closer too, but the young missionary was unafraid. She was sure now it had come to deliver a message, to tell her something of vital importance. When it came to within twenty feet or so, she knelt down on one knee, genuflecting on the hard, red earth, and slowly held out an upturned palm. The wolf began to pant as it drew nearer, as if aging with every step. Hilda bent lower still, extending both arms out in front of her, palms turned toward the heavens. The creature's breathing was severely labored now, its paces slow and languid. Hilda rested her head on the dry clay and, eyes closed, listened to the panting shadow as it came upon her. When she felt the warm breath fill her hands, she looked up, into its molten eyes, full of melancholy and longing and loss. The young woman felt a deep welling within her own chest, then a slow rumble, building under the earth. The creature's mighty head rested in her hands now, its regal snout exhaling short, shallow pants. A cooling breeze blew down the gorge, and Hilda heard the river, distant at first, then building into a raging rapid that shook the very ground beneath her. The horses brayed and reared again on hind legs. The wagons broke free, but by then it was too late. The heavens opened themselves and the rain began to pour. In her hands, the wolf lay still. Dead.

When the river finally washed over her, Hilda awoke, bathed in tears, life having slipped through her frail hands. Outside the yurt, the storm raged on. The missionary knew in that very moment she needed to return at once to Sinyang.

*   *   *

Chapter XVI

COLLECTIVE
UNCONSCIOUS

T he words circled my head as I, once again, ascended the stairwell connecting intensive care units, neo- and post-natal.

"I'm so sorry, little girl… …just the two of us… I'm so sorry…"

When I came at last to the fourth floor, shoes filled with water and heart sunk deep in my chest, I felt an urge to simply stop, to fall to my knees and, for the first time in perhaps twenty years, to give myself over to whatever it was that called the heavens home and, with neither shame nor expectation, ask that the grace of God be with me now. I imagined the scene, as though hovering above my prostrate form, that broken and lost soul, abased on the hospital linoleum, beseeching empty skies for something they could not deliver. It seemed so terribly pitiful. And yet, as the energy drained from my limbs and the air escaped my sorry lungs, I saw my quivering hands reach out and felt my knees begin to buckle. Then I heard her voice. *Evie!*

Feeling my way along the corridor, I was careful to stay one step behind hope that she might be awake, delivered from that horrible abyss, that violent gnashing and writhing, that terrible *tormenta*. Outside her door my heart stopped, as if awaiting her permission to perform its next task, to go on beating. There was Doctor Laso, and another voice and, yes…yes… Evie, too! In I burst.

"Look, here he is! Please, darling," she motioned to me, imploringly, "won't you tell them? I must see my baby, my daughter!"

I turned my shock to Laso and his unknown colleague, hoping, perhaps, to unload some fear and confusion, or onboard some clarity. His face was cement, utterly unreadable. So, too, the lab coat by his side. Back to Evie, poor exasperated Evie. Where had she been, I wondered, what had she seen down there, in that hellish no-man's-land? Was it all a dream to her, or some lucid night terror from which her tired body could not awaken? Falling through the shutters, the cold fluorescent light fell in prison stripes across her sweat-dampened sheets. I thought I saw, between the shafts, her exposed nerves, reaching up in inch-long streamers, signaling from her glistening forearms. Her hair was matted, her eyes target-red. For a second she appeared crazed, electrified, as if suspended by an aftershock. Then a calm passed through her, like a lull upon the water.

"Doctor, please." She held her voice in tightened reins. "I'm not asking for much. A mother wishes to see her child, that's all."

Apparently alive, the man to Laso's side muttered something into his clipboard. I sensed Laso nodding in the corner of my periphery.

"Evie, as I explained to your husband," he turned to me, his expression conscripting me to his narrative, as though I was somehow part of this forced separation of mother and child, "your situation right now is... dynamic. There are certain protocols... precautions, really... that we ought to follow. It's..."

Again the semi-muted sidekick murmured something.

Laso, nodding gravely: "I'm afraid it's just... not possible."

A long silence fell upon the room. Evie cast her widened, chaotic eyes around the space, first toward the doctors then, sensing the shortest pathway down to earth, to me. My soul emptied. My words became stones. She read my face in a heartbeat. Between us the silence hardened, a wall of unspoken explanation erected instantaneously. On one side of the barrier I stood, motionless, gaze falling into my useless, empty hands. I recalled the doctor's words, "situation critical... imminent and likely... multi-organ failure..."

How to tell a person, a partner, a part of your whole, that they are dying, one cell at a time? I searched Laso's face for the results of the tests, the slightest shimmering of optimism, a sliver of hope. Nothing. So what was this, then? This momentary burst of awakeness? This sortie into the realm of the living? Evie's closing act? Her final struggle against the dying of the light? Still, the silence pervaded the space.

At last, having appraised herself of the situation, having received the low flying signals and processed the unuttered information, Evie spoke. Her voice was unrestrained now, but perfectly calm. She would be in control from this point onward.

"Doctor, with all due respect, my 'situation,' as you call it, cannot be so critical that I cannot be transported, in this very bed, if necessary, the 50 feet from here to the elevator, that I might descend two floors and be delivered to my child's side. As you know full well, there is no distance in the world that a mother would *not* travel. No obstacle she would *not* surmount. And if, *if*," here she raised a hand to preempt any notion of doubt, the slightest suggestion of prohibition, "if you tell me that it is impossible, that my life now hangs in the balance, then you will be all the more respectful of my wish, given that it may well be my last..."

Even the machines seemed to halt their infernal beeping for a spell, as if in unconscious, automatic deference to Evie's speech. The physical exhaustion seemed to cloak her entire form, to weigh down on her shape, even as she made her worldly claim. Wrapping my hand in hers, she continued:

"My husband will remain by my side, as always, to give me strength. Any medical instruments you deem necessary," she made to lift her arm, but was unable to muster the desired gesture. I knew the frustration she must have felt, the imposed impotence, the helplessness of one whose own body is holding their will captive. She exhaled a long, tired breath, and continued. "These transfusion bags, or these lines, whatever on earth they are for, the nurses can rig to a wheelchair... or gurney... or whatever is needed." Evie proceeded the only way she knew how: by deciding on an outcome, then moving the heavens to ensure that her will be done. Somewhere, from deep within her, she summoned her remaining energy, found a way to feed off the internal spark. "If the floor itself needs to be removed, Doctor, or my bed lowered by crane from the window, I will see my baby."

Leaving the "else I will leave this world trying" to hang, implied, Damocles-style, over the doctors' heads, Evie turned her sweetened eyes to me and said, in a voice alloyed with pure expectation, "Now tell me, dearest, all about our little family."

* * *

From that moment, for the rest of the morning's unerring forward march, Evie maintained a singular, eagle-like focus. So intense was her concentration on her goal, her human destination, people around her began to believe not only that the shortest, most important journey of this woman's life was possible, but *inevitable*. Nurses, doctors, orderlies, the janitor, her husband, even Dr. Laso himself; we were all swept into her cause, gathered together behind her mission, like matter trailing a comet toward its cosmic fate. And arrowheading the project, from her ICU cockpit, was the only person there who had everything in the world to lose.

Having convinced Doctor Laso that seeing her daughter was a matter of inarguable predestination, a foreordination not even the gods themselves could undo, she swiftly returned to him the power and potency of his vast mind by conscripting him as Chief Medical Logistics Officer.

"This is all in your capable hands," I overheard her say to him, with an optimistic pat on the arm. "I know you'll do whatever's necessary."

Incredibly, Doctor Laso responded to Evie's instructions as though they were routine pathology results or lab tests; he immediately, automatically allocated his entire, purpose-built cerebrum to the task at hand and went about distilling the problem, working it over, imagining it from every conceivable angle, until it began taking the shape of a solution. It was sometime deep into mid-morning when, having consulted with various other doctors and administrators (both on Evie's floor and down in NICU), and rallied a squadron of nurses and conscripted a pair of wheelchair assistants, he came bursting into the room to outlay and explain his plan.

"I'm ready," was Evie's simple, direct, inevitable reply.

"We'll need a half hour or so to line everything up… to get you prepped, for the nurses to rig the wheelchair, plus coordinate with NICU and so forth… but don't worry, we'll get you down there."

"Thank you, Doctor. I knew you'd understand. I just knew you would."

Doctor Laso left the room and, at last, Evie exhaled, betraying to me the first signs of her unending relief. I watched the muscles around her eyes relax and her expression soften, as her clean white lips mouthed the words, "I will see my baby."

* * *

And so she did.

On April 23, of the year 2015, Marta's broad white staysail spirited the child into Evie's waiting arms. Completely overcome, I whispered into their soft embrace:

"Evie, my darling, I'd like you to meet your daughter, Miss Hilda Evelyn."

The instant would last an eternity in the child's eyes, her mother's naked touch transferring the boundless love only she could possibly bestow. Evie held her newborn flesh to her own heart-filled chest, skin-to-skin, cangurito-style, delivering herself entirely to peace and transcendence. Her eyes filled with tears, which flowed down her cheeks and onto the child's head, a baptism of maternal love. Evie kissed them dry, dewdrops on the soft, rose skin. For a long time she wept, overcome by the magnitude of the event, the reunion of mother and child. Deep in the solemnity of that embrace, Evie's life, past, present and future, became one. Reaching out, she took my hand in hers, bringing me into space. Through the joy and exhaustion, the love and fear, the pain and relief, she held us all together.

"Mother. Father. Daughter."

And for a perfect moment, our little family circle was complete.

* * *

Less than one hour later, back in her own room, the experience indelibly etched into memory, Evie laid her head next to mine on the clean white hospital pillow and, closing her eyes, surrendered herself to our collective unconscious.

* * *

Chapter XVII

A LETTER TO HILDA

Dear... Hilda,

There, that feels right, doesn't it? Hilda Evelyn. Just saying your name out loud brings a smile to my face. Your mother and I knew it was right as soon as we had the idea. It belonged to your great aunt (that's your grandmother's sister, on mommy's side). She was a fearless traveler who ventured to China and Mongolia way back in the 1920s. But her story will have to wait for another day, another chapter.

There is so much in this world I am looking forward to sharing with you, and this is only the beginning. Your name is an act of encouragement, a will to, like the long line of strong, independent women in your family, go forth into this life with head held high and mind open to wonder. There are horizons over which you will sail and terrain you will venture to discover all on your own, but you will always carry with you this name, which your parents call you by and which, to us, will always fill our hearts with love and admiration for, every time it passes our lips, we think of the miracle that you are and the special role you play in our little family.

In a few short months you will be in this world, alive and thriving and filling your body and soul with new experiences each and every moment. I sometimes can't imagine what it will be like, to have another life in the house, another being to nurture and care for and love. Already your mother has been such an amazing addition to my life. She has made me whole in more ways than I could ever have understood before I met her. I feel as though we are two parts of the same person, two bodies sharing one conscious experience. I guess it only makes sense that it is through that union which you were conceived. And now you're going to be here, with us, part of us, and we part of you. It feels like you are completing our circle, that you are bringing to us all your future. I'll never forget how fortune has smiled on me, my dearest Hilda, that I have you and mommy to accompany me through this journey called life.

Well, I'll be kissing your little forehead and holding your little hand in no time at all. Mommy will write to you in a little while. She's doing plenty of resting now, making sure you're all safe and sound in there. Hopefully the next time I write I'll have news on our new apartment and your very own nursery. Fingers crossed!

All my love for now,

Daddy

Buenos Aires
March, 2015

Chapter XVIII

GOING HOME

A t last, the Lord gave Hilda a sign. After waiting two agonizing days, while the heavens wept their fill, the clouds finally cleared and the rains ceased. It was late in the afternoon and, until that very moment, Hilda was unsure if she would ever get away. Doctor Ingram had insisted she delay her trip, at least until the weather turned for the better. Still, understanding her calling, he arranged for a Mongol guide to accompany her on horseback to Peking, where she would take the train the rest of the way. It would be a long and arduous journey, he warned, but in his heart, he knew she was in God's safekeeping. And so, with the sun peering faintly through the twilight clouds, it was decided. Hilda and her guide would ride the few hours down to the nearby town, where they would rest for the night before setting out again the following morning. The family gathered by the palace gates to wish the departing visitor goodbye. Even the prince and his sister joined in the farewells. Hilda was overwhelmed when the younger royal placed in her hands the brooch she had been wearing the night they first arrived.

"To keep you safe on all your journeys," she remarked, "both this one, and those to come in your long, happy life."

Hilda pressed her hands together and bowed low in gratitude. Then she pinned the glimmering piece inside her cloak and, waving goodbye to those gathered, mounted her horse and followed her guide through the gates and onto the trail. Without the wagons to delay them, they would be able to take the quicker route down the mountain.

"Be sure to stay close by your guide," Hilda recalled the doctor's parting words, "for he is a strong leader and knows well the way." She thought it apt enough advice for a woman of faith, and so committed the phrase to memory.

The way down was, as is often the case, far more difficult than the way up. Even with the guide a few paces ahead, showing the way, the rain-soaked ground was rocky and unstable. Hilda's horse often slipped and she felt herself clenching its tense muscles with her legs in order just to stay on its back. Every so often a rock would settle or roll, setting the horse stumbling a few paces forward or to the side. Hilda wrapped her arms around its strong neck and prayed it keep its balance. She even remembered a few words in Mongolian, which she whispered in its ear, as she had sometimes seen the other horsemen do. The going was slow and the sun set long before they reached flat land. Hilda focused her gaze on the guide, watching his blue-black form a few paces ahead of her, remembering the doctor's words. The sun took with it the day's warmth and a bitter cold settled on the mountainside. Hilda's knees ached and her shoulders shivered. After riding through what seemed like endless darkness, she saw a tiny glimmer of light, like a cat's eye, off in the distance. An inn! On they trudged, down the mountainside and toward the little town. At last the guide held up his fist and the horses slowed to a halt. Without a word, he dismounted and went inside. Hilda sat, sore and frozen to the bone, willing there to be vacancy. Alas, when the guide reemerged, he only shook his head and got back on his horse. Again and again this happened, inn after inn unable to accommodate them. Each time they approached a light, Hilda's hopes soared, then fell again into the depths of despair. When at long last they did come upon an inn with space, Hilda could barely climb down from her horse, so stiffened were her muscles and joints.

Once inside, she encountered an odor such as no place in the world, save for an oriental inn in the far outreaches of the countryside, could supply. On the long *kang,* from one side of the room to the other, lay what looked like a row of fattened sausages. They were men who had driven their oxen and camels and horses all the long day, their smell a confirmation of dirt and animal excrement and sodden, soaking rain.

The open fire was built not with wood, but with animal dung, and the air was thick with smoke and stench. But there was shelter. And there was heat. It would have to do. Hilda unfurled her wet tarpaulin at the foot of the kang, nearest the entrance, and the guide pegged their boots above an open fire to dry. Amidst the snoring and filth, the sound of animals outside and the pouring rain, the young missionary huddled beneath her bedding and prayed the good Lord deliver her through the night, safe and sound. She was asleep before she could complete her petition.

It was still pitch black when she felt the Mongol guide tapping her shoulder. Without a word, he handed Hilda her boots. They were so stiff she could hardly get them over her heels, but they were warm and dry. The early morning air was filled with mist, such that, at first, the riders could scarcely tell if it was raining at all. Hilda ate half of a sandwich that the Ingrams had packed for her, offering the other half to her guide, who politely declined. Off they rode, into the ashen fog. Little by little, after what seemed like several hours, the sun began to penetrate the atmosphere. It came benignly at first, like a slow smile, rolling back the mists and revealing, object by object, the surrounding landscape. Hilda was awed by the cut glass mountains, these ancient shards of earth, subjected to the intense pressures of time. She gazed at the mysterious valleys below them, still shrouded in mist, and the fathomless skies overhead, the clouds peeling back to admit the sun's gallant rays. She thought how quickly a situation can turn, from dark and treacherous to inexplicably wondrous. Night becomes day, fear turns to hope, and the path is lighted anew. Closing her eyes in deep acknowledgment of all that remained beyond her, the young missionary gave thanks and praise.

It was early morning when they finally reached Kalgan, the gateway from Mongolia to China proper. With sunshine on their faces, Hilda and her guide rode their mud-caked steeds, side by side, through the city streets. Burden bearers were coming to market from their farms and merchants were beginning to open their shopfronts. One after another, they gazed in amazement at the strange foreign woman, not comprehending why she would be riding, alone, with a Mongol guide. Hilda held her right thumb straight and high, a sign of great commendation, and the wonder grew on the local's faces. Thus they proceeded to the Kalgan mission station, where they received a warm reception and a hearty breakfast. There, Hilda was able to change into some clean clothes she had deposited on her way through earlier. She was glad to feel refreshed and human again, but felt slightly embarrassed of herself when it came time to bid her guide farewell. She handed him her fare, along with a generous tip, and thanked him as much as her patchy Mongolian allowed. The man returned a simple, pure smile and handed her his riding crop. Despite his dirty attire and lowly position, Hilda recognized in his expression a servant's graceful dignity.

"I will always remember you," she said in English, "as a fine Mongol gentleman, courteous and considerate. You do yourself much credit."

An hour later, Hilda was aboard the train to Peking. The hours flew by the window, along with the unfolding countryside and the slow emergence of the sprawling city. It was early evening when she finally reached the Ingram's home, a short rickshaw ride from the Peking station. There, in the familiar comfort of the near empty home, she chatted with the old woman servant, who happily washed and pressed the young woman's clothes and fixed her a warm supper. Before bed, Hilda drafted two telegrams; one to be sent to the Ingrams the very next morning, informing them of her safe arrival; the other to Miss Anderson, to say she would be back in Sinyang in time for the commencement of the school year, a few days hence. Hilda could hardly suppress a tearful smile as she thought of her impending reunion with Ling. They had been so long apart. She had so many stories to share and she longed to hear her dear sister's voice and to see her delighted expressions of wonder and enthusiasm. That evening, she prayed for safe passage on the final leg of her journey.

When the stillness of night carried her off, Hilda was dreaming of embracing Ling at the mission gate, of regaling her with tales from afar, of planning their own journey together, to America, with the little red church on the hill, and the cool lake waters and the long green grass, and of her own strange life, all that had come to pass, and all that would be...

* * *

The train ride to Sinyang took two nights and a day in between. After the journey down the mountain and on to Peking, it seemed to Hilda the height of luxury simply to be able to stare out the window without having to worry about falling off a horse or finding shelter and warmth. She saw the country in a new way, now, through a lens refocused by time and experience. It had been almost seven years since she arrived in this extraordinary foreign land, a timid missionary following a calling that at once inspired and terrified her. During that time, she had borne witness to pain and suffering such as she had never before encountered. Death had ridden in on the back of poverty and disease and civil unrest. Great floods had buried entire villages, cast families across the plains, ended lives in numbers untold. Man, too, had turned monstrous, looting and raiding and slaughtering his way through a time of mass confusion and upheaval. It was a period of great change, of transition from what was, to whatever was to come next, the past folding itself into the unrelenting future. Still, there remained a timeless beauty that transcended the moment, turbulent epoch though it was, that promised deliverance for the long-suffering people. It was out beyond the hills and buried in the valleys, hidden on the winds blowing through the ancient temples, stretched across the heavens overarching.

Hilda thought herself closer to this truth now. It was like a Great Knowledge, immovable and transcendent. Not a God, as she had always known Him, but an expression of the Divine nonetheless. Something numinous, she thought to herself. For a long time, the young missionary reflected on her own personal metamorphosis, all that had changed since she stepped off the *Fushima Maru* those many sunsets ago. She was the same person, the same vessel, the same woman staring into the train window, but now she was filled with a new understanding of the world around her. She now saw herself as a part *of* the whole, not apart *from* it.

So it was with a full heart that Hilda arrived at the mission on the third day. It was late morning already, but the sky remained a dull and lifeless gray. Immediately, she noticed that the gate to the mission was unlatched and that the place seemed abandoned, hardly the atmosphere she expected to find with school set to recommence the very next day! There was an unseasonable chill in the air and it ran the length of the young woman's spine. With growing trepidation, Hilda pushed her way through the entranceway and into the main foyer. There she encountered a hunched figure, seated in a rocking chair over by the piano. The old woman struggled to her feet, but only when she held her arms outstretched and raised her weary head did Hilda recognize Miss Anderson's countenance, run deep with sorrow and commiseration. Instinctively, Hilda turned once more to the entranceway, where she did not see her dear sister, Ling, waiting. Her stomach dropped and her breathing quickened in an instant dose of panic. She turned her desperate eyes again to Miss Anderson.

"Where is…"

But the old woman only shook her head. Her lip quivered, but no tears came to her eyes. She had cried them dry. Hilda stood motionless, unable to bear the weight, unable to comprehend this unspoken message. A breeze blew through the empty gate. The old woman shivered and hung her gray head. Hilda felt her legs become numb and her words turn to cement. She, too, was shaking her head, mouth agape, unwilling to surrender to this waking nightmare.

"Where is…" Hilda could not bring herself to say her sister's name, could not form the sound on her lips. "Where is…"

The old woman shuffled closer, her wiry arms outstretched, but Hilda collapsed before she found their embrace. "My sister," she sobbed on bended knees, her own tears streaming down her face. The pain washed over her like a raging river, pummeling her into the dirt. "My dear, dear sister," she cried.

And there on the threshold, Hilda's full heart spilled onto the cruel, unswept floor.

*　*　*

Chapter XIX

ON YOUR BIRTHDAY

Dearest Hilda,

My sweet, sweet little Hilda... I just wanted to write to you because, well... to tell you I love you.

I'm probably overreacting, but just in case... in case I don't have the opportunity to tell you this later.

Please know that I love you and your daddy more than anything in the whole world. Please always love and respect him. He adores you already and he is so excited to meet you and help you along your way in life.

There, I feel better having written this down...

No matter what happens, never ever forget, your mommy loves you.

Always,

Your mommy

Buenos Aires
April 20, 2015

Chapter XX

A PART *of* LIFE

She was right there, on the other side of that door. I could almost hear her breathing, feel the rise and fall of her own nervous expectation mirroring mine. The moment was pregnant with possibility. Overdue, in fact. It was coming up on five years since Evie and I experienced our love at pre-sight moment, down there by the Mason-Dixon, at the end of that long American summer. Pre-sight, because the attracting forces had not then fused together to become one. There was ample time, space and energy... but no matter. The intervening seasons had flung us along our own individual journeys, she to Russia and elsewhere, me to Australia and back. We wrote, occasionally, but mostly we lived our separate lives, became our own separate people. Then the Fates grew cross, and crossed our paths again. Or rather, they intersected them.

We flew through night and day, respectively; she over water, in from London just that morning; me over the land, from San Diego or San Francisco or some other West Coast notion of the sublime, to touch down early evening, half a rotation later. Evie was on summer leave from university, Stateside to determine whether New York City was right for her "professionally speaking," as she told her father. This I learned on a surprise call just a few weeks earlier, when a matter-of-fact Evie had phoned me from Edinburgh "just to catch up," after all these years, and to inquire of my address in the city.

"You wrote 'Manhattan,' but I wasn't sure exactly where..."

"I'm down in the Seaport District, just south of the Brooklyn Bridge. Why," I clumsily joked (and silently hoped), "you planning on dropping by sometime?"

She was silent for a second, as if consulting her mental calendar. My heart skipped a beat when she finally said, "How about three Friday's from now? That would be…"

"The 3rd," I replied, automatically. "Your birthday."

"You remembered!" She seemed genuinely surprised. I did not tell her then that I had thought about her every year on that day for the last five years, summoned her from her various worlds. Evie in Annapolis, reading the classics under the umbrageous oaks and watching the midshipman as they hopped, one-legged, up the training hill across the fields. Evie decamped to Moscow, staying with her father while she took some time to "figure out what I really want to do." Then Evie in Edinburgh, *not* St. Andrews, because, "all those swooning American girls trying so desperately to land themselves an English prince? No thank you!" Followed by Evie in Italy, treating herself to "my first real trip in years, not counting the others." And now Evie in (impossibly, amazingly) New York City, three-weeks-and-counting from that very second. My pulse gave another jolt.

"I had an idea it was somewhere around then," I white-lied, but only because I could not gather the fortitude to declare, "It's a date!"

She chuckled, as if hearing my unspoken words anyway. Then she had to go and we fumbled through a series of awkward "see you soons." The line went quiet and, unremarkably, the conversation ended. I sat in the dark, looking out my window over the frowning East River, flowing indifferently beneath the suspended rush hour(s) traffic, the red and yellow glare streaming steadily away from me. Three Friday's might have been three light years.

And then, something magical happened. She called again, the very next night. And again the next. And the one after that. For hours on end we filled each other in on where a decade (five years hers, five mine) had gone, gradually folding one another into the present with every tale recalled. Across the wires, over the Atlantic, we were dancing cheek to cheek, reanimating the lost time, connecting the dots between then and now, setting backdrops and spinning yarn.

I remembered a postcard she had sent from Moscow during one winter stint, casually depicting the view from her father's apartment overlooking Red Square. It was covered in snow, Saint Basil's Lewis Carroll-like Cathedral dominating the vista. To me, anyway, it looked like some kind of fairytale. The view was "close enough to what I can see from my own bedroom window," as her elegant hand noted on the flipside, "which I look out from every evening, when I permit myself a single, solitary Sobraine. (When in Russia, *нет*?)"

That particular message I read (and reread… and reread…) while lying on the grass up on Burleigh Heads, overlooking the coastal stretch to which my own childhood belonged, the place I then, for almost two whole years, called home (again). On that bluff, the clear Australian summer in full swing below me, the surfers riding their waves toward inevitable shores, the smell of sausages and eucalyptus suffused in the weekend air, "the Jays" crackling over a portable radio; Evie's world seemed as far away from mine as I could possibly imagine. The blistering sun on my face, I tried to picture her days and nights in that strange and foreign land, tried to read beyond her words and into her thoughts, attempted to look out from her eyes at the marvelous wonderland that composed the film-reel scenery of her life. It seemed almost precisely contrasted to mine, as though we were speeding away from zero in opposite directions, me burning up nearing 40 degrees Celsius, she plummeting to sub 40 at the other extreme. What unseen forces, I dared interrogate the clear blue skies overhead, might bring our opposites together again, might bend and curb those departing trajectories, so that they may come full circle, return to the point of origin, and become one again?

There were other communiqués, too. A roving report from Byron Bay (mine); a triple-stamped souvenir from Bratislava (hers); and, much later, a three-pager penned on foolscap from Florence, where she found herself with a free afternoon and, as if to apprehend her thoughts after the morning's excitement, settled into the Golden View, just over the medieval Ponte Viccchio, to write her antipodean pen pal.

"Botticelli's *Birth of Venus* was worth the trip alone, though I must say, Caravaggio's *Sacrifice of Isaac* nearly brought me to tears. (Okay, so not *nearly*.) I've enclosed a postcard of the former, which was to bear this message, until it spilled over onto these post-script pages. Do forgive my rambling!"

"Forgive *you?*" I responded, a self-restrained month or so later, from a maritime-themed dive bar in midtown Baltimore, "for spiriting me away from the rustbelt grit, for guiding me through the halls of the world's great collections? I'm not sure how you hope to atone for such flagrant impropriety?"

Then came another, under my pen, three months after alighting a midnight train under Grand Central Station, "...near the tip of Manhattan's outstretched finger. I share the space with a couple of colleagues and my work pays the difference, so I almost have enough for an end-of-week cocktail, if I budget responsibly. Don't worry, though: Admission to the Met is still *gratis*. Nothing you'd want to see, of course. David's *Death of Socrates*, Gauguin's *Two Tahitian Women*, and my personal favorite, John Singer Sargent's *Madam X* [Tactfully omitted: Because it reminds me of you...] Ah, but do forgive my rambling..."

Then came the impromptu phone call, boldly, shortly thereafter. And three weeks later, there stood Madam Evie, a study in contrasts all of her own, alabaster complexion under black chiffon blouse, socialite arrived for a party of two, familiar yet mysterious, Norwegian-born, American-raised expatriate most at home abroad, framed by my opened door (5D). I felt my heart beating in counterpoint rhythm to hers as simultaneous pasts rushed forward to meet us; Evie and I, present together, the future poised to begin all over again.

* * *

Comfortably installed at Les Halles a few hours later (the one down on John Street, between Broadway and Nassau; since closed) it all seemed perfectly natural, as if this was precisely where we were supposed to be, the random, rapid-fire internationalism of the preceding years merely a prelude to the inevitability of the present, as though the bistrot two-top, set back in the mirror-paneled corner, had been reserved for us all those years ago.

"It's a long way to travel for a birthday drink," I raised my glass to meet hers.

"Well, you weren't coming to Edinburgh, were you?" And she winked.

Was it really a question? A serious one? It took me a second to imagine that as a possibility. Could I just *be* there? Like she was here? Like she was anywhere? She seemed to achieve it so effortlessly, this global, perpetual, perennial *being* of hers.

"What's it like?" I managed, eventually.

"Edinburgh?"

"No. Well, yes. I mean, what's *it* like, all of it? Russia. Scotland. Italy. Traveling around like you do. It's so…" [don't say 'romantic,' don't say 'romantic'] so… *peripatetic*."

"Hmm, not the word I thought you were going to use," she smiled, always with an eye to reading the unwritten. "But yes, it's a sort of unquenchable wanderlust, I guess. I can see that. Sure. Maybe not quite the Aristotelian component, though. Then again…"

It was as if she were considering all this for the first time, looking at her own life from someone else's point of view, genuinely curious that anyone might be awestruck by what to her seemed so effortlessly intuitive, so personally probable. Movement, to Evie, was not merely a cheap stopgap, plugging the space where boredom might otherwise settle like mold, but the road most obviously, necessarily traveled. Movement was essential, integral, inseparable from life itself. So, she sought it out both in herself, and in those around her.

"And what about you?" She took a sip of rosé champagne and I remembered, with delight, the look of quiet satisfaction that always followed her lips from the flute. "You've been to the end of the world and back since those sunny Sunday's down by the Chesapeake."

"Yeah, but that's different," I responded, trying to figure out why. "That's…home. There's nothing peculiar about going home."

She raised an eyebrow, but left the "isn't there?" dangling, something for the future to deal with. I missed this subtle skip in the record, of course, enraptured as I was by the simple fact that we were actually having this conversation in person at all. I might, at any point, have considered the other diners in the room, absently going about their regular Friday routines, embarked on their dreary, quotidian march, "the onion soup... the duck... the crème brûlée," completely unaware of the magnitude of this event unfolding in their midst, this monumental rendezvous, a shared decade in the making. How equally banal we must have seemed to them. Just a couple more faces in the crowd. But I did not consider them. Not for one second. Not for one thought. Not at all. From the moment she waltzed across the 5D threshold, so vital and immediately crucial to my life, I registered nobody but Evie. I watched her glide down the entranceway, her long-pleated skirt floating over the parquetry, midnight blouse draped upon slender shoulders, cinching slightly at the small of her back.

"Kitchen on the left..." I bumbled along behind her, "washroom just there, to the right... living room straight ahead..." as if she, Evie, worldly Evie, had never been in an apartment before.

When she reached the open space at the end of the hallway, the octagonal windows opposite directly overlooking the cable-stayed bridge, she raised her own arms by the wrists and twirled once, twice, thrice, there on the spot. Her long skirt billowed at the knees to reveal a pair of golden, gladiator-style sandals. Around the room she cast, like a night fisherman's net, her magnificent smile of grace and verve and impeccable courteousness. "Nice place," someone else might have said; only she did not. Rather, she returned directly to the very first question she ever put to me, as though it were bookmarked all along; this, the singular point from which we could now, at last, proceed.

"So here we are," she fixed her open gaze on me, then added simply, naturally, "Now where do you want to go?"

Since "Sarajevo... Sevastople... Suzuka..." (and all the rest) were still a long way off, I nominated the little French bistrot that, until that very moment, I would never have suspected I might be saving for exactly this occasion.

"Perfect!" she enthused.

"Ah, so you know it?"

"Not yet."

"Perfect it is, then."

And perfect it was; from the sound of the flutes (*santé!*) to weekends at the Met with *Madam X*; entangled ambles through brownstone canyons under the pelting afternoon rains, to endless conversations on open window sills; unhurried Pastis brunches to *"Last call!"* on Mott Street; from the last of spring to the first of fall; it was all, perfect.

* * *

And so the summer concluded without a question. We *would* return to Europe together. We *would* ramble across the continent, hand-in-hand, imperturbable, heads aloft, on toward irresistible *wherever*. For even out there, beyond the unturned page, there existed no real uncertainty, no meaningful anxiety of any sort, not with you by my side and I by yours. We *would* read each and every subsequent line aloud, threading ourselves into whatever narrative might arise, *together*. For nine short years I saw the world through your Athena gray eyes, door after door opened with curiosity's skeleton key, opportunity colliding with willfulness, forever forging ahead.

Over in Scotland, where you unfurled your masterly thesis and I corresponded with the office back on Wall & Broad, editor-at-large for *Tomorrow in Review*, a flimsy publication that barely kept the lights on, but somehow managed to pay for the next plane, the next bus, the next train. Remember that first one? The morning after your graduation (and a "resounding commencement speech by Professor Dennett," visiting that year from Tufts), the National Rail spirits us from Edinburgh (EDB) to London King's Cross (KGX), via Durham, between the Moors and the Dales. A few meals in The City, none of which (I am sorry) include dinner at The Criterion, for that will have to wait until the accounts weigh a few more pounds, and we're through the Chunnel, under the Channel, and shot, baby-faced and half-naked across Europe. We aim for the Adriatic, but get waylaid no further than Cancale, where we toss emptied oyster shells on the opalescent beach and throw back economy rosé. ("We're saving money," you tease, "just by eating them here. Look [slurp] another five euros we didn't have to spend in Paris!") In the Ville de Luminaire, we whittle away a week or two in a sixth-floor Montmartre walkup where, raiding the owner's bookshelf, you decide that the wonders of Porec's Byzantine mosaics simply cannot wait. We make it as far as Bratislava, but only after a massive detour to Tallinn because, as you excitedly point out, "there's an overnight cruise from there to Helsinki and, well… *Helsinki!*"

How *could* I refuse, my dearest Evie? I could not. I could not.

From Slovakia's capital we overnight rail right through Budapest (summers there to come) and arrive in Belgrade the following afternoon. The city is fairly bleak, but we do indulge in *that* Oblonsky-style lunch, where we end up discussing Tolstoy with the touring Czech couple at the adjacent table. You like the girl (died red hair, who agrees with you about the futility of Karenina's suicide) and so, on the strength of your hunch, we take their advice and hitch a minivan ride to Sarajevo the following day.

"Much better than Belgrade, right?"

And you are.

"Just imagine," and you do, aloud, somewhere along Ferhadijah and Ferhadija, "a city with synagogues and basilicas and mosques virtually abutting one and other, but where everyone considers himself, first and foremost, arm-in-arm, *Sarajevan*."

So I do. Imagine, that is. And it is truly liberating. Did I ever say "*Thank you*," Evie?

Enchanted by nearby Mostar, we begin blueprinting a Balkans chapter (you're devouring Ivo Andrić's *Bridge Over the Drina*), but when we arrive in Dubrovnik a few days later, the sun-broiled throngs overwhelm you and, espying a lightning special on one-ways to Istanbul, you turn the page and, thought clouds gathering into a Category 5 Hurricane Evie, begin furiously brainstorming a brand new installment. Silently apprehensive, I catch a side glimpse of your notes, "…lunch in the West, dinner in the East!" and am immediately nourished by your insatiable zest for life. "Let's do it!" So we do. Lunch and dinner in the shade of the Blue Mosque quickly becomes a weeklong cultural banquette, and when we finally do cross that tendinous isthmus, the tanker-choked Bosporus glistening beneath us, the deserts of the Middle East seem as natural a next step as drinking a glass of water.

Enter the long Arabian nights. Too many months in Dubai, where I spin PR fluff into front-page editorial for the *Gulf Times* and a chance interview with Mr. Clooney becomes "my time with Gorgeous George." You're content for a while, but relative economic freedom is "hardly worth the prohibition on holding hands in public." Then comes the "Dububble," a co-coined term all our own, and we are off again, stealing across the Subcontinent ahead of creeping Emirati censorship, an escaping duo of unpaid Bollywood extras, hot-footing it past Agra's famous mausoleum, on through Delhi's Old and New, to discover peace and filth on Maa Ganga. (And a pretty serious middle ear infection, too. Poor Evie!) As soon as you've convalesced, we hairpin around Everest in a twin-engine jet, and ride the slingshot south, across the Bay of Bengal, all the way down to the Mekong, where we explore a temple dedicated to Vishnu the Preserver, overgrown and sinking in the land of Khmer the Destroyer. At the foot of the infamous pagoda, you fall to your knees and weep under a hundred thousand skulls. Unsure quite what to do, I crouch down beside you, and pretty soon our tears are filling the Delta.

The following month in Nha Trang turns into three when the fallout from the "GFC" reaches Hong Kong and your job applications are returned, unopened, or returned not at all. You are whatever the opposite of perturbed is… sanguine, optimistic, *Evie*.

"So, we'll go to Sun Moon Lake," you declare one morning, the salt water still drying on your skin at breakfast, "and see the night sky reflected in the ink black waters. There's Taroko Gorge, too, a grand canyon made of marble. And…"

On and on we skip, past the emptying glass high-rises overlooking Victoria Bay, plunging headlong into the Taipei basin, home to seven-million souls hurtling toward Nirvana on half as many motorcycles. And all the while, you sing silly songs, "I been through the desert on a horse with no name, it felt good to be out of the rain." (Except during monsoon season, when you cheerily replace the 'out of' with your own 'drenched in.') There are visa runs, of course, imagined-border hopscotch, played every 28 days or so. Korea (Seoul, Busan and Jeju), Japan (Tokyo and

Fukuoka, twice, plus the bullet train out to soothing Nozawa Onsen), Shanghai (once when you were a brunette, twice more when you went blonde, because "C'mon, it'll be fun!") and a magnificent jaunt to Kota Kinabalu, where we ride a leaky ferry boat to that little island (you, alone, could remember the name) and feed the reef fish breadcrumbs squeezed from plastic bottles, standing in the center of a swirling, subaqueous cyclone, encircled by life itself. Underwater, overwhelmed, together in the middle of nowhere.

There were moments, of course, when things really did hang in the balance. When the rear wheel of our Hertz rental (model: Jazz, color: electric mustard) slipped off the gravel roadside, for instance, somewhere beyond "mobile coverage," high in the Omani mountains. I had been trying to turn us around, a failed eleven-point blunder, when we heard the crunch of axle on rock and felt the sudden, ten-inch drop. What were we doing out there, anyway, wadi-dipping that far from Jumeirah and that close to dusk, with a trunk full of liquor from Umm al Quwain and not a wedding ring in sight? What would we have told the rescuing authorities, had the passing Iranians not appeared first, in a dune-bashing Land Cruiser with a winch, no less?

"Ah, but they *did* appear," you nonchalantly observed, after they had towed us from the ravine, "and they *did* have a winch on their big diesel truck. And a snorkel, too!"

"And the wedding ring?"

"Let's get to that when we reach the Americas," you said, the moon, the stars, the whole damned universe in your eager eye.

And so we did, Evie. So we did.

*   *   *

"I'm off to write my vows," declared my dear fiancé, on the morning of our wedding.

"What's the order again?"

"Paper, scissors, rock?"

"You always win."

"Okay, then you go first."

I would not have wanted to follow Evie anyway, not with a hundred of our closest friends and family there to witness our Declaration of Co-dependence, as we had taken to calling our imminent and unorthodox ceremony. I suppose she knew that already, generous Evie, knew I would be nervous, and that, knowing she was to follow me, that she was right there beside me, to catch me if I fell, would calm and reassure me. (Right again, m'dear.)

It was six months since, on one knee and all, right there on Punta del Este's western boardwalk, I asked Evie if she would "consider growing old and crippled with me?" She almost fell off her engagement cane. Granted, she had not had much time to get used to it, given that she only broke her toe the previous evening. The elderly English couple at the antique store were kind enough to throw it into the deal. I could see them wincing as they watched smiling, hobbling Evie and I peruse the treasures laid out on blue felt mat, set atop the glass counter.

"This here is classic art deco style," the woman was doing the talking; the man the wincing. And talk she could. "Here, you can see the milgrain around the stone and along the top of the ring shank. And there, this lattice work, or *filigree*, is ever so detailed. Of course, sapphires were very popular during that era, often contrasted against the 'warmer' cuts of the Old Mine diamonds. This piece probably came to South America sometime around the late-thirties, early forties and…"

"Oh, don't tell us, please!" implored Evie, adding sweetly, "We'd like to make up our own story." (Even back then Evie hated spoilers, especially of a story's beginning.)

"And what happened here?" the old man motioned to Evie's foot, his curiosity finally getting the better of him.

"Just a temporary adventure wound." Evie exposed her purple pinkie toe to the man's further grimace. He wandered around the desk and returned a minute or two later.

"Here," he handed Evie a derby walking cane in Titanic blue. "To go with your new ring, should you choose it."

And so we did. Hence the engagement cane to match the ring. Still, we had agreed on waiting until we returned to Buenos Aires before deciding on the actual proposal.

"What about a favorite restaurant? Don's? Elena? Lo de Jesus?"

"Or we could pick a rooftop bar, maybe do it at sunset?"

"We haven't even worked out who's going to ask who…"

"Ok, ok. Let's just enjoy our weekend in Uruguay and worry about the whos and the wheres and whatnot when we get back."

So we went to Punta to buy an engagement ring. That afternoon, the Deco piece squirreled away in our hotel safe, we spent on the beach drinking white wine from plastic cups and watching the world passing us by. Being shoulder season, we had the setting mostly to ourselves, the long shoreline marching off into the distance, one grain of sand at a time. It was a clear day, but might have been a torrential storm for all Evie and I cared. To us, there was only the thrill of each other and the knowledge that we had embarked, directly, on a new phase in our journey together. The occasion seemed to open itself up to us, offering one of those moments in life when reflection and quiet contemplation replace the daily minutia in the mind, when the past and future stretch off into oblivion and you see yourself standing between the two, appreciating fully just where you are at that very point of existence. Reclined in a couple of faded red and white striped beach chairs, the sounds of the ocean rising and falling over the chatter of the gulls, we closed our eyes and reckoned on our place in time, the age before and to come, and the great mystery swirling outside the present. Soon enough, Evie's thoughts had drifted onto another past.

"Do you think she lived a happy life?" There was a touch of melancholy in her voice. She turned to look at me. "The woman who owned the ring, I mean. Do you suppose she felt fulfilled, when her time came? At peace?"

"I'd like to think so," I replied, trying to form an image of this mysterious woman in my own head. Evie was already ahead of me.

"The lady from the store said it was a French piece, and that it probably came down here during the war, when so many Europeans were fleeing the continent. I wonder what side she was on, the owner, what she had to do to get down here, what became of her…" A soft breeze passed across the dunes and crept out over the ocean. Along the shore, an elderly couple moved slowly towards us, then slowly away, the tide lapping at their weary, bare ankles. "I wonder why she chose to sell it,"

Evie continued, "how it ended up in that little antique store. Did she need the money? Maybe she didn't have anyone to pass it on to..."

The waves collapsed onto the shore, carrying the reflected sky over the sand, before ebbing once again to reveal the sun's glistening light.

"Maybe you'll pass it onto someone one day," I mused, with no intention other than to continue her story.

Evie thought about this a while. "Yes, I think I would like that," she said, the melancholy in her voice now imbued with a certain sweetness. "I think I would like that very much."

Later that same night, along the slow walk to dinner, I knelt down beside her engagement cane and asked my love to marry me. I just could not wait to grow old and crippled with Evie. Six months later we said, in happy, hopeful unison, "We do."

*   *   *

As below, so above.

Much as we have come to understand our world, stood atop the shoulders of so many giants, sung songs of the heart and wept tears of despair, peered into the cosmos and contemplated our origins here on earth, there reigns chaos aplenty still. We may comprehend a handful of causal relationships. A kiss that sets a hopeful heart aflutter. A shot which finds its target across an open field. In love and in war, possibilities are delivered into actuality every second of every day. Yet, so much of what constitutes our experience remains firmly beyond our grasp, relegated to the realm of spontaneous order. From the behavior of atoms to the paths of the wandering stars, the universe is brimming with acausal events, happening seemingly at random. Why, for instance, do some women develop preeclampsia? Why do the lightning clouds gather over their heads and not others? And why do some of these women live, even as others, so many others, die?

My head was full of chaos and questions, questions and chaos, as I ascended the familiar stairwell, between second and fourth floors, climbing out of one hospital room and into another. I could still feel her skin on mine, could recall the softness of her infant touch. A tiny baby girl, who did not know she was two-months early, had no understanding of what had happened during the seven days since her emergency Cesarean delivery, either to her or her mother, and who had not yet the faculty to even contemplate what might come next. She could not know what the words "spontaneous recovery" had meant to a father and, astoundingly, phenomenally, a husband weeping tears of joy and relief. Life for her was causal for the moment, a precise matter of calories ingested and grams gained and stages reached. Every passing day presented a new goal, a new equation, and a new determination. And so, second by second, cell by cell, breath by tenacious breath, this precious life pressed herself into existence, shouldered her way into the world with the impressive stubbornness of someone who does not know otherwise, to whom the question "Why not?" simply does not occur.

"It's as though she doesn't know she's premature," Marta had remarked. "She's just going about the business of living."

And so she was. Life, it seems, is still a matter of great debate. The precise moment it actually begins, to exactly when, or even *if*, it ever truly ends. Perhaps one is not entirely separate from the other. Death not apart *from*, but a part *of* life, written into its deepest code. I do not know when that moment was for Evie, when she seemed to come back to the world, but I like to think it was when she held her daughter in her arms that very first time. Watching her there, bathed in a moment of pure love, I could almost sense the vitality returning, as though she were strengthened by her daughter's own determination to live, to be. Maybe this is all a transition phase. A process by which one thing is always and everywhere becoming its opposite, a perfect reflection of itself. Night yielding to dawn, and then the long day surrendering to darkness once again.

All this and more I thought as, one step at a time, I went to see my Evie.

Chapter XXI

A LETTER FROM HILDA

Dear Margaret,

I hope it is not too early to offer you my sincerest congratulations. Your mother informed me you are with child; a girl, I am told. After quite the succession of males, my sisters and I were beginning to wonder if Papa's family tree would ever again bear the fairer fruit. Though it is far from me to question the Good Lord's plan for us, I was nevertheless elated to learn of your happy fortune, and wanted to send you correspondence at once, expressing as much.

It may seem strange to you, to receive such a message from your old Aunt Hilda. Sentimentality is not something I generally find becoming to one's character, particularly the saccharine variety so readily on display these days. In my opinion, the world would be a lot better off if we learned to value one another in accordance with our deeds, rather than our words, which so often fall short of their lofty aspirations. That being said, there are times in life when it is preferable that the heart hold forth over our impulse to pure reason, lest the tenderness of the moment be sacrificed.

I say this to you not as a woman impetuous in her youth, but as one who is older even than this present century itself (if only just), and who has certainly witnessed her due share of it, for better and for worse. Though I do not find myself wanting for experience or grand adventure, I wake to discover that, as they sometimes say in the East, my 'branches are bare.' So, as I draw near the end of my own time on God's green earth, allow me a moment of reflection, that from my past, I might perhaps impart some wisdom that shall serve you and your dear child in the very near future.

A long time ago, when I was abroad on my missionary work, a wise man told me, "All is one, and one is all." He was a kind and decent man whom others called a Christian. In reality, he was a sort of philosopher, to whom Christianity was but one part of a greater truth. He drew on ancient wisdom from the East as much as from the West, believing the two to be interrelated in a profound and mysterious way. I learned a great deal from this man, as well as from the many characters of that rewarding chapter in my life. Above all, perhaps, was the idea that, as we grow, we discover new and different ways of seeing things, perspectives which, though at first may seem oppositional to our own, may in fact be complementary to it. We learn to empathize, to see the same problem from many sides, to apprehend that commonalities are often more important than petty indulgence in our minor differences. To nurture an open mind is not always easy, and one falls prey to lazy thinking all too often. It is, however, an undertaking that yields surprising rewards, especially when they are least expected.

I hope I do not frighten you when I admit that I see this old man's face in my dreams still, and after all these years! It is sometimes difficult for a woman advanced in her years to revisit the season of her youth, when the future stretched out far before her. Yet, even as those moments are so distant, I recall them with great fondness, as if they were only yesterday. So, too, I witness the passing parade of faces, including one, a child as she appears to me now, whom I once called sister. We knew each other thusly because, though from different families and cultures, from different worlds, that's exactly what we were. I think with great fondness of many people, over the years, gone on to that other world, beyond the horizon. One can barely believe it when one's own time draws near.

I mention all this not to burden you with any melancholy of my own keeping, only to encourage you to be mindful and thankful for each moment you have with loved ones of your own, not least your precious daughter. No doubt there will be trying times, when you feel overwhelmed by the enormous responsibility set before you, or fatigued by the seemingly unending demands of the moment, but there is great strength in knowing you are never alone, even when those you love seem far, far away.

It was on that very same adventure, as it happens, from the Midwest to the Far East, that I met a princess who gifted me the brooch you find here enclosed. When she handed me the keepsake, she wished me safe passage, both on this, and on all the successive journeys of my "long, happy life." I carried her words of confidence with me, and wore her thoughtful gift through rain and shine, through the ebbing seasons of my years. I feel grateful and blessed to have, indeed, lived a long and happy life. It was not always easy going, for the path was seldom straight and the directions rarely clear, but as our faith is tested, we find our spirit grows and we discover, with the passing of time, how to become the person we were always meant to be.

So it is to you, my dear niece, that I entrust this treasured keepsake, one that was passed to me over half a century ago, and which I have kept close to my heart ever since. May it inspire in you an appetite for adventure and learning, a driving curiosity that spirits you over each and every horizon, keeps you asking questions and challenging the perceptions and norms of your own time. May your daughter grow to be a strong and proud woman, so that one day she may bear daughters of her own. And when the moment comes, may it be long from now, that you wake to find your own limbs grown weary with travel and experience, you will know well to whom you should pass this precious heirloom, a gift once to me and now to you, from beyond where the farthest sun sets.

With love and kindness,

Hilda Nilsen

Concordia University, Wisconsin

Fall, 1982

THE END

*   *   *

...Postface

O ver nine separate sessions, between the fall and winter of 1976, an 82-year old former missionary sat down with her interviewer to document a series of recordings for the Midwest China Oral History and Archives Collection. According to the original documents – copies of which sit on my desk, open beside me, as I type these words almost half a century later – the testimony includes, in part:

> [...] Initial experiences at station in Sinyang; description of language school in Peking; living and working in Peking; brief history of Sinyang; lifestyle in Sinyang; experiences as principal, teacher and bookkeeper; experiences working with thousands of flood refugees; reasons for keeping servants; description of students; bandit raid of the compound [...] memories of bound feet; evangelizing in Sinyang; sudden deaths in the missionary community; trip to Mongolia, 1922; text of *My Experiences with Bandits*, a pamphlet written by a missionary kidnapped by bandits, 1923 [...]

Frida Nilsen, the subject of the interviews, was born in 1894, in Scandinavia, Wisconsin. She died two years after these sessions, having lived a life that took her from some of the remotest parts of America's Midwest to some of the most isolated regions of Asia's Middle Kingdom. Frida's story, at turns incredible and at others all too believable, too human, served as part of the inspiration for the preceding tale.

I first came across these primary documents, hundreds of pages of typed transcripts, comb bound and spanning two thick volumes, in the summer of 2019. They were piled on my mother-in-law's already-bulging bookshelf, at the family lake house in Livingston, Texas.

Frida's story charted an epic course in its own right, spiriting our heroine, a young, naive missionary, across the Pacific Ocean to another hemisphere, and plunging her deep into the heart of a foreign land during one of the most tumultuous periods in its long history. Known thereafter as the Warlord Era (1916-1928), this was an age when bandits roamed the land in marauding gangs, sacking villages and battling for power as the post-dynastic country tore itself apart, province by province, town by town. For the long-suffering Chinese people, who endured famine and drought, plague and mass starvation, disasters man made and natural, this must have been an unfathomably challenging time to be alive. For a young missionary, an ocean away from home, it must have seemed like another world entirely.

Readers have often asked me which parts are invented, products of my own mind, and which are real, products of the forces of history. Sometimes, the answers appear straight forward; other times, I am not quite sure myself. The character Ling, for example, I invented as a companion for Frida, a flesh and blood confidante to help draw out Frida's inner thoughts and against whom I could plot her development and growth. On the other hand, the gift from the Mongolian princess, while actually a silver bracelet (not a brooch), is presently in my wife's safekeeping, as real as the metal from which it is made. One day, hopefully in the long distant future, this heirloom will be passed down to our own daughter who, inquiring of its origin, will discover herself another part of the inspiration behind the story you have just read.

Joel Bowman
Buenos Aires, Argentina ~ April, 2023

* * *